Clickbait

L. C. NORTH

PENGUIN BOOKS

TRANSWORLD PUBLISHERS
Penguin Random House, One Embassy Gardens,
8 Viaduct Gardens, London SW11 7BW
www.penguin.co.uk

Transworld is part of the Penguin Random House group of companies
whose addresses can be found at global.penguinrandomhouse.com

First published in Great Britain in 2024 by Bantam
an imprint of Transworld Publishers
Penguin paperback edition published 2025

Copyright © North Writing Services Ltd 2024

L. C. North has asserted her right under the Copyright,
Designs and Patents Act 1988 to be identified as the author of this work.

This book is a work of fiction and, except in the case of historical fact,
any resemblance to actual persons, living or dead, is purely coincidental.

Every effort has been made to obtain the necessary permissions with
reference to copyright material, both illustrative and quoted. We apologize
for any omissions in this respect and will be pleased to make the
appropriate acknowledgements in any future edition.

A CIP catalogue record for this book is available from the British Library.

ISBN
9781804992609

Typeset in 10.68/14.26pt Dante MT Pro by Jouve (UK), Milton Keynes.
Printed and bound in Great Britain by Clays Ltd, Elcograf S.p.A.

The authorized representative in the EEA is Penguin Random House Ireland,
Morrison Chambers, 32 Nassau Street, Dublin D02 YH68.

No part of this book may be used or reproduced in any manner for the purpose
of training artificial intelligence technologies or systems. In accordance with
Article 4(3) of the DSM Directive 2019/790, Penguin Random House
expressly reserves this work from the text and data mining exception.

Penguin Random House is committed to a sustainable
future for our business, our readers and our planet. This book
is made from Forest Stewardship Council® certified paper.

Praise for *Clickbait*

'A novel you inhale . . . a total stunner'
B. P. Walter

'Masterfully plotted and told with verve and humour'
Jo Callaghan

'Dark, devious and totally addictive'
Lesley Kara

'Compelling and page-turning with some
shocking twists along the way'
Catherine Cooper

'An utterly gripping thriller that explores the
addictiveness of reality TV in today's society'
Nikki Smith

'A gripping page turner that will quite literally have
you on the edge of your seat'
Glamour

'Riveting, skillful and wonderfully inventive'
Daily Mail

'I felt as though I was watching this gripping story
unfold in the media in real time; clever and captivating'
Jackie Kabler

www.penguin.co.uk

Also by L. C. North

The Ugly Truth

Also by the author, writing as Lauren North

The Perfect Betrayal
One Step Behind
Safe at Home
All the Wicked Games
My Word Against His
She Says She's My Daughter
The Teacher's Secret

EMERGENCY SERVICES CALL CENTRE, WATERLOO ROAD, LONDON

Date: Monday, 11 September 2023
Time: 5.15 a.m.

AUDIO RECORDING

Operator: Emergency. Which service please?
Caller: I don't know. I don't know. Who do I need for a dead body?
Operator: Transferring you to the ambulance service now.
Caller: I don't need an ambulance. I need the police.

THE FIRST EPISODE OF WHAT BECAME BRITAIN'S MOST POPULAR REALITY TV SHOW, *LIVING WITH THE LANCASTERS*, AIRED ON YOUTUBE IN 2007.

THE FOLLOWING IS AN EXTRACT FROM THIS EPISODE.

Living with the Lancasters
Series 1, episode 1 (2007)

PUBLISHED TO YOUTUBE: SUNDAY, 8 APRIL 2007

224.9M VIEWS

Taylor Lancaster, confessional
I'm Taylor Lancaster, but you probably already know that. I'm twenty years old, but I'm turning twenty-one next week. I'm having a huge party and you're all invited.

This is episode one of our brand-new reality show – *Living with the Lancasters*. It's a show all about us – our family – and what we get up to in our home and when we're out and about.

What do I think viewers should know about me? Well, for starters, I'm the star here. I'm the one that people will tune in to watch. I'm the one with the number-one single that put us on the map. I'm the one with the sponsorship deals and my face in the magazines. Everything that will come for my family and this show will be on my coat-tails, and I'm totally fine with that. I'm happy for them. I shine bright enough for all of us and I always will. I know the haters are going to say I'm full of myself, but that's bull. I'm a realist. I say it how it is.

Some people are born to be famous, and I'm one of them.

Locke Lancaster
Taylor said that? Why am I not surprised! Yeah, she kicked off the fame stuff with that one song, which by the way I hate. Every time it comes on the radio, another part of my soul dies. Seriously!

But look, one of us would have hit it big eventually. Taylor isn't special, she's just the oldest. She's three years older than me, and seven years older than India, so it's no surprise Mum's focus started with Taylor. Me and India will be next. And even if I'm riding Taylor's coat-tails like she said then let me tell you – it's a bumpy ride. It's not easy being the only boy in this family. Welcome to the circus that is *Living with the Lancasters*. I'm Locke and I'm seventeen years old.

India Lancaster
I'm India. I'm the baby of the family at fourteen. I'm still in school so I don't think you'll see much of me. Taylor is right. She's the star. What you need to know about Taylor is that she's always saying things without thinking. It's what people are going to love, and it's what drives Mum crazy. But Taylor works harder than all of us. Don't be fooled by any of the glamour. She's all business. It's work, work, work, 24/7 for her and Mum. You don't live in the same house with someone like that and not develop a lot of respect.

Besides, Taylor probably only said that thing about us all riding her coat-tails or whatever because she knew it would wind Locke up.

Lynn Lancaster
I'm Lynn Lancaster. You might know me as the wife of former Manchester United footballer Ed Lancaster. We were happily married for a long time. I'm now a widow, a mum and a manager. I'm forty-three, and before anyone asks, I love all my kids the same. They couldn't be more different though, and it's my job to make sure I'm getting the best out of all three of them. There is no one-size-fits-all. Taylor can be pushed and pushed. She lives on adrenaline and a

desire to be at the top of her game. But try and push Locke and he'll push right back. Locke needs to be presented with opportunities in a way that makes him think they are his idea. As for India, she's still young and figuring out who she is.

That's the beauty and the fun of what we're creating with this show. *Living with the Lancasters* has something for everyone. You're going to love us, and if you don't, then you're going to love hating us. We've got new episodes every Sunday at 7 p.m. here on YouTube.

In today's episodes, we're getting organized for Taylor's twenty-first birthday party. There's a lot to do and a lot of people to invite. Tensions are running pretty high as we try to find the perfect outfit for Taylor. She's gained some extra weight over the last few months which has pushed her up a dress size, but when the sales assistant and I try to point this out, Taylor hits the roof . . .

FEBRUARY 2023

TRANSCRIPT FROM SKY NEWS LIVE
WITH PATRICK MONAGHAN AND
AMBER CARNEY, 14 FEBRUARY 2023

Patrick: Good morning, it's 6.50 a.m. on Tuesday the fourteenth of February. You're watching *Sky News Breakfast*. I'm joined on the sofa by our celebrity reporter, Amber Carney, who's here to tell us what's been happening in the world of celebrities this week.

Amber: Hi Patrick, it's certainly been an exciting week. Hitting the headlines is a story about an episode of *Living with the Lancasters*, the popular reality TV series.

In Sunday night's show we saw the gorgeous thirty-three-year-old Locke Lancaster paying tribute to his late father – former Manchester United footballer Ed Lancaster – who died nineteen years ago this month. It was a moving tribute from the usually laid-back Locke, who finished by sharing a never-before-seen video of his father.

The home movie captures Ed Lancaster dancing at his fortieth birthday party back in 2003, before the reality TV show that catapulted the family to fame. But it's what's in the background of this home movie that has thrown the Lancasters into the heart of a media storm this week.

Patrick: I believe we're able to show a clip of the video on the screen behind you, Amber.

[On-screen video clip from *Living with the Lancasters*, series 17, episode 7]

Amber: So, you can see here that on first glance we've got Ed dancing with a group of people in the Lancaster family home in West London. It looks like the kind of lavish party we've come to expect from the Lancasters over the years. We can see a lot of champagne bottles and a lot of glitzy party props.

But if we look to these people here in the corner of the screen, we see Ed's wife, Lynn. Who appears to be in a rather heated discussion with . . . Bradley Wilcox.

Patrick: That's Bradley Wilcox, the teenager who disappeared in the summer of 2003 and remains missing?

Amber: He not only disappeared in the summer of 2003, but on this night that we are watching here. Bradley was just eighteen when he attended Ed Lancaster's birthday party, but later the very same evening, Bradley went missing on his walk home. Twenty years on, no one has any idea what happened to the teenager that night.

His disappearance made headlines at the time, but with no new leads in the police investigation, interest quickly dried up. You have to remember that this was before Taylor Lancaster's hit song, 'Girls Girls Girls', in 2006, and before the family's reality show started the following year. So, the Bradley Wilcox investigation didn't grab public attention in the same way we can expect it to now with this potential new evidence.

Patrick: Are the Lancasters really that famous? I think I recognize Ed Lancaster's name more than his family.

Amber: [Laughing] Have you been living under a rock for the last decade, Patrick? This family – Lynn, the mum, and three children, Taylor, Locke and India – are Britain's most recognized family, second only to the Royals. *Living with the Lancasters* is now on its seventeenth series. And while the show has seen a downturn in viewers in recent years, it's still one of the most popular British YouTube channels, with over 5.7 million subscribers in the UK alone. And Sunday's episode showing missing teen Bradley has already been viewed over ten million times. These numbers really show how popular the Lancasters still are.

This 2003 party video could have huge significance for Cassie Wilcox – Bradley's sister and last surviving relative, who is still searching for answers about what happened to her brother twenty years ago.

Extract from National Newspaper, 15 February 2023

TIMELINE QUESTIONS FOR MISSING TEEN

A twenty-year-old video of missing teen Bradley Wilcox is now being investigated by the Metropolitan Police. The video, which was filmed on the night of Bradley's disappearance, has called into question the timeline of Bradley's last known movements around retired Manchester United player Ed Lancaster's fortieth birthday party in 2003.

Witnesses at the party told the original police investigation that they had seen Bradley leave the Lancaster home in a taxi which took him to Richmond, West London, shortly before midnight. Police believed that Bradley disappeared on foot during his walk home from Richmond to East Twickenham in the early hours of the following morning. However, in a previously never-before-seen video from the party, shared during this week's episode of *Living with the Lancasters*, Bradley is seen still at the party after midnight, throwing the previous police assumptions into question.

Bradley's sister, Cassie Wilcox, has always questioned the witness statements in the original investigation. 'People have been lying since day one. This video proves without a shadow of a doubt that Bradley never left the Lancaster house in that taxi. It's time for the police to investigate my brother's disappearance properly. It's time for the Lancaster family to stop lying.'

A spokesperson for the Metropolitan Police said: 'The disappearance of Bradley Wilcox has remained an open investigation. Any and all new evidence will be investigated, including the recent video shared online.'

While no one from the Lancaster family was available to comment, Taylor Lancaster posted the following message on Twitter on Monday night:

I can't believe we've had a video of Bradley in our loft all this time and didn't know!!! Bradley was a close friend of mine and I'm still deeply affected by his disappearance. My heart goes out to his family. #BradleyWilcox #Missingperson #LivingWithTheLancasters

ONE WEEK LATER

TRANSCRIPT FROM SKY NEWS LIVE
WITH PATRICK MONAGHAN AND
AMBER CARNEY, 21 FEBRUARY 2023

Patrick: Good morning, we're joined now by our celebrity reporter, Amber Carney. Amber, what's been hitting the papers this week in terms of celebrity news?

Amber: I've got a selection of the papers here, and as you can see, it's still all about the Lancasters this week. We've got 'LANCASTER LIARS' from the *Sun*. The *Mirror* has gone with 'LIAR LIAR LANCASTERS', and the *Daily Mail* is asking 'WHERE IS BRADLEY?' We've also got Bradley Wilcox's sister Cassie dominating these articles, which all focus on the disputed timeline surrounding Bradley's disappearance, and whether Lynn Lancaster lied to the police in the original investigation.

Of course, the question everyone wants answered is not just whether Lynn lied, but whether the Lancaster family know more about Bradley's disappearance than they're letting on.

Patrick: Has there been a statement from anyone in the Lancaster family?

Amber: Not yet, Patrick, which is very surprising for them. We usually see Lynn Lancaster as the official spokesperson for all things *Living with the Lancasters*, but it's been radio silence from them, and no mention of Bradley Wilcox or the media storm at all in last Sunday's episode, despite a whopping fifteen million people tuning in to watch. My guess is that they're keeping quiet and hoping this story dies down very soon.

Patrick: Thank you, Amber. We're joined now by Cassie Wilcox, the younger sister of Bradley Wilcox. Cassie runs a missing persons charity, Never Give Up, and is working on a social media campaign called #JusticeForBradley.

Cassie, thank you for joining us. What can you tell our viewers about your brother, Bradley?

Cassie: Bradley wasn't your typical eighteen-year-old. He wasn't bothered about parties or clubbing. He never drank. He was really dedicated to his studies. He had a place waiting for him at Cambridge to study law when he went missing. He really wanted to use his degree to help people in trouble.

Patrick: What do you say to claims that Bradley simply ran away that night in 2003? Perhaps the pressure of his future got too much?

Cassie: Anyone who says that is quite frankly an idiot and a liar. They didn't know my brother. Those lies were started by Taylor and Lynn Lancaster to stop the police from investigating what really happened to my brother the night of their party.

Patrick: That's quite a bold—

Cassie: It's the truth. A word the Lancaster family wouldn't have a clue about. They've been lying about my brother's disappearance for twenty years, and now finally there is proof that Bradley didn't leave that party when they said he did, and what are the police doing about it? Nothing.

Patrick: I believe they're investigating—

Cassie: What does that even mean? No one has spoken to me about it. I want to know what the police are doing. What have they found? I want the truth about my brother. The Lancasters have been lying for twenty years and they've got away with it because they're rich and famous. We know they lied and yet they're carrying on with their lives like nothing has happened. Where is the justice for Bradley?

Patrick: Thank you, Cassie. I understand it's difficult—

Cassie: No, you don't. I'm sorry, but you don't have a clue what I've been going through for the last two decades. I won't stop until I get the truth. So either the police do something or I will. These—

Patrick: Thank you, Cassie. That was Cassie Wilcox—

Cassie: Don't do that. Don't cut me off. It's exactly what everyone has done for years. I've been completely ignored and pushed aside. My brother is not a headline about that family, he's a human being. He deserves justice. You're all the same. You—

Patrick: We'll be back with today's top news stories after this short break.

JULY 2023

To: Tom@TomIsaacInvestigates.com
From: Cassie_Wilcox@BlueInternet.com
Subject: My brother – Bradley Wilcox
Date: 18.07.23

Dear Tom,

My name is Cassie Wilcox. I'm the sister of Bradley Wilcox who went missing after attending a party at the Lancasters' home in 2003. I'm guessing you saw the news in February about the video and Bradley? Since then, nothing has changed. And that's why a friend recommended I contact you.

I run a missing persons charity called Never Give Up, and we have a social media campaign called #JusticeForBradley, but it feels like we're shouting into the void. I don't think the police are doing anything. The papers have moved on. I keep phoning all the media outlets but no one will return my calls. I got a bit angry on Sky News and now everyone thinks I'm crazy. I'm not! I'm just frustrated.

I've watched all of your investigations on your YouTube channel and I think you're a brilliant investigator. How you got that puppy farmer crying in the final interview was amazing! And I'm not just saying that because I really need your help.

My brother's disappearance killed my parents and ruined my life. All I want is the truth.

Can you please help me?
Best regards,
Cassie Wilcox

To: Cassie_Wilcox@BlueInternet.com
From: Tom@TomIsaacInvestigates.com
Subject: RE: My brother – Bradley Wilcox
Date: 20.07.23

Hi Cassie,
OMG you won't believe this but I was just thinking about your brother last week and wondering if I could do a docuseries on what happened to him. It was meant to be!

I would love to help you. I'm just finishing a series on MP expenses in Westminster and then I was planning to have a break, but Bradley's disappearance feels too important. I can totally understand why you're feeling frustrated.

Let's talk next week!

Tom x

PS I'm not sure if your friend mentioned this or if you remember me, but I went to St Dunstable's School too. I was in Locke's year and we used to be friends. I haven't seen him for years though and it wouldn't affect my investigation. I'd be completely impartial. My whole ethos at *Tom Isaac Investigates* is about uncovering the truth, but I felt like I should mention it.

PPS I remember Bradley from school a bit. He helped me get on the rugby team when I was in year seven and he was in his final year.

To: Tom@TomIsaacInvestigates.com
From: Cassie_Wilcox@BlueInternet.com
Subject: RE: My brother – Bradley Wilcox
Date: 20.07.23

Hi Tom,

Thank you so much! I'm so grateful for any help you can give me.

Thanks for letting me know about your connection to Locke. I don't remember you from school I'm afraid but I was in Taylor's year so I would've been three years above you. I actually think it's a good thing that you know/knew Locke. Maybe the Lancasters will be more willing to talk to you than they are to a stranger (or to me!!!).

Best wishes
Cassie x

PS I've stayed in touch with the original detective on Bradley's missing persons case. His name is Badru Zubira. He's retired now but still has a lot of insight and contacts, and I think he'll help you.

IN 2022, #LWTLFAVMOMENTS TRENDED ON SOCIAL MEDIA. FANS OF *LIVING WITH THE LANCASTERS* USED A GREEN SCREEN TO SHOW THEMSELVES SITTING ON THE LANCASTERS' PINK CONFESSIONAL SOFA AND RECOUNTED THEIR FAVOURITE MOMENTS FROM THE SHOW.

2022 trending video: #LWTLFavMoments

@EvelynSpires_DancingQueen

I hate it. Never watched an episode in my life, but my little sister is obsessed with it. She even had a *Living with the Lancasters* themed party where everyone had to dress up as one of the family.

[Laughing]

I went as Lynn. She's easy. She always wears a miniskirt and blouse and a lot of bling. I stuck all these little affirmation notes to my body too like the ones she'd stick on the mirrors in the house. 'You are worthy of success.' 'We make our own luck.' 'Money will come my way.' All that crap.

I can see why it's so popular. Something a bit different. Sunday nights are so tedious, aren't they? Thinking about work or school – the week ahead. The Lancasters are a distraction from the mundane.

@Felicity_Spires21

OK, carrying on from my big sister's video, I'm totally up for doing a *Living with the Lancasters* Favourite Moment. So what have I loved most about the show? I think it was Taylor and what she did with la tierra. I'm studying fashion at St Martin's now probably because of watching

Living with the Lancasters growing up. My favourite ever episode was the evening before Taylor had this big fashion event, showing off her designs for retail buyers. And when she unboxed the clothes, they'd used one of the earlier designs. Taylor had this absolute meltdown – screaming and shouting. It was so funny. But then she got her sewing machine out and spent all night unpicking the stitches herself and redoing them. I know some of the stuff on the show is exaggerated but you could see how tired Taylor was the next day. That was real.

@JackBurns_FilmBlogger

Living with the Lancasters is totally addictive viewing. I didn't start watching it until series 6 and binged every episode over two weeks.

There is something for everyone. The super-stressed busy mum, the fashionista, the lazy brother, and the awkward teen who blossomed into a gorgeous model. Their antics and their fights are insane. They're a mad, rich family whose show paved the way for an entire generation of reality TV like *The Only Way is Essex* and *Made in Chelsea*. Who'd have thought the average person would enjoy watching a family of elitist, shouty, spoilt brats so much. Even when Lynn had breast implant surgery and filmed it for the show. It was gross and yet you couldn't look away.

The whole show is like a car skidding on ice. You have to find out whether they'll crash in a ball of flames or manage to carry on. I can't believe the stuff they get away with.

AUGUST 2023

Tom Isaac Investigates: What really happened to Bradley Wilcox?

Episode 1: Everything we want to know!!!

PUBLISHED ON YOUTUBE AND SPOTIFY:
FRIDAY, 4 AUGUST 2023

LOCATION: TOM'S STUDY

Tom

Hi everyone, welcome to *Tom Isaac Investigates*. I'm the voice of the people. You tell me where to dig and I dig. Together we've exposed the MP expenses scandal, school dinner nutrition, and of course our most famous case – together we uncovered the arsonist known as Singe, who was burning down empty factories across the East London and Essex area. Rot in jail, Anthony Price.

Not to mention puppy farming in Wales last year, which led to me adopting my one-eyed wonder, Snowy, who is snuggled on my lap right now.

But I don't work alone. You are as much a part of *Tom Isaac Investigates* as I am, so get digging, get talking, and put everything in the comments. I read them all and together we expose the truth behind the nation's biggest secrets. I can't do this without you, TIs. So comment, comment, comment, or if you need to get in touch privately, then you'll find my contact details on my website. And in case there are any new subscribers out there wondering what the heck I'm talking about, my TIs are you – my lovely viewers. You are like my own private eyes helping me to investigate – except it's 'Tom's Investigators' not 'Private Investigators'.

[Laughing]

Today is the start of our biggest docuseries to date. I have one question for you – what really happened to Bradley Wilcox? The missing eighteen-year-old who was last seen at Edward Lancaster's fortieth birthday party twenty years ago.

Let that sink in for a moment.

Twenty years.

Two decades of Bradley's family wondering every minute of every day where he is and what happened to him that night. Two decades of not knowing.

Not a single sighting or phone call home. No addresses or bills registered in Bradley's name. Nothing.

There is so much mystery surrounding this case. It really does seem like Bradley disappeared into thin air.

And of course, at the centre of it all is the nation's most famous family – the Lancasters. These people are more than a family. They are an empire. They have their own clothing range, la tierra, and their own underwear line. They model, they endorse, they dominate the magazine pages and headlines, and every Sunday evening at 7 p.m. millions of us tune in to their YouTube channel to catch up on the latest episode of *Living with the Lancasters*.

I have so many questions. Especially for Lynn and Taylor. They were at the party the night Bradley disappeared and both told the police that they saw him leave. The big question here is this: how much do they know about Bradley's disappearance? Did they lie to the police twenty years ago? And if so, why? And what were Lynn and Bradley talking about in the now-famous 2003 party video?

I don't know yet if anyone from the Lancaster family is going to talk to us, but full disclosure: I went to school with Locke Lancaster and we used to be friends. Here's a photo of me and Locke from 2006 to prove it.

Don't ask what I was doing with that bleach-blonde French crop.

That was when I was in boy band True Dimension, which you know I do *not* like to talk about. Embarrassing!

And of course, those of you who are *Living with the Lancasters* fans will know that I featured in an episode way back in 2007, attending Locke's eighteenth birthday celebrations at Cirque Le Soir in Soho. What does this mean? It means I'm hoping to get us access.

It also means that I remember Bradley a little bit from my time at school. I remember him going missing and the effect it had on the local community. So this investigation feels personal to me.

We need to uncover the truth. The Wilcox family need answers. They need justice. Which is why Snowy and I are in my little study doing some research. And, yes, I know I promised you at the start of my last docuseries in the spring that I would be back in my own place this summer, but honestly, since moving home to Mumsie's house to save up to buy somewhere, it's been really lovely. And Mumsie loves having me here.

But back to the case. I have lots of guests lined up for Bradley's investigation, including celebrity psychologist and body language expert Olivia Hatton-Smith, who will be giving us her opinion of the people behind the Lancaster brand.

I also have retired police officer Badru Zubira lined up to talk to us. Badru was the lead detective on the 2003 missing persons case, and he'll be talking us through the original police investigation. And Bradley's sister, Cassie, will be sharing her memories of Bradley and the night he disappeared. Plus a whole host of other people connected to Bradley and the Lancasters.

This is my first historical docuseries. It won't be easy. We're going to be asking people to remember very specific details about events that took place two decades ago, when most of us can't remember two months back.

But you know me – it's dig dig dig and follow the leads. One thing is for sure, by the end of this series, we – my lovely TIs at home watching and commenting – and the world will know what really happened to Bradley Wilcox twenty years ago. We will find the truth and we will get justice!

Join me on Fridays at 7 p.m. right here on *Tom Isaac Investigates*. And don't forget to like and subscribe.

To: Lynn@LivingWithTheLancasters.com
From: Tom@TomIsaacInvestigates.com
Subject: Interview request for Tom Isaac Investigates
Date: 05.08.23

Hi Lynn,

I'm not sure if you remember me. I'm an old school friend of Locke's. I used to come over after school to swim sometimes and I was at Locke's 18th birthday party in Soho. I'm a huge fan of the show!

Anyway, I'm an investigative journalist now with my own podcast and YouTube channel (*Tom Isaac Investigates*). I'm recording a new docuseries on Bradley Wilcox and I'd love to chat to you and Taylor about what you remember from the night of the party.

I appreciate that you're probably really busy, so I can be flexible on a date and time. I'd love to hear your side of things from that night.

Cheers,
Tom x

2022 trending video: #LWTLFavMoments

@SazBennett881

Favourite episode ever – series seven. When they hired that cruise boat in the Caribbean. It was like an episode of *Rich Brits Abroad*. So funny when Lynn got the runs from eating prawns on one of the beaches and had to run into this wooden shack that she thought was a toilet. Turns out it was just a changing room, but it was way too late.

[Laughing]

Taylor had to lend her her sarong.

And then they got on the boat and left Locke behind in St Lucia while he was buying the booze. That was Taylor's fault too. She told the captain to go. They only noticed when Lynn went to make rum cocktails, and they had to turn around and go back for him. He was fuming. I thought he was going to push Taylor overboard.

Tom Isaac Investigates: What really happened to Bradley Wilcox?

Episode 2: The night of the party, part I

PUBLISHED ON YOUTUBE AND SPOTIFY:
FRIDAY, 11 AUGUST 2023

Voice of Sebastian Haworth

Bradley was a really good mate. The best. I would say that he was always someone who seemed happy to be on the outside of the friendship group. Never the centre of attention. Never loud or anything. But he could be really funny. It was like he wouldn't speak for an hour and then he'd just come out with something that would have us all in stitches. He wasn't one of the in-crowd like Taylor and Cassie, but everyone liked him.

LOCATION: WILCOX FAMILY HOME

Tom

Bradley Wilcox was just eighteen years old when he disappeared on Saturday, 2 August 2003.

With a place waiting for him at Trinity College, Cambridge, to read law, Bradley had a bright and promising future ahead of him. But on a warm August night twenty years ago, Bradley disappeared without a trace.

I'm in the living room of Bradley Wilcox's family home in East Twickenham. Behind the camera is my trusty cameraman, Javi, back to lend a hand with the filming.

Javi, make sure you capture this fireplace. As you can see from all the photos, TIs, it feels a bit . . . like a shrine, if I'm honest. For those listening on my podcast, this place has a nan's living room feel to it. The carpet is black with yellow flowers on it, floral print sofas too.

Lace covers on the backs of the chairs. I feel like I've stepped back in time. There's a gas fire and a fireplace and . . . is that . . . yes, it is, it's wallpaper made to look like bricks. I have never seen that before.

I've got to say, I'm a bit surprised by this house. It's nothing like I thought it would be. Cassie and Bradley were friends with the Lancaster family in 2003 and attended the same private school – St Dunstable's – so I think I was expecting something bigger and grander.

I was three years below Taylor and Cassie but I remember they were the 'it girls' of the school, and this is not a house I ever would've pictured Cassie living in.

The Wilcox family might only live a few miles from the Lancaster mansion, but it feels more like a hundred from where I'm standing.

Voice of Sebastian Haworth

Bradley was someone you could rely on. I remember once, I spent a week in hospital having my appendix out. Bradley took notes for me on all the classes I missed, even economics. He didn't study economics, but he went to those classes just so he could take notes for me. I think about that a lot.

Tom

Every surface in this room is literally covered with memorabilia. There are a lot of swim trophies and I can see two Kindness Cups from school. I remember they only gave one out each year to one person in the entire school. It was a big deal to get one. I'm not surprised Bradley has two. He was in the final year of school when I joined as a weedy eleven-year-old.

Bradley used to come along to the after-school rugby training we were all forced to do. There were a bunch of us who'd never played before and we were really struggling. Bradley arranged for us to have extra practices with him at lunchtimes just to help us out. I even made the rugby team.

There are a lot of gold photo frames here too. Bradley as a baby, Bradley as a schoolboy. Look, here's Bradley at a pool holding a swimming medal.

Voice of Sebastian Haworth
Bradley loved swimming. Practically every memory I have of him is with wet hair and smelling of chlorine. I once saw him competing for the school. He looked so happy in the water. You wouldn't catch me up at 5 a.m. three mornings a week back then.

Tom
It's weird seeing these different shots of Bradley. We're all so used to seeing that one photo – Bradley in his dark green sixth form uniform. The official school photo used by all the papers. Posed and proper.

These pictures are like opening a window into someone's life. I'm seeing such a different side. Look at this one – it's Bradley dressed as Dracula for Halloween. He must have been about ten here. And this one as a young teenage boy with his arm slung around Cassie at a Christmas dinner table. They look so alike. That glossy brown hair, big toothy smiles. People must have thought they were twins.

Bradley is so good-looking in these later photos. He could've been one of those all-American sports stars. All perfect teeth and a muscular frame. There's a photo here with an eighteenth birthday banner in the background. He looks so happy. He's holding up his wrist and showing off a big silver watch. It must've been his birthday present.

It feels really tragic that the photos all stop after that. I can't see any recent photos here at all. Not even of just Cassie. You get a sense in this room of how this family's life stopped dead the day Bradley didn't return home from the Lancaster party.

INTERVIEW BETWEEN TOM ISAAC AND CASSIE WILCOX

Tom

I'm sitting on the sofa now with Bradley's younger sister, Cassie, who I think it's safe to say has been the driving force in the social media campaign #JusticeForBradley.

I was just saying to my viewers, Cassie, how sad it is to look at these photos because they all stop around Bradley's eighteenth birthday.

Cassie

It's a lot of photos, isn't it? My mum put them up on the one-year anniversary of Bradley's disappearance. I think she gave up on him coming home then. She stopped leaping out of the chair every time the doorbell went.

Tom

It's incredibly heart-breaking. I don't think I could look at them in this room every day.

Cassie

The truth is, I rarely come in here. I don't actually think I've sat in here since my parents died. My mum passed away four years ago and my dad three years ago. They were still young, both in their sixties, but I think the not knowing what happened to Bradley ate them up, hollowed them out. They loved Bradley so much. We all did.

This photo was the last one my parents took of Bradley. He'd just opened his birthday presents and got the watch he'd wanted. It was one of those Seiko Kinetic diving watches with all the dials. Dad got it engraved with 'Happy 18th Birthday Son' on the inside—

[Pause]

Sorry. Some of this stuff is still hard to talk about.

Tom

Of course it is. Why don't you tell me a bit about Bradley? I only have a few memories of him from school but I remember him being really caring and kind.

Cassie

That sounds like him. Bradley was a quiet person. A real thinker. But he wasn't unhappy. He had a job as a lifeguard at our local swimming pool. I remember every Friday after his shift, he stopped at the supermarket on the way home and picked up a bunch of flowers for our mum – not the expensive ones, something small – carnations or daffodils, if it was spring, and a bar of Cadbury's Fruit and Nut for our dad. Bradley was always doing stuff like that.

I used to struggle with my maths homework. I'd tear my hair out about it but I never asked for help. I was only a year younger than Bradley and there was a bit of competitiveness to our relationship – only from my side though. Bradley didn't need to compete with me. He was always better.

He used to do his homework in his room, but I did mine at the kitchen table, and one day he just came down with his books and sat down beside me to work. It took me a while to realize it was always on the days I was doing maths. He'd gently point things out, like, he'd say, 'Maybe try dividing that fraction first.' And I'd look up and he'd be leaning over his work like he'd not even spoken.

I know I'm making out like Bradley was this perfect person. And of course, we bickered sometimes. He got annoyed with how long I spent in the bath and I'd moan at him for never taking the bins out – literally never. He would do anything to avoid that job. But he really was the nicest guy. When he didn't come home that night, it was like . . . I can't even describe it. It was like the world around us just crumbled into dust.

One of the awful things about losing my parents is that they died without knowing the truth about what happened to Bradley. I feel a lot of guilt about that. Right from the start, they were out of their depth with everything that was going on. It was hard for them to get out of bed every morning, let alone keep hounding the police and the papers to carry on asking questions. I took that job on. But after a while, it was always the same responses and I . . . I . . .

Tom

You got on with your life.

Cassie

Yes. Which makes me feel really bad.

Tom

Oh Cassie, it's completely understandable. I won't pretend I knew Bradley well, but from what you've told me, I don't think he'd have wanted you to give up your whole life for him.

Cassie

He'd have done it for me.

[Pause]

I moved away. That's terrible, isn't it? I just couldn't stand the sadness any more. It was like this house had a dark cloud hanging over it. I took a PA job in Sheffield in my mid-twenties. It was only when Mum died that I moved back here to help Dad out.

I guess after he died too I could've sold this place and moved back to Sheffield. I had a nice life up there. I had friends and hobbies. I was captain of my local netball team. It's nothing, is it? But I enjoyed it. When Dad died, it was like losing another connection to Bradley. It felt like I was the only person in the world who knew he'd ever existed. That was when I set up Never Give Up. I found strength in helping others, I guess.

And I know people will think it's weird, me living here. A

thirty-seven-year-old woman living in her parents' house with no life, no friends, completely obsessed with my brother. It's sad. Even I can see that, but . . . this is Bradley's home too. I can't move away or get on with my life. If he comes back and I've sold this house, he won't know where to go, will he?

Tom
Do you think he will come back? Do you think he's out there somewhere living a whole different life?

Cassie
Not really.

Tom
You don't sound convinced.

Cassie
Everyone knows Bradley was a straight-A student. Our parents were so proud of him. But I look back now and wonder if that's what he wanted. He'd argue with our parents sometimes. Stupid stuff about wanting to take a gap year and them saying they couldn't afford it and he couldn't throw his one chance at a career away. Our parents sacrificed a lot to send me and Bradley to St Dunstable's. I have no idea how they paid the fees. Bradley got a big scholarship when he was twelve which helped, but I didn't.

It must have been a lot of pressure for Bradley. They wanted so much for him. So sometimes in the middle of the night, I like to pretend to myself that he ran away. That he's out there somewhere. That he's happy. But in the morning, I remember that Bradley would never do that to my parents or to me. We're a close family. We *were* a close family, I should say. I was the wild one who stayed out all night. Bradley was the sensible one. He wouldn't have left without telling us. That whole running away story was created by the

Lancasters when they spoke to the police. They didn't have the first clue about Bradley. They were just protecting their own backs.

I've always believed that something bad happened to Bradley that night. But there was no evidence. Nobody wanted to listen to me. The papers thought I was a nutter. DS Zubira – the detective on Bradley's case – was kind, but what could the police do? Everything pointed to Bradley leaving the party.

It was only in February this year when the old video of Ed Lancaster's party emerged that we all found out the Lancasters had lied that night. To me. To the police. To everyone.

Tom
Tell me about Ed's fortieth, Cassie. You were friends with the Lancasters too. I remember you and Taylor being close at school.

Cassie
I'm the reason Bradley knew them. Taylor and I were best friends. We were in the same class from when we were four years old. One day she forgot her bag and I lent her my favourite My Little Pony pencil and we were instant best friends.

We were always hanging out at Taylor's house. Look around you – it's not much contest, is it? They had a tennis court and a pool and a massive garden to play in, a ton of rooms to hang out in.

Every time I was at Taylor's, there were always people there. Football types and business contacts of Ed's, friends, people Lynn was trying to impress for one thing or another. Before the iPhone came along, Lynn would go everywhere with a hot pink Filofax in one hand and a BlackBerry in the other.

The Lancasters were always throwing parties. Drinks, dinners, barbecues. Christmas, Easter, Halloween, everyone's birthdays. Lynn would use any excuse. Like, at the start of the summer they'd have a pool opening party, or there was a time when India lost her last baby tooth and Lynn threw a dinner party to celebrate.

Lynn was a total social butterfly. We all see that side of her on their show and it's exactly how it was twenty years ago. They even threw me a birthday party every year and I wasn't even family, although they always treated me like I was.

That's one thing I'll say about Taylor and all the Lancasters actually – they never made me feel poor. Never brought up how little I had or how crap my clothes were. Taylor shared everything with me.

I'm rambling. Sorry. Nobody's ever wanted to know all this stuff before. It's always been just the facts about the hour Bradley went missing and that bloody taxi journey.

Tom
Oh darling, it's all so awful. Please believe me when I say, *we* want to know everything!

Cassie
OK. So the party in August 2003. Lynn had been planning it for months and was going all out. Catering staff dressed in togas, champagne fountains, the works. Nothing was too much.

Taylor and I were seventeen. Bradley was eighteen. He didn't have much to do with the Lancasters. Sometimes in the summer holidays when we were younger, he'd bike over or get the bus and come collect me and stay for a swim in the pool. We didn't pay him much attention. He was always just my dorky older brother. That's how it was anyway, until earlier in that summer in 2003.

It's hard to say how it happened. Looking back, it felt like it was this overnight thing. Bradley wasn't a dork any more. He was suddenly this broad-shouldered hunk that all the girls fancied. It was like all that swimming suddenly paid off.

Taylor played it cool, but she started asking about him a bit. 'What's Bradley up to this weekend?' 'Does Bradley want to come to the cinema with us? Invite him if you want.' Then a few weeks before Ed's birthday party, she just said: 'Hey, Bradley should come too.'

I got the impression she was hoping to make a move on him at the party, and maybe that's one of the reasons I didn't go.

And that's the thing that always gets me – how close I came to going to the party. Even on the Saturday morning, I remember sending a text to Taylor and asking her if it was all right if I stayed over because I'd changed my mind and was going to come, then changed my mind again. All these years later I still feel this wrenching pull of indecision in the pit of my stomach.

Everything would've been different if I'd gone to the party that night.

Everything.

My parents.

Me.

Bradley. Especially Bradley.

LOCATION: KENSINGTON GARDENS

Tom

I'm just back from talking to Cassie and as you can see I'm out walking Snowy. She needed the exercise and I needed to clear my head, except I can't. Today was incredibly intense. Being in her house, listening to her talk, you can see what Bradley's disappearance has done to Cassie and to her parents before they died. Cassie talked about a dark cloud over the house and I really felt that.

People die, people go missing. We see it in the news every day, but talking to Cassie, learning about Bradley and the absolute devastation that has been left behind because of one night, one person, has really hit home. I'll never scroll past a missing persons story again.

It's strange because I do feel connected to this case more than any other investigation I've done. Seeing the photos of Bradley and remembering him was really hard, so I can't imagine how Cassie must feel every day. You can see it's taken its toll. Cassie is nothing like I expected. I remember her being really popular. If she and

Taylor were walking down the corridor at school, you got out of their way. She really was one of the 'it girls', but it's clear her brother's disappearance totally changed her life too.

Bradley didn't just have a bright future ahead of him. He had a family who loved him. He was the centre of their universe, their lynchpin. When he disappeared, they fell apart.

What do you think so far, TIs? Put everything in the comments. Together we can find the truth, and I really mean that. Remember it was a TI comment about a friend of a friend who was obsessed with fire that led to us finding the arsonist, Anthony Price. And another comment that led to the puppy farm in Wales and me adopting Snowy.

I said at the start of this episode that it was like Bradley disappeared into thin air on his walk home from that party. But people don't just disappear. There were a hundred people at that party. Someone knows what happened to Bradley. Someone has been keeping quiet for twenty years and I'm going to find them.

Tom Isaac Investigates: What really happened to Bradley Wilcox?
Episode 2: The night of the party, part I

PUBLISHED ON YOUTUBE AND SPOTIFY:
FRIDAY, 11 AUGUST 2023

658 COMMENTS

LWTL_No1Fan
I am dying! This is going to be your best investigation yet. CAN'T WAIT!! I'm desperate to know more about the Lancasters and what they knew.

Katy Shepard
My heart is breaking for Bradley's family. I need to know what happened that night!! I already have so many theories!

SyfyGeek90
Tom, you have to speak to the Lancasters ASAP! Bet they know more than they're letting on!

> **TrueCrime_Junkie1001**
> They've spent over a decade on a FAKE reality show! As if any of them are even capable of telling the truth now. We need to build up the evidence first before interviewing them, like Tom always does.

TI_BiggestFan
Poor Cassie. No one believed her all this time. I'd be so angry if I was her.

> **SyfyGeek90**
> Hardly surprising no one listened to her, is it? You can see from that house how poor they were. The Lancasters were rich and powerful even before the fame. The Wilcox family didn't stand a chance.

Katy Shepard
The Wilcox kids went to private school with the Lancasters. Hardly poor!

SyfyGeek90
Compared to the Lancasters, they were poor. I'm not trying to be mean. Just saying it how it is.

JulieAlexander_1
I feel sorry for Cassie. Even before Bradley disappeared, it seemed like he was the golden boy and his parents only had eyes for him. Must have been tough.

Ernie Martin
Seeing Tom without his beard is too weird!

Wendy Clarke
I like it. He looks like a young Robert Downey Jr. I really want to set Tom up with my brother.

TrueCrime_Junkie1001
That's not what these comments are for.

Ernie Martin
God, you TIs take this stuff way too seriously.

TI_BiggestFan
Keep digging, Tom. Time to expose the lies.

LancasterFANMAN
Be careful, Tom! This family is powerful. They destroy anyone who tries to bring them down . . .

To: Tom@TomIsaacInvestigates.com
From: Lynn@LivingWithTheLancasters.com
Subject: RE: Interview request for Tom Isaac Investigates
Date: 12.08.23

Hi Tom,
Sorry, but I have no space in my schedule for an interview right now.
  Good luck with the show. We have all been deeply affected by Bradley's disappearance.
  Regards,
  Lynn

TRANSCRIPT FROM SKY NEWS LIVE
WITH PATRICK MONAGHAN AND
AMBER CARNEY, 14 AUGUST 2023

Patrick: It's nine thirty-seven on Monday the fourteenth of August. You're watching *Sky News Breakfast*. Up next, I'm joined on the sofa by our celebrity reporter, Amber Carney. Amber, what's been happening this week?

Amber: Well, Patrick, I'm going to start by telling you what's not been happening in the world of celebrities, and that's the launch of la tierra Naked for Men – Taylor Lancaster's latest underwear line. The launch was supposed to be taking place on Friday in Leicester Square. We saw press invites sent out months ago with the usual Lancaster flair, but just hours before the event was due to go ahead, it was cancelled.

Anyone watching Sunday night's episode of *Living with the Lancasters* will have heard Taylor on the pink confessional sofa blaming the cancellation on manufacturing delays. However, I wouldn't be surprised, Patrick, if the real reason was a lack of retailers willing to stock the new underwear line.

The Lancasters have been facing increasing backlash since the 2003 Bradley Wilcox video was released in February. They lost their show's sponsor in March. In April, they saw their lowest viewing figures since series three. We then saw Locke Lancaster suspended from his co-hosting role on the *Xtra Factor*, while India was replaced at the last minute in a Calvin Klein perfume campaign.

I think it's safe to say that the cracks in the Lancaster empire are starting to show. We have la tierra clothes pulled from high street stores and now the cancelled launch. And there's also Lynn making headlines just yesterday after she was caught on camera screaming at shoppers in Waitrose who confronted her about Bradley's case.

It's hard to see how things could get any worse for the Lancaster family right now.

EXTRACTS FROM INTERVIEWS RECORDED
BY THE METROPOLITAN POLICE
BETWEEN 22–24 FEBRUARY 2023

Location: Twickenham Police Station

Taylor Lancaster: I get why you have to ask us this stuff but I really don't know how I can help you. I'm completely gutted Bradley went missing after my dad's party, but it was twenty years ago. It all feels like a blur now. Especially with my dad dying so suddenly the following year. I really don't like to think about that part of my life.

Locke Lancaster: We were having a clear-out of the loft. It was for the show. A look back at our childhood kind of thing. I found all the old home movies Dad recorded. Dad was pretty obsessed with making home movies. It's one of the things I remember most about my childhood. He used to do these New Year's Eve interviews with all of us. Where do you see yourself this time next year? What do you want to be when you grow up? It was just a bit of fun.

Sorry, the DVDs, yes. Dad died in February 2004, and Mum sorted his stuff out that spring. I think the DVDs got put in the loft then and we all forgot about them. Up until I found the video of Dad dancing, I didn't know there were any recordings from his birthday party, let alone that one would have Bradley Wilcox in the background.

India Lancaster: I was only ten in 2003. I wasn't at the party. I was told to stay upstairs in my bed all night.

Lynn Lancaster: I'm more than happy to give a statement but I'd like some time to consult with my lawyer first.

2022 trending video: #LWTLFavMoments

@Vicki_LondonWeddingPhotography

Love love loved *Living with the Lancasters* when I was growing up. I used to have to watch it in secret under my duvet at night on my iPad because my mum caught one of the episodes and decided it wasn't appropriate.

It was the one when India was at that modelling shoot for the lacy underwear. It was pretty early on. I think she'd only been modelling a few months. She didn't want to wear the sets they were asking her to put on. I didn't blame her. It was see-through and skin tones. She might as well have been naked. And then Lynn got, like, really nasty about it and basically made India do it. Telling her if she didn't, then her career as a model was over and no one would take her seriously if she started out as a diva.

India was practically in tears by the time they did the photos. They came out beautiful. Really moody, but I couldn't look at those images without remembering how much India hated doing it. It was pretty sad.

Yeah, so my mum decided that *Living with the Lancasters* was toxic and didn't let me watch it after that, even though I still did.

Tom Isaac Investigates: What really happened to Bradley Wilcox?
Episode 3: The night of the party, part II

PUBLISHED ON YOUTUBE AND SPOTIFY:
FRIDAY, 18 AUGUST 2023

Voice of Sebastian Haworth
The last time I saw Bradley was the day he went missing. I bumped into him in the supermarket and invited him to the pub that night. He really wanted to come but he felt like he couldn't get out of the party. That's the thing I'll always remember about Bradley. He was a stand-up guy. He always stuck to his commitments.

LOCATION: TOM'S STUDY

Tom
Welcome back to *Tom Isaac Investigates*. Before we dive into today's episode, I've just got to say how crazy this docuseries is. Normally, aside from you, my lovely TIs, no one pays much attention to what I'm doing until I present the evidence to the police and they arrest the bad guys. But in this case, Bradley Wilcox and the Lancasters have been headline news now for the past six months. And look what happened last week – I got mentioned in 'What to Watch' in the *Sun*.

As if I didn't feel this mega weight of pressure to get answers for Cassie, I now have the press holding their breath to see what I find. Sorry, sorry. I'm being dramatic. As Mumsie said as we were drinking my favourite WC2 coffee this morning – the best and only way to start the day – this is really good for me and my channel. WC2 are sponsoring this episode. You can grab a twenty per cent discount code for their super-tasty products in the show notes.

On today's episode, we're going to take a deep dive into that fateful night of Ed Lancaster's fortieth birthday party and Bradley's disappearance.

One of the things that's been bugging me about Bradley's disappearance is why he was at the Lancasters' party in the first place. After talking to Cassie last week, as well as Bradley's childhood friend Sebastian Haworth, I feel like I've got to know Bradley and so it's surprising to me that he would go to Ed Lancaster's birthday party. This was a boy who liked swimming at 5 a.m. and quiet nights in the pub with friends, but who didn't drink. So what led him to attend a large and wild party for a family he barely knew?

I'm leaving in a moment to meet Cassie in the exact spot where the police believed Bradley got out of the taxi having left the Lancasters' party. We're then going to walk down to the riverside and continue our interview.

LOCATION: RICHMOND RIVERSIDE, LONDON
INTERVIEW BETWEEN TOM ISAAC
AND CASSIE WILCOX

Tom

I'm here by the River Thames in Richmond with Cassie Wilcox. We can see the White Cross pub behind us, and in front of us we've got a calm stretch of the river. It's a popular footpath for both tourists and locals, and it's obvious why. On the opposite riverbank, there is a long stretch of leafy green trees and cute riverboats moored up. And it was here, a little over twenty years ago, that Bradley was believed to have disappeared.

Saturday the second of August 2003 was a warm and cloudless night. The moon was just a sliver in the sky when, shortly after midnight, a taxi dropped a group of young men in King Street, just two roads away from here, where they planned to attend a nearby nightclub.

Two witnesses at Ed's party claimed Bradley was one of those passengers. And one witness in the taxi told police that Bradley left the group at King Street and walked down Water Lane, which is the road you can see just behind me. The police believed Bradley then walked along this stretch of riverside in the direction of Twickenham bridge and towards home.

And it was in this exact spot on Monday the fourth of August, less than forty-eight hours after Ed Lancaster's party, that two police diving teams began searching this stretch of the river. They were looking for a body. They were looking for Bradley Wilcox.

The water is a murky green and, despite looking calm, there is a fast current just beneath the surface. It's hard to believe anyone would ever want to swim in this river even on a warm summer's evening, and yet that's exactly what the police believed happened to Bradley.

That must have been an agonizing time, Cassie. What was going through your mind when you learnt the police were searching for a body?

Cassie
There are no words. They were the worst days of my life and when I look back now, I feel . . . this . . . this anger burning through me. This rage. I get breathless with it. My jaw clenches, my chest physically hurts. I can't control it. What was it all for? The river search put my family through hell.

Tom
Can you take us back to the night of the party? You were Taylor's best friend, and close to the Lancaster family. You regularly attended dinners and sleepovers and even holidayed with the family, but you said in our last interview that you didn't go to Ed's fortieth for a few reasons. What was the main one?

Cassie

[Sighs]

I was seventeen and I was dating this guy who at the time felt pretty out of my league. He was my first proper boyfriend. I thought it was love and I was completely wrapped up in him. It was Taylor who introduced us, actually, at a barbecue. I think Ed knew his dad. He was another one with more money than sense, but at that point in my life I was really drawn to the lifestyle, that entitlement, everything I didn't have but saw at school or at Taylor's house every day.

By that August, we'd been dating for three months, but he was busy a lot of the time so we'd probably only been on around ten dates and some of them were in a group. I hadn't brought him home or introduced him to my parents or Bradley. He thought I was Taylor's neighbour and I was working up the courage to tell him the truth. So stupid now I look back, but like I said, I was seventeen and thought it was love.

This guy – is it OK if I don't name him? I don't want to drag him into this.

Tom

Of course. That's completely fine.

Cassie

So the guy's parents were celebrating their twenty-fifth wedding anniversary with a dinner at this mega-fancy French restaurant right on the Thames near Butler's Wharf. I couldn't believe it when he asked me to go and I was gutted it was the same night as Ed's birthday party.

I thought we'd go to the party together and . . . oh, it doesn't matter now.

I was going to tell Da— the guy – I couldn't go to the dinner but

Taylor convinced me I should. She was like, 'Cass, my mum has parties every other week. When is the next time you're going to eat at . . .' wherever. I can't even remember the name of the restaurant.

The guy really wanted me there and Taylor said I should go, so I did. The family of this guy had an apartment in Westminster and they were having an after-dinner drinks thing, so the plan was that we'd stay at the apartment rather than travel home late.

I was really torn. I wanted to go to Ed's party, but I was so focused on not wanting to appear rude or ungrateful.

It's funny, but at the time I thought Taylor was being so nice, encouraging me to go to the dinner. She knew how much I liked the guy and didn't want me to miss out on seeing him. With everything that came later, I wonder now if Taylor planned it so I'd be out of the way.

Tom

What do you mean, 'planned it'? The dinner?

Cassie

My invite to it, yes. Here was a guy I'd been on a few dates with, inviting me to a really important family event when I hadn't even met his parents yet. Don't you think that's odd? Unless of course you consider that this guy and Taylor were friends.

Taylor had this way of asking for things that made it hard to say no. What if she convinced this guy to invite me to the dinner to get me out of the way because she wanted Bradley to herself? It's one of the many things I'd like to ask her.

You know, it wouldn't even surprise me if she set up the whole relationship with this plan in mind. Taylor was always a few steps ahead of me. And the guy never called me again after that night. Not that I was interested in anything but finding my brother at that point.

Sorry, I'm sounding paranoid, aren't I?

Tom

I totally get what you're saying. And hey, we've all seen what Taylor is like on *Living with the Lancasters*.

Tell me about Bradley going to the party.

Cassie

He really didn't want to go. I loved all the glamour and shine of the Lancasters, but I think Bradley always felt uncomfortable with it. So when I said I wasn't going to Ed's party, Bradley said he'd stay home. Then, the day before the party I get a call from Taylor. She's chatting normally about what she's wearing to the party and asking me what I'm wearing to the dinner and did I want to borrow anything. Then she said, 'Oh, by the way, is Bradley there?' And I said he was. So she asked if she could have a chat. 'A super quick word,' she called it. That's what she always said when she wanted something from you. 'Can I have a super quick word?'

I put Bradley on the phone and three minutes later he's making faces at me but laughing too and saying, 'OK, OK, I'll be there.' I wasn't surprised. Like I said, it was hard to say no to Taylor.

Tom

At what point did you realize something was badly wrong?

Cassie

I got a text from Bradley at around eleven on the night of the party. It said: 'Things are really messed-up here. I'm coming home. Need to talk ASAP.'

I didn't have a clue what Bradley meant and I'd had a couple of glasses of champagne by that point. I wasn't drunk drunk but I wasn't thinking clearly either. I sent a reply saying I'd talk to him in the morning. And that was the last time I heard from my brother.

Tom

At the time, reading the message, what did you think Bradley meant by 'things are really messed-up here'?

Cassie

I certainly wasn't thinking that he was in any kind of trouble. I guess I assumed Bradley had fallen out with Taylor. Maybe she'd tried to kiss him and he'd turned her down. Maybe she caused a scene. We've all seen her temper on the show. There's nothing fake about that. She was always flying off the handle about the littlest things, but she calmed down just as quickly.

I hate myself for this now but I remember being more concerned about my friendship with Taylor and worrying that she'd be annoyed with me over Bradley.

Tom

And what happened the morning after the party? When did you realize Bradley was missing?

Cassie

I called Bradley at about nine on Sunday morning but his phone was off. I assumed he was sleeping or already at the pool training. Then, late morning, I got a call from Mum to say Bradley hadn't come home.

I wouldn't say I was worried at that point. Bradley was eighteen and while it was unusual for him to stay out and not tell our parents, there was a first time for everything.

I caught the bus home and on the way I called Taylor to catch up on the gossip from the party. When she didn't pick up, I called the Lancaster home phone. It rang and rang and I guessed everyone was sleeping off hangovers.

Bradley hadn't turned up by the time I got home and Mum was worried. She kept looking at the clock and then at the door as if willing Bradley to walk through it. Dad was more relaxed. He said: 'Let the boy have a bit of freedom. He's moving out next month.'

After lunch, I phoned the pool to check if Bradley had been there. Then I phoned his friends but none of them had seen him. So at about three o'clock when we still hadn't heard, I rode my bike over to the Lancasters'.

Tom

What were you thinking at that point? How worried were you?

Cassie

The truth is that I don't remember being worried at all. If anything, I was more annoyed that Bradley was upsetting Mum. But something made me ride my bike over to their house when I could easily have called them again, so maybe there was a niggling sense of something being not right.

I rang the front doorbell when I got there, which again was unusual because normally I went straight round to the back door and let myself in. I don't know what made me do it differently that day.

Lynn answered the door in full tidy-up mode, which to Lynn meant getting a cleaning team in and telling them what to do while she drank coffee. There were caterers packing up and a removal company carrying out fake gold statues.

Lynn was all, 'Hi Cass Cass –' that's what she called me – 'we missed you last night.' And I came straight out with it and asked if Bradley was there. Lynn looked a bit perplexed and shook her head, and I burst into tears, which was more tiredness and frustration than worry, I think.

Lynn ushered me into the kitchen, sat me down at their breakfast bar and got me a can of Diet Coke. She seemed genuinely worried about Bradley. I remember her exact words to me. She said: 'I'm sorry, Cass Cass, Bradley jumped in a cab at eleven forty-five heading into town with a group of lads he met.'

I think I was so deflated by her words that I didn't twig until later how rehearsed her answer was. I mean, she didn't even 'um' and 'aw' over it. There must have been over a hundred people at Ed's party, not to mention a lot of champagne. The whole house still stank of booze and cigarettes, and yet she knew without a moment of hesitation the exact time the brother of one of her children's friends had left.

Then Taylor walked into the kitchen in these hideous white silk pyjamas she was always wearing. She looked really awful. Properly green like she was hungover and hadn't slept. She was trying to convince one of the cleaners to drive to McDonald's for her. I asked her about Bradley, and do you know what she said?

Tom
Oh my God, what?

Cassie
She said, 'Bradley left in a taxi at eleven forty-five.'

Tom
The same answer Lynn gave.

Cassie
Yes. I think about that a lot. About how naive I was. How stupid. If only I'd realized then. If only I'd questioned them, pushed for answers, maybe they'd have let something slip. I know that's what your TIs will be thinking, but you have to understand that the Lancasters were like my family. It was Lynn who helped me when I got my period, and Ed who taught me how to tie a Windsor knot in my tie for school.

I completely trusted them. There wasn't a single doubt in my mind that they were telling the truth. I rode home and told Mum to call the police.

Tom

Did you talk to Lynn and Taylor about the text Bradley sent the night before?

Cassie

No. I was too focused on finding him. At that point, I had no reason to think that anything bad had happened to Bradley during the party, especially when the third witness came forward claiming Bradley was in the taxi with him.

As far as I was concerned and as far as the police were concerned, Bradley left that party and travelled to Richmond.

LOCATION: KENSINGTON GARDENS

Tom

I'm out walking Snowy again. I keep thinking I'm going to get some fresh air and then go home and record these last bits of the episode but then all this stuff just pops into my head and I have to talk about it.

Lynn and Taylor would later tell the police that they saw Bradley leave the party in a taxi with four players from Crystal Palace football club who were heading to a nightclub in Richmond. Three of the four footballers stated that they were too drunk to remember. Only one – Dale Peterson – confirmed Bradley was with them. It's this version of events that became the primary focus of a police investigation that would subsequently lead nowhere.

But thanks to the 2003 party video released by Locke in February, we know that Bradley wasn't in that taxi.

Why did three people lie about seeing Bradley leave the party? What happened at Ed's party that made Bradley send a text to his sister at eleven o'clock, telling her that things were really messed-up?

And what were Lynn and Bradley talking about when they were caught in the background of the video?

I might not be able to ask Lynn or Bradley that final question right now, but there is someone who can help to answer it. Tune in next Friday at 7 p.m. for the truth behind the party video.

Tom Isaac Investigates: What really happened to Bradley Wilcox?
Episode 3: The night of the party, part II

PUBLISHED ON YOUTUBE AND SPOTIFY:
FRIDAY, 18 AUGUST 2023

1,144 COMMENTS

LWTL_No1Fan
I could totally feel Cassie's anger as she was talking about Bradley's disappearance. If it was me, I'd have done something about it.

SyfyGeek90
Tom, have you contacted Taylor, Locke and India as well as Lynn? Where were they during the party? Maybe they know something.

> **Wendy Clarke**
> Yeah, but I've just done the maths and Locke was 13 in 2003 and India was only 10. Not sure how much help they'll be.

Katy Shepard
On the day Bradley went missing there were fifty sightings in south-east England of unidentified flying objects. We can't ignore all the evidence out there that Bradley could have been abducted by aliens. How else does someone disappear without a trace? Anyone else thinking this?

> **Ernie Martin**
> Just you.

LancasterFANMAN
Better watch out, Tom! The Lancasters have a lot of fans and support still. Getting close to them could be dangerous for you.

VIDEO RECORDING FOUND DURING A
POLICE SEARCH OF THE LANCASTER PROPERTY
ON 13 SEPTEMBER 2023

Evidence item no: 139

Description: Extract from home video recording, 31 December 1995

Taylor's interview

Ed: So, Taylor, here we are in the hot seat on another New Year's Eve. Tomorrow it will be 1996. How old are you now?

Taylor: I'm nine, Daddy. You know that.

Ed: Ah yes, that's right. Nine. And what do you want to achieve next year?

Taylor: I want to beat you at chess without you letting me win. And I want Cassie to come for a sleepover every week.

Ed: [Laughing] OK then.

[Background voice] **Lynn:** Sit up straight, Taylor. You're on film.

Taylor: Yes, Mummy.

Ed: It's a home movie, Lynn.

[Background voice] **Lynn:** It's a home movie now but we don't know what it will be one day.

Ed: So, Taylor, what do you want to be when you grow up?

Taylor: I want to be a grandmaster. I want to be the world chess champion.

[Background voice] **Lynn:** Oh honey, that's not a job. You want to be a singer or an actress, remember? That would make Mummy very happy.

Ed: She can say what she likes. She's nine years old.

Locke's interview

Ed: It's New Year's Eve, 1995. How old are you, Locke?

Locke: Nearly six and a half.

Ed: And what do you want to achieve this year?

Locke: Er . . . Don't know. Eat lots of chocolate.

Ed: Good answer. And what do you want to be when you grow up?

Locke: Tractors. I want to drive tractors.

Ed: You don't want to be a footballer like your daddy?

[Background voice] **Lynn:** [Laughing] He's six. If Taylor can be a chess player, Locke can drive tractors, Ed.

Ed: Fair point.

Locke: I don't like football. It's boring.

Ed: [Laughing] OK then. Tractor driving it is.

India's interview

Ed: Hello, sweetheart. Can you tell the camera how old you are?

India: Two.

Ed: That's right, darling. Well done. And do you know what you want to be when you grow up?

India: Mummy.

Ed: You want Mummy now or you want to be a mummy?

India: Mummy.

Ed: I bet you want to be as beautiful and as lovely as your mummy, don't you?

[Background voice] **Lynn:** Oh Ed, you goof. Come on. We need to get ready for the dinner party. People will be arriving in a few hours.

Ed: In a sec. Take a seat, Mrs Lancaster.

Lynn: Me?

Ed: Go on.

Lynn: Fine.

Ed: So it's New Year's Eve, 1995. How old are you?

Lynn: Too old.

Ed: You're not.

Lynn: I'm thirty-one. That feels old.

Ed: And what do you want to achieve this year?

Lynn: I want to find a drama school for Taylor and Locke and I want to have lots of parties and meet lots of interesting people.

Ed: And what do you want to be when you grow up?

Lynn: [Laughing] I just want the kids to have all their dreams come true.

Ed: With you as their mum, nothing will stand in their way.

To: Lynn@LivingWithTheLancasters.com
From: Tom@TomIsaacInvestigates.com
Subject: RE: Interview request for Tom Isaac Investigates
Date: 20.08.23

Hi Lynn,
Thanks for your reply last week. I understand how busy you must be right now. I want to reassure you that I'm not out to interrogate you. This is about hearing your side of the events that took place in your home on 2 August 2003. The press have been extremely critical towards you, Taylor, Locke and India. Perhaps telling your side of the story will put an end to the negativity?
   Cheers,
   Tom x

2022 trending video: #LWTLFavMoments

@BrentwoodGolfingEquipment

My favourite episode was pretty early on. It must have been series one or two. Taylor got invited to a club opening and then got hammered on tequila and could barely stand up straight when the club owner started doing his speeches. Taylor was supposed to say a few words but Lynn ended up doing it for her and everyone in the club was like, *what the fudge?*

Then Taylor passed out on the sofa in the VIP lounge and was sick all over India's revision notes. God knows what India was even doing there. She was revising for some exam, I think.

I stopped watching it about series six. It got too commercial. I liked it better when it was really amateur. It was funnier. Besides, Taylor's pop-brat routine got a bit tedious. I caught an episode the other day and she was still exactly the same. Expecting everyone to run around after her. She's in her thirties now. It's sad.

@KTHunterGrand

Favourite moment has to be when Taylor got turned away from the business-class lounge at Heathrow for wearing joggers. Her face.

[Laughing]

She was fuming.

She wouldn't accept it, would she? Kept arguing with the attendant that they weren't joggers, they were la tierra loungewear, and 'don't you know who I am?'

'I'm never flying with your airline again.'

And to be fair, she didn't. After that it was always a private jet.

That got a bit tedious, though, to be honest. Every time she met anyone she was trying to impress she'd always say, 'I only fly by private jet now. It's more pricey but worth it, you know?'

Tom Isaac Investigates: What really happened to Bradley Wilcox?

Episode 4: The 2003 party video – What are we seeing?

PUBLISHED ON YOUTUBE AND SPOTIFY:
FRIDAY, 25 AUGUST 2023

LOCATION: TOM'S STUDY

Tom
This is episode four of *What really happened to Bradley Wilcox?* I did have this whole opening planned about how we're away and flying with this docuseries, but something has happened and . . .

[Pause]

To be honest, I'm a bit thrown. Ten minutes ago, the doorbell went and when I answered it, there was no one there, but . . . sitting on my doorstep was this bouquet of dead roses and this . . .

[Pause]

This brick. There was a typed note wrapped around the brick. The note says: 'I warned you the Lancasters have a lot of fans. Keep digging, Tom, and the next time you see this brick it will be smashing into the side of your head.'

[Pause]

I'm in complete shock. My heart is still racing and I feel sick. This was on my doorstep. Someone has come to my home. They know where I live. I can't believe it. Nothing like this has ever happened before.

I'm going to take this note and this stuff to the police now and record the rest of this episode later.

Tom Isaac Investigates: What really happened to Bradley Wilcox?

Episode 4: The 2003 party video – What are we seeing? (cont.)

PUBLISHED ON YOUTUBE AND SPOTIFY:
FRIDAY, 25 AUGUST 2023

Tom

I'm back. The police have started a case file and are going to look at any possible CCTV on the street and surrounding areas. I'm still deeply shocked, but I'm also angry. In fact, here's a message for the person who left that threat for me.

[Pause]

If you think you can scare me off that easily, you are wrong. All you've done is made me more determined to find Bradley and uncover whatever secrets you obviously seem to think the Lancasters are hiding.

Starting right now.

Voice of Cassie Wilcox

Not a single day has gone by in all these years where I haven't thought about the night of the party. Where I haven't agonized over it, clawed through my memories and what we were told about Bradley, looking for something else, some clue we'd missed, doubting how well I knew my own brother, wondering if I could have done anything differently. All those hours, all these years, and what was it all for? Nothing. Everything we thought, everything we were told was a lie.

Tom

Today we're going to do a deep dive into the party video. This is the video that Locke shared on *Living with the Lancasters* back in

February that reignited Bradley's missing persons investigation and created some serious negative press for the Lancasters. It's had a huge knock-on effect on the Lancaster family's lives. Viewing figures are down, they've lost the show's sponsor and Taylor, Locke and India's careers are suffering.

[Extract from *Living with the Lancasters*, series 17, episode 7]

Locke Lancaster
Today is the anniversary of the day my dad died. He was forty years old. Only seven years older than I am now.

I was fourteen when he died and it really hit me hard. Dad was an actual football legend who so many people loved. When he retired from playing, he became a football agent. It wasn't for the money. Dad was determined to help talented footballers get to the top clubs. He was always pressuring the FA to put more rules in place to protect the lads in youth football.

He was a football legend but he was a legend to me, too, just for being my dad. I really looked up to him.

He used to take me with him on these really long drives in his Porsche 911 Carrera. There was always an errand, something Mum wanted picking up, or a new player he wanted to watch. I look back now and I'm like, wow, that was just an excuse, right? To get out of the house and spend time together – to chat one to one.

I miss him so much.

I was talking to Taylor and India about doing something special next year. It'll be twenty years since he died. I can't wrap my head around that. It still feels so fresh. We were thinking of a charity football match or a party. Talking of parties, I was digging around in the loft the other day and I found this really funny video of my dad dancing at his fortieth birthday party. Check it out! I think I look so much like him here.

Tom

According to Taylor and Locke, their dad enjoyed making family videos. So why didn't the police know about this video? This is a question I'll need to ask the detective who worked the case when we speak.

I'm completely speculating here, but my guess is that the police had no idea the camera or the party video existed. You have to remember that this was in 2003, a whole four years before the launch of *Living with the Lancasters*. Close friends and family may have known of Ed's love of shooting family videos but there's no reason the police would have. In today's world, one of the first things a police officer is going to ask witnesses is if they have videos or photos on their phones, and no wonder! We're always snapping away. But back then, it really wasn't a thing, which is why this video has sat undetected, maybe even hidden, for the last two decades.

It may have taken twenty years to come to light, but once it was posted, it took only minutes for the Lancasters' world to implode. The comments on the video started almost immediately.

[YouTube comments from *Living with the Lancasters*, series 17, episode 7]

Is that Bradley Wilcox in the background?
OMG it's Bradley Wilcox. I bet this is the last footage of him ever. 💔
Look at the time stamp on the video!!! It says 00.15 on 03 August. Didn't Bradley leave the party at 11.45 p.m.?
    Just checked. Yes he did.
    But he didn't!!!!!
    OMFG! The police need to see this!!!

Tom

I've watched the video a thousand times at least. I'm sure we all have. That living room with the red and gold sofa pushed up against the wall. The makeshift dance floor strewn with party popper streams. Glasses and champagne bottles on every surface. Not to mention the gold statues of two Greek goddesses either side of the doorway.

And at the back of the room, a staircase and a doorway leading to a different part of the house, and of course, Bradley Wilcox and Lynn Lancaster. The video is time-stamped 12.15 a.m. and we can also see a clock on the wall showing the same time, so there can be no doubt that this footage was filmed a full thirty minutes after the taxi left.

Here is the interview I recorded yesterday with celebrity psychologist and body language expert Olivia Hatton-Smith, who's going to take us through exactly what is taking place between Bradley and Lynn.

ZOOM INTERVIEW BETWEEN TOM ISAAC AND OLIVIA HATTON-SMITH

Tom
Olivia, thank you for joining me.

Olivia
My pleasure.

Tom
I read your book, *Behind the Image: What celebrities don't want you to know*, last year and found it super fascinating, and you really are a world leader on body language, so I'm desperate to speak to you about what we're seeing between Lynn Lancaster and Bradley Wilcox. I know you're up to speed on what's going on, so can you talk us through what we're all seeing, please?

Olivia

So I've spent several hours watching this video frame by frame and I'm going to share my screen now so we can watch it as I'm talking.

What we've got here is a large living room area and the focus of the video is this group of people here, dancing, and in particular this person – Edward Lancaster. I could go into great detail about the movement of the dancers and their demeanour, but it doesn't take an expert to know that everyone in this group is drunk.

But it's what the person recording this video has inadvertently captured in the background that we're interested in. If I pause the footage here, we can clearly see that beyond the dancers, in the corner of the room beside a staircase, is a young man who we know is Bradley Wilcox standing with a woman – Lynn Lancaster. Lynn is talking to Bradley as she's making a drink. We can't see the table but it looks like a spirit mixed with a lemonade or a tonic.

If I press play again, then right here we see Lynn's hand move over the glass as though she might be dropping something into it. Unfortunately, a dancer stumbles across our view so it isn't clear what that something is or even if that's what we're seeing. What I can tell you, though, is that Lynn is trying to shield her actions. Perhaps from Bradley. Perhaps from any potential onlookers. See how her shoulder hunches as she leans forward. That's a classic secretive posture. Her head movements are jerky which suggests whatever is happening here is making her nervous.

And then the dancer moves away and we see she's holding a glass out to Bradley.

Tom

And what does their body language tell you about what we're seeing?

Olivia

That's an excellent question. If I just rewind the video a fraction and focus on Bradley, I can tell you that this is a person who is feeling very uncomfortable. He's shifting position and picking at his nails. We can see from his facial expression that he's not smiling. His lips are visibly pinched which suggests a high level of tension or discomfort.

And then moving forward again, we have Lynn holding out a glass and talking to Bradley. When people are relaxed we expect to see smiles and laughter, we would see a certain amount of movement between both people. Shoulders are usually lifted, heads are raised. There would be nodding and body touching; hair flicking is common for women, whereas men tend to touch their jawline. We're not seeing any of that here. I obviously can't tell you what's being said, but I can tell you that it's an intense conversation.

Bradley is stood with his back to the wall. He's not leaning so much as pressing his whole body against it as though he wishes he could take another step back. His body is slightly turned away from Lynn which suggests he's not open to their conversation. Bradley is showing all the signs of someone who wants to be somewhere else.

In contrast, Lynn is leaning forward. Her lips are moving very fast so we know she's talking quickly. See how she's gesticulating her free hand near her face. We do this movement when we want our words to carry more weight.

In my expert opinion, Lynn is trying to convince Bradley to calm down and take the drink, and based on how Lynn is looking over her shoulder – here and then here – I'd say she's anxious no one sees her do this.

Bradley does eventually take the glass reluctantly. He's looking at the liquid, his forehead furrowing. Lynn even touches the glass as though wanting to tip it into his mouth.

I would say that social conventions kick in here. Bradley is only eighteen. He is young. He is used to respecting adults and doing what he's told. We know this from his school reports. I would say that he feels compelled to drink it so as not to appear rude, and he does then drink it.

LOCATION: TOM'S STUDY

Tom
Wow. That was so interesting. Olivia has really hammered home exactly my feelings on the video – that something weird was going on between Bradley and Lynn.

Why was Lynn so keen for him to take that drink? Did she put something in it, and if so, what? Only two people can tell us the answers to these questions and one of them hasn't been seen for twenty years. I am so desperate to talk to Lynn and find out what happened to Bradley after this video was shot.

Join me next week where I track down the third witness – Dale Peterson – who, in addition to Lynn and Taylor, claimed to have seen Bradley get in the taxi with him and his friends, and then walk away when they got to Richmond. He lied to the police about that night and I want to find out why.

Tom Isaac Investigates: What really happened to Bradley Wilcox?
Episode 4: The 2003 party video – What are we seeing?

PUBLISHED ON YOUTUBE AND SPOTIFY:
FRIDAY, 25 AUGUST 2023

5,787 COMMENTS

Wendy Clarke
OMG Tom. That threat is so scary. I hope you're OK!

Katy Shepard
What if Bradley saw something or did something that night and the Lancasters gave him a shit ton of money to run away and never come back? If someone offered me a million pounds, I'd be straight out the door.

> **SyfyGeek90**
> Where did he go then? His passport was still at home.
>
> **Katy Shepard**
> As if people like the Lancasters don't have ways around passports.
>
> **SyfyGeek90**
> They're not super spies! Just because you're rich, it doesn't mean you've got criminals on speed dial. Ed wasn't even a businessman. He was an ex-footballer and a football agent. Hardly one of the Kray brothers.

KMoorcroft58
Bradley could've got a flight to somewhere in the UK without needing a passport and then got a private yacht anywhere in the world. They don't check passports at every marina.

Katy Shepard
Just checked and there's a private airfield less than an hour away from Hampton Wick where the Lancasters live. It's called Blackbushe. I remembered it because Taylor used it once when she flew to Paris for a fashion thing. Worth checking out if any flights left the day after the party??

LancasterFANMAN
I did try to warn you, Tom. Don't mess with the Lancasters or someone might mess with you . . .

TI_BiggestFan
You are a despicable human being!!! Hiding behind an anonymous name and threatening Tom. He is only trying to find the truth and help Cassie.

JulieAlexander_1
Have you seen this, Tom? Might be worth getting the police to track this user's IP address.

EXTRACTS FROM INTERVIEWS RECORDED
BY THE METROPOLITAN POLICE
BETWEEN 22–24 FEBRUARY 2023

Location: Twickenham Police Station

Taylor Lancaster: The video was a complete shock. Perhaps you saw the show of us looking through our childhood things? No. OK, well it was part of an episode.

Locke found the one of the party and Dad dancing and thought it would be fun to share as a tribute to mark the anniversary of his death. None of us even twigged that Bradley was in the background of the video until some of our fans commented on it.

Locke Lancaster: I vaguely remember Bradley. I think he came to the house a few times to pick up his sister, Cassie, who was friends with Taylor. But I was only thirteen and wasn't allowed at the party.

Sorry, just to be clear, I was there – in the house, but not at the party. Me and India were upstairs the whole time. It was adults only and we were too young. We watched films and went to bed.

India Lancaster: No one ever told me anything. I was like Macaulay Culkin in *Home Alone*. The little kid everyone forgets about. The first I knew about Bradley being missing was when the police came to the house the Monday after the party and spoke to Mum and Dad.

Taylor Lancaster: The timings? I don't know what to say about that to be honest. It was all so long ago. I swear I remember seeing Bradley with those other lads – the footballers. They were going clubbing in Richmond and I thought Bradley grabbed a lift with them.

Lynn Lancaster: I've written a statement which I'll now read.

Bradley Wilcox was invited to my late husband's fortieth birthday party by my eldest daughter, Taylor. He had a few drinks and then he got into a taxi with a group of four footballers from Crystal Palace.

Sorry? No, I don't remember their names. I gave officers in the original investigation a list of party guests in attendance. I didn't keep a copy.

At the time of the party and up until Monday the thirteenth of February this year when I checked comments on series seventeen, episode seven of *Living with the Lancasters*, I believed, as previously stated, that Bradley left our home in that taxi. I now assume Bradley changed his mind and got out of the taxi after I saw him get in, and he remained at the party.

We had fireworks in the garden shortly before 1 a.m. and all the guests left soon afterwards. I can only assume that Bradley either got a lift with one of the guests leaving then or walked home.

VIDEO RECORDING FOUND DURING A
POLICE SEARCH OF THE LANCASTER PROPERTY
ON 13 SEPTEMBER 2023

Evidence item no: 142

Description: Extract from home video recording, 31 December 1998

Taylor's interview

Ed: Here we are again in the hot seat. It's New Year's Eve, 1998. How old are you, Taylor?

Taylor: Twelve.

Ed: Twelve going on twenty-one.

Taylor: *Daa-aad.*

Ed: [Laughing] Sorry. What do you want to achieve this year?

[Background voice] **Lynn:** Hang on, Ed. Taylor, move your hair away from your eyes. We want the camera to see your beautiful face.

Taylor: Better?

[Background voice] **Lynn:** Much better.

Ed: So . . .

Taylor: I want to get a part in the school play. It's *Alice in Wonderland*.

[Background voice] **Lynn:** You want to be Alice, don't you?

Taylor: Mum, one of the older girls will get that.

[Background voice] **Lynn:** With that attitude they certainly will. You've got to want it, Taylor. You want to make Mummy and Daddy proud, don't you?

Taylor: OK, Mum. I want to be Alice.

Ed: And what do you want to be when you grow up?

Taylor: An actress.

Locke's interview

Ed: Here he is. My boy. Welcome to the hot seat, Locke. It's New Year's Eve, 1998. How old are you?

Locke: I'm nine.

Ed: And what do you want to achieve next year?

Locke: I want to score lots of goals.

Ed: Good answer. What do you want to be when you grow up?

Locke: A footballer.

Ed: Keep practising and you will be.

[Background voice] **Lynn:** Don't you want to be an actor, Locke? Miss Debbie said you've got a lot of potential. I think you'd be a lovely actor.

Locke: Maybe. I'd rather play football like Dad.

India's interview

India: I'm India Lancaster. It's New Year's Eve, 1998. I'm five years old. Next year I want to solve a mystery and I want to stop doing drama classes. And when I grow up I want to be a detective.

Ed: I see.

[Background voice] **Lynn:** A famous detective?

India: No, Mummy. A police detective. Can I stop going to Miss Debbie's drama school on Saturdays? It's boring.

[Background voice] **Lynn:** No, you need the lessons.

India: Why?

Lynn: You just do.

Ed: Surely if she's—

[Background voice] **Lynn:** We've talked about this, Ed.

Ed: You're right. Come on, India. Let's go get you ready for bed.

India: Can I come to the party?

[Background voice] **Lynn:** Not this year, honey. It's time for your medicine.

SEPTEMBER 2023

TRANSCRIPT FROM SKY NEWS LIVE
WITH PATRICK MONAGHAN AND
AMBER CARNEY, 1 SEPTEMBER 2023

Patrick: You're watching *Sky News Breakfast* on Friday the first of September. The time is eight fifty-four. Before today's top stories, Amber Carney joins us to share the celebrity news hitting the headlines this week.

Amber: Thank you, Patrick. Reality TV star Lynn Lancaster is in the spotlight again this week. She was seen walking into Twickenham Police Station with her solicitor on Monday to answer questions on the Bradley Wilcox missing persons investigation, triggering headlines like 'Make Her Talk' and 'What is Lynn Hiding?'

Several stories include a source inside the police investigation claiming that Lynn is refusing to answer questions, and until she tells the police what, if anything, she knows, the investigation into Bradley's disappearance has stalled again. Which is frustrating news for the police and, of course, for Bradley's sister, Cassie Wilcox.

Patrick: This story has been dragging on now for six months. Can we expect a conclusion any time soon?

Amber: It's hard to say. There's a real pressure-cooker feeling among members of the press at the moment. It's certainly difficult to see how Lynn can continue her campaign of silence.

2022 trending video: #LWTLFavMoments

@BengyBold888

We'd all sit around the computer on a Sunday night to watch the show. My mum and my two sisters and me all crammed into a tiny box room where the computer lived. Then later on, an iPad balanced on Mum's lap on the sofa. It's so much easier now with smart TVs.

My sisters loved India and all the modelling stuff she did. There was one photoshoot where the whole family came along to watch and the shoot director put them all into hair and make-up and instead of the photos being of just India lying on a bed with a sheet draped over her, all four of them were squeezed into this double bed wearing matching tartan pjs. The expression on their faces was hilarious, like even they were all thinking WTF. That was pretty funny.

I don't know why I liked the show. There was something normal about them. Like, you could tell that at the end of the day they were a family who loved each other even if they did fight all the time. That was me and my sisters. It made us appreciate what we had, I think.

You know they never apologized to each other on the show? It was like, well, we're family so even if we fight, we're going to get on. We did that too. They didn't hold a grudge, even when Taylor answered Locke's phone while he was in the shower and then forgot to give him the message, and he missed this big meeting with a breakfast show TV producer. That fight was massive.

Tom Isaac Investigates: What really happened to Bradley Wilcox?
Episode 5: The third witness – what did they see?

PUBLISHED ON YOUTUBE AND SPOTIFY:
FRIDAY, 1 SEPTEMBER 2023

LOCATION: TOM'S STUDY

Tom

Welcome back to *Tom Isaac Investigates*. Before we start today's episode, I want to say thank you for all of your messages and kind words after I received the threat last week. Yes, I am taking it seriously – I've installed a doorbell camera – but no, it's not going to stop me.

In fact, I've tracked down Dale Peterson, the third witness to tell police that he not only saw Bradley get in the taxi, but also travel with the group to Richmond and get out again.

Let's think about that for a moment.

We know from the police investigation that the cab was logged by the taxi firm's computer system as having arrived at the Lancaster house at 11.45 p.m. The taxi travelled to Richmond and stopped outside a nightclub on King Street at 12.17 a.m.

So how was Bradley back at the party at twelve fifteen talking to Lynn? It's not possible, which is why I'm keen to chat to Dale today and find out why he lied to the police.

Dale is a taxi driver himself now and would only speak to me if I was a paying customer, which means Javi and I are about to spend the afternoon in the back of a taxi, driving the streets of Slough. Let's see what Dale has to say, shall we?

LOCATION: TAXI, SLOUGH, BERKSHIRE (20 MILES WEST OF LONDON)
INTERVIEW BETWEEN TOM ISAAC AND DALE PETERSON

Tom

Dale Peterson has just collected us from Slough train station and we're sitting in traffic heading towards the town centre.

Dale, thanks so much for talking to us today. As I said on the phone, I'm an investigative journalist trying to uncover what really happened to Bradley Wilcox the night of Ed Lancaster's fortieth birthday party in August 2003. You told the police back then that Bradley was in the taxi with you when you left the Lancasters' home at 11.45 p.m., which makes you the last person to see Bradley before he disappeared. What can you tell us about that night?

Dale

Er . . . yeah. I told this all to the police a few months back. I really want to help and everything, but I got nothing new, man. I know about the video that came out and I guess I was mistaken about Bradley being in the taxi. It was so long ago and I was pretty drunk that night.

Where do you want to go?

Tom

Anywhere is fine. Just drive around. Why were you invited to Ed's party?

Dale

Ed was my agent – he'd got me a new contract at Crystal Palace the year before the party – they were in the First Division at the time so it was a good level. I wasn't fussed about going to the party but Lynn invited me and it was free food and booze so me and a couple of the other Crystal Palace lads Ed represented went along.

Lynn was sort of like Ed's PA or gatekeeper, it felt like. She took my calls and booked stuff with me, but she didn't do the deals, so I thought going to the party might give me a chance to chat to Ed one to one about my career.

I wasn't getting a look-in for the first team and felt I was running out of time to get my shot, you see. That's the kind of thing your agent should help with. I wasn't always a fat slob. I used to be really fit. I could've gone all the way – I was a striker – but I never got that right place, right time moment. Then I got a knee injury at twenty-five and realized I didn't have shit to my name.

Tom

I'm sorry to hear that. What can you tell us about the party? Who was there?

Dale

No idea. It looked to me like a bunch of old people pretending they weren't old. I know it was Ed's birthday, but it felt more like Lynn's party. She was in this strapless gold dress and greeting everyone like we were all her long-lost friends. From what I could tell, Ed didn't give a toss. For the entire time I was there, he pretty much stayed in the corner, talking to a group of blokes.

Tom

I hear the theme was gold?

Dale

Ha! The theme was 'Look how much money we have', but yeah, we were all supposed to wear gold. I didn't have anything so I bought this really cheap gold-looking chain necklace from the market. Probably looked like a total wanker but that's nineteen for ya. It's like I tell my boy – kids have no idea how easy they've got it until it ain't easy any more. Not that he ever listens to me.

Anyway, there was gold everywhere. A gold carpet leading up the front steps of the house and into this massive entrance hall. They even made the pool water look like it was gold liquid.

I suppose it would all be considered a bit tacky now, but I remember being impressed.

I probably spent the first ten minutes just looking around the place with my mouth hanging open, but after that it all got a bit hazy. There was champagne everywhere. Bottles stacked in ice buckets people could just take. Trays of gold champagne flutes being carried round by half-naked male waiters. You couldn't move without someone topping up your glass.

We got there about nine, and by ten I was pretty hammered. We'd just finished pre-season and had the first game of the season coming up, so it wasn't too professional, but – you know – nineteen and not getting a look-in. Anyway, everyone was hammered. It was carnage. Dancing, laughing, swimming. They had these canvas tents in the garden set up as changing rooms with swimwear of every size. I'm pretty sure some people were going into those changing rooms together for some privacy, if you catch my drift? It was that kind of vibe.

At about eleven, me and my mates decided we wanted to go clubbing. Most of the women were either too old or out of our league and we were all single and wanted to pull. So we booked a taxi to take us into Richmond. My mate Tonko knew about this nightclub we could get into for free. The taxi arrived and we left. That's all I remember. As soon as I got into the club, I was doing shots.

Tom
And at what point during the evening did you meet Bradley Wilcox?

Dale
Er . . .

[Pause]

I'm not sure. It was so long ago.

Tom
You told the police several days after the party that you remember Bradley getting into the taxi with you. Can you tell me about that memory?

Dale
Yeah. I did say that when the police called me, and I did genuinely believe it.

Tom
You believed it or you remembered it?

Dale
Remembered. I remember him getting into the taxi.

Tom
And travelling with you to King Street, Richmond?

Dale
Yes. Look, we almost done or what?

Tom
I just have a few more questions if you don't mind. The taxi firm – Richmond Rides – had a computerized booking system and GPS on all of its taxis. So we know with absolute certainty that the taxi arrived at the Lancaster home at 11.45 p.m. on the night of the party and drove away from King Street at 12.17 a.m.

Dale
If you say so. I wasn't looking at the clock. Don't expect to get asked this stuff twenty years later.

Tom
What I'm wondering, Dale, is how Bradley could be in the taxi with you at the same time that he's seen on film still at the party talking to Lynn.

[Pause]

Tom
Dale?

Dale
Like I told the police in February, I've no idea, mate. I must've been mistaken.

Tom
I don't think you were mistaken at all. I believe you lied to the police when they asked you in the days after Bradley's disappearance, and I believe you've been lying for twenty years. The evidence is all there on the video, Dale. So why did you lie?

[Inaudible mumbling]

Tom
What was that?

Dale
I didn't lie, OK?

Tom
But you weren't mistaken either, were you? What happened, Dale? You can tell me. I just want the truth for Cassie. She has spent over half of her life not knowing what happened to her brother that night. Doesn't she deserve some answers?

[Pause]

Dale

Yeah, yeah, she does. Look, I've never told anyone this before – not 'cause I was trying to hide something or anything like that. I just never thought it was relevant, but maybe it is.

[Loud exhale]

So, the Monday after the party I got a call from Lynn. She starts off like she's calling all the guests to thank them for coming to the party. Real friendly, lots of chit-chat. Then she said, 'Ed really enjoyed your chat on Saturday. He sees something in you, Dale. You remind him of what he was like as a young player. He thinks Palace are mad for overlooking you – thinks there'll be Premier League interest if he puts some feelers out.'

I was stoked. Football was all I was good at, and finally my agent was giving me a chance to move up.

Lynn goes on to say that Ed is good friends with a scout at Tottenham who he knows saw me score in pre-season. Says he'll be speaking to the scout and the Tottenham manager soon.

Tom

Did she mention Bradley to you on that call?

Dale

Yeah, yeah, sorry, I'm getting to it. So, Lynn said she'd call me soon about Tottenham, that she knew there weren't long left in the transfer window et cetera, and we're wrapping up the call when she mentioned that lad. She said, 'By the way, you know that boy, Bradley, who jumped in the taxi with you? He's gone missing. The police are looking for him and they'll probably give you a call. We're all very worried.'

I started saying that I didn't remember him being in the taxi and Lynn got a bit funny with me. She said, 'How can you not remember? I saw him get in right behind you. If you don't remember something that happened two days ago, maybe you're not as reliable as Ed thought you were. How drunk were you? You have to be disciplined to make it at Premier League level.'

So really quick I was like, 'Oh yeah, that guy. I remember.'

Then after a bit I started thinking maybe I did actually remember that. I was pretty wasted but I had vague memories of someone chatting to us as we were booking the taxi and asking if they could get a lift with us.

When the police came to see me on the Monday night, they said they had two witnesses that saw Bradley get in the taxi and leave the party, and so I told them that I was really drunk but yeah, I remembered Bradley getting in the taxi too. God's honest truth, I thought that was what happened.

Tom

And did Lynn or Ed ever call about the Tottenham move?

Dale

Yeah. I was getting nervous because the window was about to shut and I hadn't heard anything, then right near the end of the month she text me just like she said she would. Said the manager was keen but the board had said they'd only give him money for one more player and he'd chosen someone else. I was gutted and went to their training ground anyway, just in case I could change his mind, but security wouldn't even let me through the gates.

It was humiliating, man.

Tom

Let me make sure I've got this right. Lynn calls you and dangles a chance for all of your dreams to come true right in front of you, under the condition that you remember Bradley was in the taxi with you? At what point did it occur to you that you were played?

Dale
I dunno if I was, to be honest. Me and Ed did chat at the party about my future and I was a great footballer. I was in the same youth team as Ashley Cole in the mid-nineties, and I was a better footballer than he was any day of the week. It was just bad luck that move didn't come off, and then the manager got sacked before the transfer window opened again.

Ed was still working on getting me something else but then he died, didn't he?

Tom
It sounds like you lied to the police because you thought it would help your career. A career that meant everything to you, so perhaps that's understandable.

Dale
Yeah, exactly. Football was my dream. And it wasn't like I was the only person, right? When you're told over and over that something happened, you believe it. I was wasted that night. Lynn told me Bradley got in the taxi. And the police told me they had another witness too. Why wouldn't I believe them? I didn't want to be the idiot who couldn't remember. So maybe I sort of convinced myself because, like you said, my career meant everything to me.

I've felt bad for years about what happened. I believed that lad was in the taxi. I believed I was the last person to see him that night. Maybe if I hadn't been so drunk, I'd have remembered something that could've helped him. Turns out, I hadn't needed to worry though, hey? Not that I'm saying I lied. I just . . . I convinced myself of something.

Tom
Why didn't you tell the police after the video first emerged in February?

Dale
I dunno. Probably didn't want to get in trouble, like. But I feel bad for that lad's sister. It's not exactly like I'm living the high life here, is it? Might as well do one decent thing now.

To: Tom@TomIsaacInvestigates.com
From: Lynn@LivingWithTheLancasters.com
Subject: RE: Interview request for Tom Isaac Investigates
Date: 01.09.23

Hi Tom,

I'm thinking I should talk to you. The press are not going to stop hounding me until I say something. This has got completely out of hand! But if I'm going to talk to anyone, I'd rather it be someone who knows us and isn't out to draw blood.

I think you'll be very interested in what I have to say about Cassie. She's not who she seems!

I assume you're fine to provide the questions in advance for approval?

Lynn x

To: Lynn@LivingWithTheLancasters.com
From: Tom@TomIsaacInvestigates.com
Subject: RE: Interview request for Tom Isaac Investigates
Date: 01.09.23

Hi Lynn,
Great to hear from you. Of course, that all sounds fine. Let me know when would suit you for the interview.
 I'd love to talk to Taylor as well, if that's possible?
 Thanks,
 Tom x

Tom Isaac Investigates: What really happened to Bradley Wilcox?

Episode 5: The third witness – what did they see? (cont.)

PUBLISHED ON YOUTUBE AND SPOTIFY:
FRIDAY, 1 SEPTEMBER 2023

LOCATION: SLOUGH STATION

Tom

Dale has just dropped us back at Slough station. We have . . . six? Yes, six minutes before our train back to London, and so I'm recording this conclusion now because it's Friday and I know a lot of you will be waiting at 7 p.m. to see this episode, and I don't want to disappoint you.

So, what did you think of Dale?

We knew of course that he'd lied to the police, but we didn't know, until a few minutes ago, *why*. According to Dale, he was coerced by Lynn into falsely telling the police Bradley was in the taxi. What he did was not only wrong, it was illegal, but I've come away feeling sorry for Dale. He had these big dreams to be a footballer and clearly his life hasn't panned out how he'd hoped. That doesn't excuse what he's done, of course!

The big question we need to ask now, is why – why did Lynn ask Dale to lie? And in the last few minutes I've had email correspondence with Lynn about a potential interview. This is really exciting, guys. Lynn hasn't spoken publicly or, from what we can tell, to the police about the night of Bradley's disappearance, but it looks like she might talk to us.

In the next episode, Cassie and I meet with retired police officer Badru Zubira – the lead detective on the 2003 investigation into Bradley Wilcox's disappearance. I really want to understand where the police investigation went so wrong, and I have *a lot* of questions.

Tom Isaac Investigates: What really happened to Bradley Wilcox?
Episode 5: The third witness – what did they see?

PUBLISHED ON YOUTUBE AND SPOTIFY:
FRIDAY, 1 SEPTEMBER 2023

7,131 COMMENTS

LWTL_No1Fan
I literally spat my coffee out when he said, 'I've not told anyone this before.'

> **TI_BiggestFan**
> Tom always gets them talking!

TrueCrime_Junkie1001
Lynn was definitely covering up for something. But what?

JulieAlexander_1
Things aren't looking good for Lynn. Hard to see how she'll talk her way out of this one. I wonder if the threat came from her?

TrueCrime_Junkie1001
Where is the original taxi driver who picked those boys up from the party? I assume the police spoke to him as well? Tom, can you track him down?

> **Katy Shepard**
> Just because Bradley didn't get in the taxi, it doesn't mean he didn't leave the party later. Why are we all assuming Lynn is the bad guy? I still think he might have run away.

Wendy Clarke
Why didn't the police spend any time questioning the Lancasters about Bradley's text? He literally told Cassie something bad was happening.

To: Tom@TomIsaacInvestigates.com
From: Cassie_Wilcox@BlueInternet.com
Subject: Latest episode
Date: 02.09.23

I knew it! I *knew* Lynn got to Dale.

I could kill him right now! I could kill Lynn, for that matter!

I wish I could say I can't believe the lengths that woman has gone to in messing with the police investigation into Bradley's disappearance but I don't think anything can surprise me about this family any more.

See you Monday,

Cassie xx

EXTRACTS FROM INTERVIEWS RECORDED
BY THE METROPOLITAN POLICE
ON 4 SEPTEMBER 2023

Location: Twickenham Police Station

Lynn Lancaster: As I've said now on numerous occasions, no, I don't remember the conversation with Bradley on the video. It was twenty years ago. I was talking to everyone that night.

No, I don't remember Dale Peterson or any conversation with him. Maybe you should be asking him why his memory is suddenly crystal clear when he's previously claimed he'd been drinking heavily on the night of the party.

Are we done? Because, quite frankly, this is a waste of my time and it's a waste of your time. This is a witch hunt orchestrated by a sad, attention-seeking woman.

Yes, I mean Cassie Wilcox. If anyone should be questioned by you, it's her. If I didn't feel sorry for her over Bradley going missing, I'd sue her for defamation. Her lies are damaging our brand. She's always been jealous of Taylor. She'd do anything to bring us all down.

I'm not answering any more questions.

Jonathon Cartwright, Solicitor: I refer you to my client's earlier statement.

Taylor Lancaster: OK, so I didn't actually see Bradley get in the taxi, but I knew he was planning to leave and he was talking to those lads earlier in the evening about getting a lift with them. Mum said she saw him get in and I know it was naughty to say I saw it too but . . . er . . . could I have a moment alone with my lawyer now please?

VIDEO RECORDING FOUND DURING A POLICE SEARCH OF THE LANCASTER PROPERTY ON 13 SEPTEMBER 2023

Evidence item no: 145

Description: Extract from home video recording, 31 December 2000

Taylor's interview

Ed: Taylor, come on. It's your turn first.

[Background voice] **Taylor:** In a sec, Dad. I'm just getting ready.

Ed: Ready for what?

Taylor: This.

Ed: I see. And are you ready now?

Taylor: Yes. You may start.

Ed: It's New Year's Eve in the year 2000. How old are you, Taylor?

Taylor: I'm fourteen years old.

Ed: What do you want to achieve in 2001?

Taylor: I want to be the most popular girl in school.

[Background voice] **Lynn:** You already are, sweetheart.

Taylor: I can be more popular, then.

Ed: You don't want to be the lead in the school play again?

Taylor: I don't need to want that, Dad. The part is mine.

[Background voice] **Lynn:** Good girl. I'm very proud of you, Taylor.

Ed: All right then. And what do you want to be when you grow up?

Taylor: I want to be famous.

Ed: Famous for what? Acting?

Taylor: I don't care. As long as I'm famous. Can I go now?

Ed: Sure. Hey, Cassie, stop hiding in the doorway and come sit down. You can have a go.

Cassie: Um . . . OK.

Ed: Cassie, how old are you?

Taylor: Dad, you know she's the same age as me.

Ed: All right. You're fourteen. What do you want to achieve next year?

Cassie: I want to get into top set in maths like my brother is.

Ed: Maybe you could take Taylor with you, too.

[Background voice] **Lynn:** [Laughing] Taylor doesn't need maths for her future.

Ed: So, Cassie, what do you want to be when you grow up?

Taylor: Cassie is going to be my assistant, aren't you, Cassie? You can reply to all my fan letters.

Ed: I'm sure Cassie has bigger plans than that?

Cassie: I don't know what I want to be yet. Sorry.

Ed: That's OK. You're still young. You have plenty of time to decide.

Taylor: Yeah, unless you live in this family, and then you have to know from the moment you're born. [Laughing]

Locke's interview

Ed: It's New Year's Eve, the last day of the year 2000. Locke, how old are you?

Locke: Eleven.

Ed: And what do you want to achieve this year?

Locke: I want to get back into the first team at Wick Rovers. I don't like playing in the second team. We always lose.

Ed: Anything else?

Locke: No.

Ed: What do you want to be when you grow up?

Locke: A footballer.

Ed: Have you got any back-up ideas?

[Background voice] **Lynn:** Ed, leave it.

Locke: Leave what?

Ed: I just don't want you to put all your eggs in one basket, Locke. I'm not sure you even enjoy playing football. You seem a lot happier doing the drama stuff.

Locke: Why don't you just tell me I'm a rubbish footballer? I know that's what you think.

Ed: That's not true.

Locke: Yes it is. India heard you telling Mum last week.

Ed: Locke, wait. Come back.

[Background voice] **Lynn:** Let him cool off for a minute.

Ed: I shouldn't have said that about him. I never meant for him to hear it. We need to be careful what we say. Eavesdropping on a conversation about Locke is one thing. If any of them find out—

[Background voice] **Lynn:** Ed, the camera is still on.

India's interview

Ed: It's New Year's Eve, 2000. India, tell the camera how old you are.

India: I'm seven years and nine months old.

Ed: What do you want to achieve in 2001?

India: I'd like to stop doing acting lessons and I'd like to create a new detective club at school.

[Background voice] **Lynn:** India, we've talked about that. Miss Debbie's drama school is good for you.

India: Sorry, Mummy.

Ed: What do you want to be when you grow up, India?

India: Same as last year and the year before that. I want to be a detective. Or maybe a scientist.

[Background voice] **Lynn:** I thought you wanted to be a model. You've got the perfect bone structure. It would make Mummy very happy if you said you wanted to be a model.

India: I want to be a detective, a scientist and a model.

EXTRACT FROM EVIDENCE COLLECTED
BY THE METROPOLITAN POLICE FROM THE
LANCASTER PROPERTY ON 22 NOVEMBER 2023

Item No: 1

Description: Notebook titled 'Detective's Notes 1 by India Lancaster, age 8'

Thursday, 29 March 2001

It was my birthday yesterday. Mum and Dad got me a Dictaphone. It's the same kind reporters and private detectives use for interviews and to make notes. I'm going to use it every day and write up what I hear in my detective's notebook.

Overheard conversation (recorded and transcribed):

Dad: Darling, can you listen to this soundbite for my TV interview tomorrow?

Mum: Sure. What are you going to say?

Dad: Youth football needs a massive overhaul to protect the rights of young and often vulnerable men who will do anything to play football. Managers, agents, clubs and the footballers themselves need to continue to put pressure on the FA.

Mum: Sounds good. You could add – 'That's why I became a football agent. To protect talented young individuals.' You want to remind them that you are the hero who's come to save them.

Overheard conversation (recorded and transcribed):

Taylor: Why do I have to go? I don't know anything about football.

Mum: It's a TV studio. There will be lots of people there. You don't know who might be on the lookout for talent.

Taylor: Fine, I'll go. But we'd need to go to Harvey Nics on the way home. I've run out of lip balm.

Notes

Mrs Simpson is coming to babysit tomorrow because Mum, Dad and Taylor are going to a TV studio. I will use this time to look for clues about Dad's golf trips. Why does he only get a bad back when he plays golf in this country but not in Portugal?

Tom Isaac Investigates: What really happened to Bradley Wilcox?
Episode 6: The detective

PUBLISHED ON YOUTUBE AND SPOTIFY:
FRIDAY, 8 SEPTEMBER 2023

LOCATION: BADRU ZUBIRA'S KITCHEN, BRIGHTON
INTERVIEW BETWEEN TOM ISAAC, CASSIE WILCOX AND BADRU ZUBIRA

Tom

Welcome back to *Tom Isaac Investigates*. In this episode we're going behind the scenes of the 2003 police investigation and what went wrong in the days, weeks and months that followed Bradley Wilcox's disappearance.

As you can see, I'm sitting at a breakfast bar in a bright and open kitchen overlooking the sea near Brighton, one of my favourite places on earth. One day I will drum up the courage to move out of Mumsie's house and maybe even London, my second favourite place on earth.

That noise in the background is Snowy playing in the garden with a beautiful black Labrador called Fenton. I've brought with me my favourite WC2 coffee. They've got a new roast called Fina Galeras. It's from Colombia and it's absolutely heavenly. This episode is being sponsored by WC2 and you can find a discount code in the show notes.

Sitting beside me, I have Cassie, and opposite us is Badru Zubira, the lead detective on Bradley's original missing persons case. I thought it would be good to have Cassie with us for this interview to share her memories on what was happening from the family's perspective.

I've just told Badru about my chat with Dale Peterson. Badru has called a colleague who is working on the investigation into Bradley's disappearance, and Cassie and I are both a bit emotional so bear with us.

Cassie
Sorry. I'm fine. It's just . . . at this point in time, twenty years later, you don't expect to make breakthroughs. I didn't think I had any hope left inside me. I've not wanted to believe we'd ever actually find anything this time around.

[Exhales]

Plus seeing Badru again is quite unsettling. No offence, Badru.

Badru
None taken. It's good to see you, Cassie. You're looking very well.

Cassie
I'm looking a mess, but thanks. You haven't aged a bit.

Badru
The benefit of losing all my hair in my twenties is that there's nothing to go grey.

[Laughing]

Tom
When was the last time you saw each other?

Cassie
It was probably about three months after Bradley's disappearance. I remember you knocking on the door, and knowing it was you before Dad was even out of his chair. You had this special knock, like a firm, hard . . .

[Knocking]

Dad led you into the living room and I wanted to go in too but something held me back. The walls were so thin I could hear everything you said anyway, and so I stayed in the kitchen making a beef stew and just listened. I think I knew what you'd come to say and I wanted to cry so badly but I was trying to hold it together for Mum.

You said you'd exhausted all avenues of the investigation, and that while the case would remain open, until a new lead presented itself you'd been moved to work on other things. Basically, you told us it was over.

Badru
A difficult conversation to have with family members, but always best to do in person and to be direct and clear.

Cassie
My dad appreciated that.

Badru
I won't pretend to understand how difficult things have been for you and your family, Cassie. I truly hope this time around, you find the answers you're looking for.

Here, my wife made some apple cake. Help yourselves.

How do you want to start, Tom?

Tom
Would you mind introducing yourself to the viewers?

Badru
Sure. My name is Badru Zubira. I was with the Metropolitan Police from 1993 to 2018 and left the force as a Deputy Assistant Commissioner, which is a few rungs up the ladder from my police constable

days in the nineties. I spent the majority of my career as a detective and, since retiring, I've continued to work with the Met and Sussex Police as a civilian consultant. I get called in for major incidents when they need more bodies working cases, or when certain investigations have stalled and they want a fresh pair of eyes.

In August 2003, when Bradley Wilcox was reported as a missing person, I was working out of Twickenham Police Station as a detective sergeant and took the lead on the investigation.

Tom
What can you tell us about Bradley's missing persons case?

Badru
The main problem we faced was the lack of actual evidence. All we had were three witnesses who saw Bradley leaving the Lancaster residence in a taxi on the night of Saturday the second of August. The taxi didn't have a dash cam or CCTV but we were able to confirm the time of the booking with their online tracking system, so we knew the time the taxi left the Lancaster home.

The taxi driver was one of the first people we spoke to. Unfortunately, he wasn't helpful. He remembered the call out to the party. He told us that there were a lot of people standing in the driveway smoking or talking. It was dark and it was his last job of the night.

He pulled up and straight away the side door was opened and a group of loud party-goers got in. He described them as male and drunk. The taxi was a people carrier capable of taking up to eight passengers with seats behind seats, and the driver said that the group crowded into the back seats and were jumping around and shouting, and all he was focused on was getting them to their destination before they were sick.

We asked him if there were four or five people in the taxi, and he said he thought there were six based on the noise levels, and he couldn't give a description of any of them. He dropped the group on

King Street in Richmond without making any stops. They paid in cash, and he drove away.

Tom
Was there any CCTV on King Street?

Badru
Yes, there was, but again, we didn't get lucky. The angle wasn't right for where the taxi stopped. The street was busy with groups queueing for one of the nightclubs or just standing on the street talking. It was a hot evening and there were a lot of pub-goers milling about after closing time.

Despite a lack of CCTV footage or corroboration from the taxi driver, we still had witness statements from Lynn and Taylor Lancaster and from Dale Peterson, giving us every reason to believe at the time that Bradley had been in the taxi that night. This gave us three possible theories.

One: between leaving the taxi and reaching his home, which was a twenty-minute walk from Richmond to East Twickenham, Bradley met an unsavoury character, some form of altercation ensued, and Bradley was killed. With this assumption we believed Bradley's body was thrown in the river.

Two: during the course of Bradley's walk home, he went into the river voluntarily and accidentally drowned. We knew from interviewing party guests that there was a lot of alcohol at the party. The taxi driver also confirmed that the young men he took into Richmond were all very drunk. It was a logical assumption that Bradley could have consumed too much alcohol and made a bad decision that led to his death.

Cassie
I'm sorry, I have to interrupt here. Bradley would never have gone in the Thames. He was a strong swimmer but he wasn't stupid. He was

a lifeguard. He understood the dangers of the current better than most people and never swam in anything but a pool. He also didn't drink alcohol. He tried a beer when he was fifteen and it made him really sick. Mum had an intolerance which meant she couldn't touch a drop without getting really ill, so Bradley thought he might have it too and never drank again. So there was no way he was drunk and went for a swim.

Badru
These are valid points and they were taken into consideration at the time. His job as a lifeguard also gave us cause to speculate that Bradley may have seen a person or animal in trouble in the water and lost his life in an attempted rescue.

Our third and final theory was that Bradley ran away. We knew from speaking to you, Cassie, and several of his friends, that Bradley was under some pressure to fulfil his family's dreams for him. He was an exceptional student who was due to leave for university the following month. Several of his friends told us that Bradley had complained of arguing with his parents about wanting to travel the world and pursue a different career. Possibly as a surf instructor abroad.

Cassie
With what money? Seriously? What money did you theorize that Bradley used to run away? It was farcical. Bradley never turned his phone back on after that night. He didn't access any of the savings he had from nearly three years of working as a lifeguard. He'd saved every penny for university. If his plan was to run away to Thailand, why didn't he take the money out? And his passport is still in our mum's sideboard. He did not run away. Only people with private jets and infinite pots of money would think he could possibly have run away. And don't get me started on the fact that Taylor was one of the people who told you that. She wasn't Bradley's friend. She barely knew him.

Badru

You're absolutely right, Cassie, but we wouldn't have been doing our jobs if we hadn't considered every possibility. We took these factors into account at the time which is why we focused predominantly on theories one and two. A diving team spent three days in the river.

Cassie

They were the worst days of my life.

Badru

After three days, we called off the river search. It was quite possible that our theory of Bradley going in the river was still correct, but that we weren't able to find his body. With a strong current, a body could easily be swept out to sea.

Tom

You mentioned earlier that there was CCTV on King Street.

Badru

That's right, and some streets nearby. Sometimes during an investigation, you get lucky with CCTV and sometimes you don't. In Bradley's case, we didn't. At 12.21 a.m. we had a camera by the river pick up the silhouette of a lone male walking in the direction of Bradley's home. That same camera caught a second male walking in the same direction several minutes later. It was my belief at the time that the first image was Bradley, and the second image, his attacker. I believed up until very recently that Bradley was mugged on his way home.

Tom

You believed he was dead?

Badru
Yes. I always agreed with Cassie that Bradley wouldn't run away. My team combed CCTV footage of railway and bus stations. We checked airports, ferries. We had missing persons posters up. There was not a whisper, and even in 2003, it was virtually impossible to disappear without a trace.

Tom
One of the questions I've been wanting to ask since I first started investigating this case, and something my TIs have picked up on too in the comments on the episodes so far, is why wasn't more done to question Lynn and Taylor's witness statements?

Badru
I understand the question and I also understand the frustration, really I do. This was my case. Finding Bradley was my responsibility. It's a cliché, but every detective has an unsolved case that haunts them for the rest of their life. Bradley's disappearance is my case.

With the benefit of hindsight and the new evidence which has emerged this year, I can look back and wish I'd done things differently. But at the time, my team called everyone on the guest list provided to us by Lynn Lancaster, and no one remembered seeing Bradley after the taxi left.

There was no evidence to suggest anything untoward happened at the party. We interviewed every guest we knew had attended and no one reported any fighting, any crying, or any blocks of time when Lynn or Ed weren't attending to the guests. We asked these questions, we looked for red flags and there weren't any. We had no reason not to believe the three witnesses.

Tom
What about the text message that Bradley sent Cassie at 11 p.m., which read—

Badru

'Things are really messed-up here. I'm coming home. Need to talk ASAP.'

I remember.

Of course we considered it. But the wording is vague. We had to take into account that the picture we were building of Bradley was of a studious and quiet young man. It was very possible that the text he sent Cassie was about the raucous nature of the party.

Tom

What did you think when you saw the party video earlier this year?

Badru

It was a gut punch. Even after twenty years, it hurt.

On one hand, I was happy for Cassie. I knew the video would reignite the investigation both publicly and with the Met, but I was deeply frustrated too. We'd wasted hours of police work on the wrong information, and obviously I had to question if I'd done everything to the best of my ability back then.

But it's important to remember that in all police investigations there is limited time and limited resources. Often we have to make difficult calls on which evidence to follow. Policing is not an exact science either. I can look back and say, 'Yes, we should have questioned the witnesses' reliability,' but in any given case, in any given moment, we are all just doing the best we can with what we're given.

I know this isn't going to make you feel any better, Cassie, or any victim of a crime who feels let down because a case remains unsolved, but it's the truth.

Cassie

Thanks. I'd be lying if I said there weren't times when I blamed the police. Not you specifically, Badru, but more a general frustration at the lack of resources. But there really is only one person to blame – or group of people, I should say – and that's the Lancasters. They are the ones who lied about Bradley, who convinced someone else to lie, who've spent the last twenty years building an empire and pretending like neither Bradley nor I ever existed. They are the ones who deserve to pay.

Tom

We know that Lynn and all three Lancaster siblings have been questioned by the police, but it's been nearly seven months since the party video first exploded online. Can you give us any insight into what's happening inside the investigation now, Badru? Can we expect any more progress or are the police at another dead end?

Badru

I can only speculate as I'm not part of the active investigation.

There are many challenges with historical investigations. It's not as easy as they make it look on the TV shows.

The release of a time-stamped video will have thrown out all previous assumptions, which meant the team investigating Bradley's disappearance were back to square one. The team would have begun a new timeline of events that evening. They would've reviewed witness statements and looked for new witnesses, which is another issue with historical investigations. It's not easy finding people who remember a party from twenty years ago in enough detail to be helpful.

Tom

You know more about this case than anyone, Badru. If you were investigating it, what theories would you be working on right now?

Badru

Like the original investigation, I'd be considering the possibility that Bradley left the party of his own accord, but with a different timeline of after midnight and a different route home. I'd be considering whether Bradley was the victim of a crime on this journey.

Unfortunately, any road traffic cameras or CCTV footage would have been deleted long ago. But I believe this is a theory the police are working on. Last month there was an appeal for information from anyone out in the Richmond and Twickenham areas on the night of August second or the early hours of August third, 2003. It's always a long shot and takes a lot of manpower to wade through the volume of calls that are invariably received.

Cassie
It's also possible he didn't leave the party at all.

Badru
Yes, that's possible, but I will say again that there was no evidence in the original investigation to suggest anything untoward happened during the party.

Cassie
But something must have happened, because my brother didn't come home that night and he didn't leave the party when they said he did. So where is he? Where is Bradley?

To: Tom@TomIsaacInvestigates.com
From: Lynn@LivingWithTheLancasters.com
Subject: RE: Interview request for Tom Isaac Investigates
Date: 04.09.23

Hi Tom,
Come to the house on Monday at 8 a.m. I'll tell you everything you want to know.
   Lynn x

Tom Isaac Investigates: What really happened to Bradley Wilcox?
Episode 6: The detective (cont.)

PUBLISHED ON YOUTUBE AND SPOTIFY:
FRIDAY, 8 SEPTEMBER 2023

LOCATION: CASSIE'S CAR, MOTO SERVICES, PEASE POTTAGE, M23

Tom

We've just pulled into some services on the way back from Brighton. Javi and Cassie have gone to get sandwiches, but I wanted to stay in the car with Snowy so I could record my thoughts while they're fresh.

It was fascinating seeing behind the scenes of the police investigation into Bradley's disappearance. I really expected to be told today about police failings, staff shortages and where the investigation went wrong. But talking to Badru made me realize that the police did what they could with the information they had. Would things have been different if three people hadn't lied about seeing Bradley leave the party? Absolutely. But that didn't happen.

We must speak to Lynn.

I feel certain now that she holds the key to Bradley's disappearance. She was seen on video arguing with him after midnight, and then not only did she lie to the police, but she convinced Dale to lie, and maybe Taylor too.

I just this minute received an email from Lynn confirming our interview for next week. That's right! Lynn Lancaster is going on record answering questions about the night of Ed's fortieth for the very first time, and she's doing it with us. This is big, TIs. Join me next Friday at 7 p.m. for the answers we've all been waiting for.

LOCATION: TOM'S STUDY

Tom

I'm adding this final section to the episode because I've just arrived home from Badru's interview expecting to see Mumsie ready for our dinner out. She's had her hair done today and we always go out on hair days. But instead, I found her on the sofa super upset. Why? Because when she left the hairdresser's today, she found a note in her bag.

This note.

It says, *If Tom doesn't stop investigating the Lancasters then he won't be the only one to get hurt.*

[Pause]

This threat is . . . I don't even have the words. We've called the police and we're waiting now for someone to come and take a statement.

Mumsie is so shaken and I'm . . . I'm upset and also absolutely furious.

Someone out there wants me to leave the Lancasters alone so badly that they've come to my house and threatened me, and then they snuck into my mum's hairdresser's and put a note in her bag while no one was looking. That is . . . really scary and really serious. This person knows where we live and, more than that, they are watching us, they know our routines.

Tom Isaac Investigates: What really happened to Bradley Wilcox?
Episode 6: The detective

PUBLISHED ON YOUTUBE AND SPOTIFY:
FRIDAY, 8 SEPTEMBER 2023

10,567 COMMENTS

Wendy Clarke
OMG Tom. You and your poor mum. Sending my love.

TI_BiggestFan
Be careful Tom xx

Katy Shepard
Maybe it's Bradley making the threats because he doesn't want to be found.

> **Ernie Martin**
> More likely to be Lynn.

LWTL_No1Fan
So excited Tom is talking to Lynn in the Lancaster house!! I hope he gets to talk to Taylor as well.

> **TrueCrime_Junkie1001**
> And get justice for Bradley too!!

TRANSCRIPT FROM SKY NEWS LIVE
WITH PATRICK MONAGHAN AND
AMBER CARNEY, 10 SEPTEMBER 2023

Patrick: It's Sunday the tenth of September. I'm Patrick Monaghan and you're watching *Sky News Breakfast*. We're going live to Amber Carney from outside the home of Lynn Lancaster.

Amber: Good morning, Patrick. Rumours have been circulating among the press that an arrest could be imminent for Lynn after Dale Peterson – a key witness claiming to have seen Bradley Wilcox leaving the Lancaster home on the night he disappeared in 2003 – retracted his statement. Dale has since been questioned by police.

We can see that all is currently quiet in the Lancaster home behind me, but I'll be reporting here throughout the day as this story unfolds.

Patrick: Are we expecting a public statement or comment from Lynn or any of the other Lancasters today?

Amber: While nothing would surprise me about this family, I think the answer to that is no. In Friday's episode of *Tom Isaac Investigates*, investigative journalist Tom Isaac revealed the rather surprising news that he will be talking to Lynn in a tell-all interview in the coming week.

Dozens of photographers and press have been camped outside the Lancaster home in West London for weeks now, and it's no exaggeration to say that we are all holding our breath waiting for Lynn's interview to land on Friday. It really can't come soon enough if the Lancasters have any chance of salvaging their reality show ratings after over ten million people unsubscribed from the channel this week alone.

Will Lynn shed any light on Bradley's disappearance? Will she tell Tom Isaac what she and Bradley were arguing about in the 2003 video? I, for one, will be tuning in on Friday to find out.

Tom Isaac Investigates: What really happened to Bradley Wilcox?
Unpublished recording

RECORDED MONDAY, 11 SEPTEMBER 2023, 7.30 A.M.

LOCATION: LANCASTER HOME, HAMPTON WICK, TOM'S CAR

Tom

I've just pulled up outside the Lancaster home and had to capture this on my minicam. There is something going on. It's still pretty early in the morning, but there are three police cars and an ambulance parked on the long driveway leading up to the Lancaster house.

Wow, there are a lot of journalists standing across the road too. There must be twenty of them at least, and it looks like they've been here all night. That's dedication. Someone – the police, I guess – has put a barrier up, so the press must have been moved back from the house at some point.

Look, a police officer has just stepped outside the front door. I'm going to talk to him and find out what's going on.

[Car door opening]

[Car door closing]

[Voices shouting]

'Tom?'
　'Tom Isaac?'
　'Are you here to interview Lynn?'
　'Why are the police at the house, Tom?'

[Footsteps]

OK, that was surreal. I can't say I've ever been heckled by journalists before. It feels weird that they know who I am.

[Pause]

I hope you can all hear this. I'm holding the camera discreetly in my right hand and keeping it by my side in case the police officer doesn't like a camera in his face, and I'll describe what I'm seeing. I'm walking up the driveway of the Lancaster home. I'm sure everyone is familiar with the house. It's a huge detached red-brick, Georgian-style mansion. It's even more magnificent in real life than on the show. The driveway is that sweeping circular kind with a patch of lawn and an actual fountain in the middle.

Another police officer has just stepped out of the iconic black front door that we all know from the opening credits of the show. I can see a few people standing around in the entrance hall but no sign of Lynn or any of the Lancaster siblings yet. I'm wondering if there's been some kind of incident, like a break-in. The hate on social media for the Lancasters has been pretty intense—

Oh, two paramedics have just appeared in the doorway. They've got a gurney with them but it's empty. Hopefully that means no one has been badly hurt.

Voice of police officer: Can I help you, sir? We're asking all members of the press to remain behind the barrier please.

Tom: I've got a meeting with Lynn Lancaster this morning.

Voice of police officer: I'm afraid I can't let you any closer to the house.

Tom: But I've got a meeting. Perhaps if someone could let Lynn know I'm here.

Voice of police officer: I suggest you go back to your car and reschedule.

Tom: Can you tell me what's happened? Is everyone OK?

Voice of police officer: I'm going to need you to move away from this property please, sir.

Tom: Of course. No problem.

[Pause]

That was weird. I'm walking back down the driveway now. Slowly. I'm trying to catch a glimpse of what might be going on inside the house. There's a dark blue unmarked van pulling in now with two people inside. And the police officer is waving them up to the house.

Hang on, the front door is opening again. It's Locke. God, he looks a mess. I'm going to say hi while the police officer is distracted.

[Footsteps]

Tom: Locke.

Locke: Tom? Long time. What are you . . .? Did I call you?

Tom: No. I'm interviewing your mum at eight. Is everything OK?

Locke: No.

[Pause]

Locke: There's not going to be an interview, mate.

Tom: Are you sure? Lynn did tell me to—

Locke: She's . . . she's dead. Mum's dead.

[Crying]

Tom: Oh mate, I'm so sorry. Shit. I don't know what to say.

Locke: Yeah. I can't . . . Sorry. I'm not thinking straight.

Tom: Of course. I'll get out of your hair. Is there anything you need?

Locke: I have no idea.

[Pause]

Locke: I was going to call you, you know? About the Bradley thing you're doing. We should talk. Just . . .

Tom: Not now. Maybe we could talk in a couple of days. Is there someone who can make you a cup of tea?

Locke: Yeah. Don't worry. I'm good. I just came to get some fresh air. I should . . .

Tom: Sure. If you need anything, call me.

LOCATION: TOM'S CAR

Tom: Oh my God. Lynn's dead.

[Loud exhale]

Just . . . Wow. I wonder what happened. Oh, Javi has just pulled up. I need to tell him to go home. I can't believe this. There is a lot to process here. I don't know how she died, but for it to be on the same day she was going to record her first interview about Bradley and the party, and with the entire country waiting to hear what she was going to say – I mean, it can't be a coincidence, can it?

One thing is for sure – this is a massive blow for learning the truth about what really happened to Bradley Wilcox.

Living with the Lancasters
Series 4, episode 1 (2010)

PUBLISHED TO YOUTUBE: SUNDAY, 3 JANUARY 2010

Lynn Lancaster, confessional

I get asked a lot about what makes me such a driven person. I think people don't get it, they don't understand me, but I don't understand them either. What parent isn't motivated to want the best for her kids? What kind of person isn't prepared to take that extra step? It's those people I don't understand.

That's what I tell journalists when they ask me. I say, 'I'm just a mother who will do whatever it takes to get the best for her children.' That's the soundbite they want to hear, but there's more to it than that. I've been thinking about it a lot as things have taken off for us. We're at the start of series four and I'm no longer being called crazy or stupid. People no longer think I'm going to disappear and be forgotten like a silly fad. Instead, they are taking notice of us and what I'm building here, and that makes me think about how it all began. So, I thought I'd use my confessionals this series to talk about that – my life.

So why am I so driven? Any psychologist worth their salt will point a finger to childhood, and they won't be wrong in my case. I grew up as an only child in a nice house in Tunbridge Wells, Kent. It was a banal semi-detached in an estate of matching houses. The kind of estate that has a little park and playground in the middle and a school at the edge. Middle-class suburbia, I suppose some might call it.

But nothing in my life as a child was mine. Nor was it my parents'. We had expensive clothes, a decent car. I went to private school, too. But we weren't rich. In fact, we were incredibly poor. We had nothing except the handouts given to us by my uncle – my dad's brother. He was a businessman and he was rich. Filthy rich.

He gave my dad a job at his company and he kept him in a low position for his entire life – no promotion – despite the fact that I think my dad was actually a rather smart man. My uncle paid for my school fees and the car and house, but every month we had to go to my uncle's house for lunch and basically kiss his arse, and every single time he would idly threaten to take it all away. We had to be grateful. We had to be subservient.

I hated it all. I'd rather have had nothing and been poor than taken his money, but my parents wanted me to have a nice life, just like I do for my own children, and I will never resent them for that. It all sounds like some awful fairy tale or a Scrooge-type Disney film, doesn't it? A rags to riches story where my uncle dies and leaves us all his money and I promise to be better than he ever was. Well, that didn't happen. My dad didn't get a penny when my uncle died.

I grew up watching my uncle and how he treated those around him, including my parents, and I learnt two things: money equals power. And power is everything.

I told myself that when I was older, *I* would be the rich and powerful one. I decided I would work harder and better than everyone else to get what I wanted and I would do that until my final breath on this earth. And that's an ethos I still live by. That is the foundation of *Living with the Lancasters*.

[Laughing]

I know I sound rather dramatic. But that's the truth. That's why I'm driven. That's why I want to build not just a Lancaster brand, a household name.

No.

I want a global empire. And I'm going to get it.

Extract from National Newspaper, 12 September 2023

REALITY TV STAR LYNN LANCASTER FOUND DEAD IN HOME

Lynn Lancaster (59), star of popular YouTube channel, *Living with the Lancasters*, has been found dead in her home in the early hours of 11 September.

The announcement was made by Lynn's youngest daughter, India Lancaster (30), via a video message posted on Instagram: 'I can't believe I'm saying this . . . My mum died last night. I got a call from Taylor at like five this morning and came straight over. We're not sure what happened. The police are here now.'

A statement from the Metropolitan Police has yet to confirm a cause of death: 'The body of a 59-year-old woman has been discovered at a home in West London. The woman's next of kin have been informed and an investigation is underway to determine the cause of death.'

The widow of former footballer Ed Lancaster, Lynn rose to fame starring in her own reality TV series, *Living with the Lancasters*, alongside her daughters, Taylor (37) and India, and her son, Locke (34).

Recently, Lynn has been at the centre of a police investigation into missing teen Bradley Wilcox, who disappeared after attending a party at the Lancaster home in August 2003.

TRANSCRIPT FROM SKY NEWS LIVE
WITH PATRICK MONAGHAN AND
AMBER CARNEY, 15 SEPTEMBER 2023

Patrick: In today's top stories, the Metropolitan Police have announced a murder investigation is now underway into the death of reality TV star Lynn Lancaster. We're going live to outside the Lancaster home with Amber Carney. Amber, what's been happening in the investigation into Lynn's death?

Amber: As you know, Patrick, Lynn was found dead in her swimming pool in the early hours of Monday morning by her daughter, Taylor. In the last five days speculation has mounted over the cause of death with fans taking to social media to suggest Lynn's death was the result of suicide. Suicide was also widely speculated in the mainstream media as well, with many believing that Lynn was driven to take her own life due to the growing turmoil for the Lancaster family after the Bradley Wilcox missing persons case was reopened in February. Lynn was also facing mounting pressure to speak publicly about Bradley's disappearance.

About five minutes ago we saw police officers arrive and enter the Lancaster home. This has followed after an announcement by the Metropolitan Police this morning that a coroner has ruled Lynn's death as suspicious. Details are still emerging, but we now know that a near-fatal dose of prescription sleeping tablets, Zalpodine, was found in Lynn's body, alongside bruising around her neck and shoulders.

Patrick: I believe the police have someone in custody.

Amber: Yes, that's right, Patrick. The police also announced that they have a thirty-seven-year-old woman in custody, helping police with their enquiries. While no names have been released, the speculation online is that this woman is Taylor Lancaster, who was alone in the house with Lynn the night of her death.

Patrick: And what about the other Lancaster siblings?

Amber: There has been no word on social media from either Taylor, Locke or India after India's announcement of her mother's death on Monday. For the past week, the Lancaster home has been surrounded by members of the press hoping to catch a glimpse of the children, but so far they've been keeping a very low profile.

And in connected news, the viewing figures of YouTube channel Tom Isaac Investigates have skyrocketed, jumping from thousands to hundreds of thousands in just a few days as the nation clamours for more details about not just Bradley Wilcox's disappearance but also Lynn's murder.

EXTRACTS FROM INTERVIEWS RECORDED
BY THE METROPOLITAN POLICE
BETWEEN 13–22 SEPTEMBER 2023

Location: Twickenham Police Station

Taylor Lancaster: Like I've said now so many times, my alarm went off at 4.45 a.m. That's the time it goes off every day. I have such a busy schedule so I have to get up early to work out for a couple of hours in the gym before the day properly kicks off or there just isn't time.

I threw on my gym stuff – la tierra of course. It provides perfect support for all my curves while making me feel sexy too.

What? I am sticking to the facts. Anyway, I went down to the kitchen to get my smoothie. I remember it was freezing, which was odd because the heating is normally on, and that's when I realized the back door was open. Not just unlocked, but actually wide open.

I thought Lynn had forgotten to shut it properly the night before. She didn't always remember to lock up, which was really frustrating. You probably have this on record somewhere already, but we had a superfan in the garden once trying to crash the show. We've had weirdos standing outside the house too, but she never took security seriously.

So I went to shut the back door and that's when I saw her – Lynn. She was face down and just . . . floating. Like a starfish. And even though I knew she didn't like swimming and never went in the pool, my first thought was that she was having an early swim and at any second she would start moving and come up for air. It took my brain a few seconds to twig that she was in last night's clothes, which is when I realized she was . . . dead.

I totally freaked out. I called India and then Locke and told them to come home, and then I called you.

No, I didn't go in the pool. It didn't cross my mind to do CPR. It was obvious she was dead and I didn't want to touch her.

I know I should've dialled 999 straight away but India and Locke are my family. I needed them with me. I couldn't tell a complete stranger our mum was dead before I'd told them.

India answered straight away but Locke took ages to answer the phone. Like five minutes of calling. And I knew his phone wasn't on Do Not Disturb because Lynn always programmed family to cut through that. We always had to answer the phone to each other.

I don't really remember what happened next. I totally shut down. I just sat at the breakfast bar in the kitchen and stared out the window and then you arrived.

Is that it? Are we done now?

Locke Lancaster: I slept over at my girlfriend's house – TV presenter, Kelly Lacey. Taylor called me and I got to the house about six thirty. Mum's body was just lying by the side of the pool. She didn't . . .

[Clears throat]

Sorry. She didn't look like Mum. She was all bloated. Mum would've hated anyone seeing her like that.

India Lancaster: I actually rent a little flat in Richmond with a couple of old school friends about twenty minutes from the house. I stay there once or twice a week if it fits in with filming. That's where I was on Sunday night – in the flat with my friends. It has a personalized key fob entry and exit system on all floors, so you can check that.

I got a call from Taylor at 5 a.m. on Monday. She told me Mum was dead and I went straight home. I arrived the same time as the first officers.

Cassie Wilcox: I'm not sure why you're even asking me this. What does it matter where I was that night? What motive did I have to kill Lynn? Ask Tom Isaac about it. He was meeting Lynn the morning she died and she was going to tell him what happened to my brother. Why on earth would I kill her before then?

Tom Isaac Investigates: What really happened to Bradley Wilcox?
Episode 7: A quick update

PUBLISHED ON YOUTUBE AND SPOTIFY:
FRIDAY, 15 SEPTEMBER 2023

LOCATION: TOM'S STUDY

Tom

Hello and welcome back to *Tom Isaac Investigates: What really happened to Bradley Wilcox?* It's Friday the fifteenth of September and this should've been a huge turning point in our investigation. This was the episode where we were finally interviewing Lynn Lancaster about what she remembers from the night of the party. Guys, I had so many questions. I didn't sleep a wink the night before the interview because I was going over and over everything I wanted to ask, and every possible follow-up.

But, of course, very sadly, Lynn died on Monday, just hours before the interview was meant to take place.

I still can't believe it.

I keep asking myself if my interview with Lynn is connected to her death. I mean, I've got an email on my phone where Lynn promises to tell me everything I want to know. And literally hours before we were due to talk, she's murdered.

It's really made me think about who's been threatening me. What if it wasn't a fan of the show? Someone wanting to protect the Lancasters. What if the person who threatened me also killed Lynn? I keep asking myself, is there something about Bradley's case and the Lancasters that someone doesn't want me to find out? It's made me completely obsessed.

Lynn's death massively changes things for my investigation. It started as a historical case about a missing teen who disappeared twenty years ago at the house of Britain's most famous family. Now, it's happening in real time.

I'm not giving up on uncovering the truth about Bradley Wilcox. He is my priority. Cassie needs answers and Bradley needs justice. These facts will never change, but now we also need to consider who killed Lynn Lancaster, and how, and if, these questions are connected.

I've got lots to plan and organize so I'm taking a short break from recording, but I will be back very soon. And if you're new here, don't forget to like and subscribe!

Text messages, 16 September 2023

Tom
Hey Locke,
   Just wanted to say how sorry I am about your mum.
   If there's anything you need, let me know.
   Mumsie has made her famous chicken casserole. She remembered it was your favourite.
   I'll drop it round tomorrow.

Locke
Thanks mate. That would be epic. I used to love your mum's cooking!
   Everything has gone crazy and we've had to get out of London. The press wouldn't leave us alone.
   I'll call you tomorrow.
   I haven't forgotten I want to talk about your investigation stuff too.
   Tell your mum thanks so much from me!

EXTRACTS FROM INTERVIEWS RECORDED
BY THE METROPOLITAN POLICE
BETWEEN 13–22 SEPTEMBER 2023

Location: Twickenham Police Station

Taylor Lancaster: I don't know why you're so convinced it's murder. She could have taken those tablets herself and fallen in the pool.

Seriously, are you even considering accident or suicide? Because if someone killed her then they wanted me to take the blame, which doesn't make any sense. Why would anyone do that?

I suppose . . .

[Pause]

Look, I don't want to point the finger here, but you know Cassie Wilcox hates me, right? She's always been jealous of me. Even when we were kids. Then her brother went missing and she totally blamed me. If anyone had a motive to kill my mum and frame me, it was Cassie.

Locke Lancaster: You're investigating my mum's death as suspicious, right? There's no way Mum killed herself. Have you spoken to Taylor? Did she tell you they were arguing all of that Sunday?

India Lancaster: I really don't know what happened to Mum. I'm not sure what to think. Maybe I don't want to think about someone hurting her because it's just so awful.

Taylor and Mum were both so stressed out about la tierra going under. The shops had stopped stocking it. Website sales were massively down. There has been so much negative press about us and it was really getting to Taylor. They were arguing a lot about what they were going to do. Mum thought a public interview would smooth everything out, but Taylor thought that it would only make things worse. She wanted to record something on the show instead. Things were getting pretty heated between them when I left to go to my flat, but honestly, that wasn't anything new. They argued a lot.

I keep thinking, everyone has a breaking point, don't they?

Cassie Wilcox: Where was I on Sunday evening? I was home in bed. No, I don't have an alibi. Do I need a lawyer?

Extract from National Newspaper, 25 September 2023

TAYLOR CHARGED IN LYNN LANCASTER MURDER

Reality TV star Taylor Lancaster has been charged with the murder of her mother, Lynn Lancaster, who was found dead in her home in the early hours of Monday 11 September.

Police arrived at the Lancaster home shortly before 4 p.m. yesterday after a two-week investigation into Lynn's death. Police were seen leaving the house with Taylor Lancaster in handcuffs. A spokesperson for the Metropolitan Police has confirmed the charges.

OCTOBER 2023

TRANSCRIPT FROM SKY NEWS LIVE
WITH PATRICK MONAGHAN AND
AMBER CARNEY, 4 OCTOBER 2023

Patrick: Welcome back to Sky News on Wednesday the fourth of October. It's time to join Amber Carney live from outside the Old Bailey, where Taylor Lancaster has appeared in court for the first time since being charged with the murder of her mother, Lynn Lancaster.

Amber: I'm standing by the steps of Britain's most famous courts, where just moments ago Taylor Lancaster pleaded not guilty to the charge of murder.

As you know, Patrick, a post-mortem found a near-fatal dose of Zalpodine – a prescription sleeping tablet – in Lynn's body. It was reported yesterday that a prescription for that drug has been discovered in Taylor's name.

But what really caused a stir in the galleries just now is the ruling by the Honourable Malcolm Pritchett, denying bail. Taylor has been remanded in custody at HM Prison Bronzefield in Surrey until her trial, which has been scheduled for early next year.

There has still been no statement from Locke or India since their sister's arrest and both were notably absent from today's proceedings.

Patrick: Amber, does this mark the end of the Lancaster brands and show?

Amber: Lynn's death certainly spells the end of *Living with the Lancasters*. We've not seen an episode of the show since early September, but public interest in the family is showing no sign of diminishing. News of Taylor's arrest has even been reported in America and Australia.

2022 trending video: #LWTLFavMoments

@CupcakeHeavenRus

The first episode I ever watched was the one where Lynn made India stay home from school with this plan to home-school her. It was totally nuts. India was clearly super smart and was revising for exams. She sat down at the kitchen counter and said, 'OK, Mum, teach me advanced trigonometry' or something like that. And Lynn actually had a pretty good go at it, but then Taylor came in carrying a sewing machine and wanted help with something and India went back to school the next day. India is my favourite Lancaster. She doesn't seem to have the same massive ego the others do.

@Julie_RogersBlogger

The episode I remember most was when Taylor and India were both up for this cover shot for *Cosmopolitan* magazine and they chose India. Taylor had this massive sulk and India offered to turn it down. You could tell she actually didn't mind and just wanted Taylor to shut up. But Lynn wouldn't hear of it. She even sent Taylor to her room to calm down. A thirty-three-year-old woman being sent to her room. She was acting like a brat though.

Then she came down and apologized and acted like she was happy for India and it was all fine.

But obviously it wasn't. On the day of the shoot, India suddenly gets this text from Locke saying his car has broken down and can she go and pick him up in the middle of nowhere. She rushes off and you can tell she's going to be late for the shoot. Lynn was having total kittens about it. Then Taylor let down Lynn's car tyres and hopped into her own car and headed off to the shoot.

Taylor had nicked Locke's phone and sent that text to India to get her out the way knowing she'd do anything for him and made sure her mum couldn't step in.

They put her on the cover obviously. And the weird thing was, no one ever mentioned it again. It was like it never happened. I studied a doctorate in psychology and we used Taylor as a case study for a narcissist.

EXTRACT FROM INTERVIEWS RECORDED
BY THE METROPOLITAN POLICE
BETWEEN 13–22 SEPTEMBER 2023

Location: Twickenham Police Station

Cassie Wilcox: It was a genuine mistake. I'm sorry. I completely forgot that I went out for a drive that night. You're right, that is my car on the traffic cameras. I wasn't going anywhere in particular. I was just driving. I do that sometimes when I get a bit stir-crazy in the house. I find driving is a good way to escape my thoughts.

I drove around for a few hours. Then I went home around midnight.

To: Warden@HMPrisonBronzefield.gov.uk
From: Tom@TomIsaacInvestigates.com
Subject: Request for use of filming equipment in agreed interviews with Taylor Lancaster
Date: 13.10.23

Dear Mrs O'Dwyer,

Thank you for your time on the phone on Wednesday and agreeing to my request to interview Taylor Lancaster privately for the purpose of my docuseries.

As requested, please find attached all the necessary completed forms and paperwork from Taylor and her legal team, a list of equipment we will be bringing into the prison, and photocopied ID for myself and my cameraman, Javi Bernard.

I look forward to hearing from you with a start date for our interviews, and once again would be grateful for your expediency in this matter.

Best regards,
Tom Isaac

Tom Isaac Investigates: What really happened to Bradley Wilcox?
Episode 8: The shocking childhoods of the Lancaster children!

PUBLISHED ON YOUTUBE AND SPOTIFY:
FRIDAY, 13 OCTOBER 2023

Extract from *Living with the Lancasters*, series 9, episode 36 (2015)

Taylor Lancaster, confessional

People assume that because we fight all the time we hate each other, which is, like, so stupid. We're a super-close family. We fight all the time because we care about each other. Yeah, I screamed at Locke today. Anyone in my situation would have done the same. We had a photoshoot scheduled with *HELLO!* magazine to promote the show and our autumn line for la tierra. The shoot was at the house and was scheduled for 9 a.m.

Mum and I had been up since five getting the living room completely perfect. Even India helped for a bit. And where was Locke? He was in bed sleeping off a hangover.

Then he was late for make-up and made the photographer wait around for him. It was lazy and it was rude. Locke thinks all he has to do is show up and everything will fall into his lap, and that's not how the world works. He's completely blind to the hard work I put into things.

Do I want to kill my family some days? Of course. Especially my mum [laughing], but I know they want to kill me too. I totally get that I'm high-maintenance. I have these standards I expect from everyone around me, but I set the same standards for myself, too. No one in this family works harder than me.

LOCATION: TOM'S STUDY

Tom

Welcome to *Tom Isaac Investigates*. I'm Tom Isaac and I'm the voice of the people. You tell me where to dig and I dig.

Gah! I have so many new followers and I really don't know how to start this episode. So much has happened since my last update a month ago.

Lynn is dead. Taylor is in prison awaiting trial for her murder. And Locke and India are in hiding, and who can blame them. Social media has gone into an absolute frenzy over this case.

The trajectory of our investigation has completely changed. It's no longer just about what really happened to Bradley. We also need to know who killed Lynn Lancaster. Was it Taylor? I don't know . . . yet! We are going to find out. But whether Taylor is innocent or guilty of murdering her mother is only part of this docuseries. This family is riddled with scandals and secrets. Plastic surgery, dodgy diet pills, and let's not forget Taylor Lancaster's fake wedding. If we're going to find out the truth, we need to go back to the start.

We need to understand who the Lancasters are and what drove them towards a life in the spotlight. Only then can we begin to piece together what happened to both Bradley and Lynn.

As I said, Locke and India are in hiding. Nobody knows where they are. They have deleted their social media accounts and they aren't speaking to anyone.

[Pause]

Except me. We are going to their secret hideout. Sounds very Batman, I know. They are giving us full access.

Of course, we need to speak to Taylor as well. I'm desperate to know how the nation's queen of glamour, who is rarely seen without stilettos and some serious contouring, is coping in prison.

Is she the only person alive who knows what might have happened to Bradley? Does she hold the clues that will lead us to the truth? More on my interviews with Taylor later. Right now, here's my interview with Locke and India. I don't want to give anything away, but I will say that Locke and India reveal some jaw-dropping secrets about the show, and about what kind of mother Lynn was.

LOCATION: LOCKE AND INDIA'S TEMPORARY HOME (LOCATION UNDISCLOSED)

Tom

I'm in the living room of Locke and India's secret new home, ready for our first interview. Locke has asked me not to share any details about the location of the house I'm in, or anything about our journey. We weren't exactly bundled into the back of a van with black hoods thrown over our heads, but let's just say, we didn't take the most direct route either. Considering the media storm currently surrounding the Lancasters, we had to be careful we weren't followed.

The living room we're in is pretty ordinary. The kind of room you'd expect from a mid-budget holiday rental. There's an eclectic stack of books on the shelf, pictures of beach landscapes hanging on off-white walls. Nothing to offend. There is none of the luxury about this place that we've come to expect from this family, unlike this coffee in my hands, which is pure heaven. It's WC2 coffee, of course. I bought some for Locke and India along with some of their super-tasty shortbread biscuits. Once again, I'm grateful to WC2 Coffee for sponsoring this episode. Discount code in the show notes.

You'll notice that I'm not standing by any windows and that there is nothing that gives away where in the country I am right now. Is this secrecy overkill? I think to understand that question, we need to piece together exactly what Locke and India have been through since the death of their mother last month, and where their heads are at right now.

INTERVIEW BETWEEN TOM ISAAC, LOCKE LANCASTER AND INDIA LANCASTER

Tom

Locke and India, thank you so much for agreeing to take part in my docuseries investigation. It feels very strange to be sitting opposite the both of you. For the benefit of my podcast listeners, Locke and India are side by side on a blue two-seater sofa.

India

Thanks for being here, Tom. I just want to say that I'm really sorry. To Cassie and to everyone who wants the truth about what happened to . . . Bradley.

[Crying]

Sorry. I feel like I've got no right to be upset but it's all so awful. We've had the year from hell and Mum died. It's obviously nothing to what Cassie has gone through for all these years.

I knew about Bradley being a missing person. I was ten when it happened and remember the police at the house, but as an adult it didn't cross my mind that we as a family should do more to raise awareness of his case and keep the investigation going.

Tom

Thanks, India. I realize this is your first interview since your mum's death last month. How are you both?

India

Up and down. We've barely spoken to anyone for three weeks so sitting in front of a camera again feels very strange.

Locke

Yeah. It's freaky. *Living with the Lancasters* ran for sixteen years. That's a long time to have a camera follow you around.

Gotta say, I miss the confessionals. That place was like therapy for me. It's where I really sorted through my feelings. I've been going pretty stir-crazy without it.

India

Maybe if you came for a run with me like I keep suggesting, you'd feel better.

Locke

No way. I wouldn't be able to keep up. Besides, you run in the middle of the night, and nothing is getting me doing that.

Tom

There's one thing I want to clear up before we properly dive in, and that's about our relationship. I've received some criticism on social media for taking on this docuseries, as I'm seen as someone who can't be impartial because of my friendship with you, Locke. So before we start, can you both tell my viewers when we last saw each other?

India

I didn't actually know we'd met at all, but Locke mentioned the other day that you used to come over for dinner after school sometimes, so we probably did meet but I don't remember you.

Locke

What about my eighteenth birthday party at that club in Soho. Didn't you meet Tom then?

India

I was fifteen years old. I wasn't there. I was revising for my GCSEs.

Locke
Well, aside from bumping into you the other day, my eighteenth was the last time I saw you, Tom. We've had the odd comment on each other's socials since, but nothing much. You're looking good, man. Glad to see you ditched the blonde.

Tom
Thanks. And you understand that my job as an investigative journalist is to follow the clues and uncover the truth wherever it might lead me in finding out what happened to your mum? Whatever the consequences might be.

Locke
That's why we're doing this too. We want the truth as much as you do – about Mum and about Bradley.

India
And if this is the last time we ever sit in front of a camera then I want it to be honest.

Locke
You think this is our last time in front of a camera?

India
You don't?

Locke
Yeah, maybe. I guess there are some things you can't come back from. Even for us. Hard to see Taylor returning to any kind of fame, no matter what happens next.

Tom
On the topic of Taylor, can I ask if either of you have visited her?

Locke
No, we haven't.

India
We'll go when things settle down a bit. Taylor is . . . er . . . very one-track minded and it's not always easy to get through to her, to talk rationally.

Locke
I can't believe they didn't give her bail—

India
Locke.

Locke
Yeah, yeah. I know she's our sister and all that. I guess if you boast about having access to a private jet whenever you want it, the courts aren't likely to let you hang around at home while they get stuff sorted for the trial.

India
Locke doesn't mean to sound so heartless. We love Taylor, but we're all dealing with a lot right now. Same storm, different boats and all that.

Tom
You say different boats, and yet I can't help but feel as though you and Locke have put yourselves in a kind of self-imposed prison, in a way. You said you've barely spoken to anyone for weeks and you've deleted your social media accounts. I'd like to understand why you've gone to such lengths.

India
It honestly felt like our only option. There was, and still is, so much to deal with. It's like our world has fallen apart. We couldn't stay at the house because ... because it was a crime scene, and with the photographers and journalists everywhere, we felt trapped. Everyone wanted a piece of us. And even when we were inside, away from the cameras, the hate started pouring in across our social media channels. We couldn't escape it and it left us no space to deal with everything going on.

Locke
It was pretty intense. Like, we – me and India – right? We're victims here. What did we have to do with Bradley Wilcox? Nothing! What did we have to do with Mum's murder? Nothing. We both have alibis but it's like, because we have the same surname as Mum and Taylor, we must be guilty.

India

[Loud exhale]

Locke, you understand where people are coming from. They're angry. They want justice for Bradley. We can't separate ourselves from the brand any time it suits us.

Locke
People are treating us like we should be sitting alongside Taylor in prison, and I don't think that's fair.

India
Maybe we should have done some interviews earlier on before the where-are-the-Lancasters hashtag and headlines kicked off.

Tom
Why didn't you?

India

In the first few days after Mum died, we didn't know what to do. Mum was this massive force in our lives. She was our mum and our business manager and our PA. She made all of the decisions. Without her, I think we sort of panicked, didn't we, Locke? Fight or flight and we chose flight. It feels like so much more than grief that we're trying to process right now. I'm not sure I know who I am without Mum.

[Pause]

God, this is hard. Sorry.

I know it sounds dramatic and quite ridiculous for a thirty-year-old, but we all lived together, we worked together. Wherever I went, Mum was there to keep things on track. So on top of the grief, it's been a huge challenge to sort through my feelings on no longer having that constant in my life and having to make decisions for myself.

Locke

Yeah, and on top of that, it's knowing it will never be like it was. The show was our life and now it's gone.

Tom

I've always been a massive fan. *Living with the Lancasters* ran for sixteen years. You've spent over half of your lives on the show, and I've always wondered, did you always enjoy it?

Locke

When it was about all of us, a family – absolutely. When we were sidekicks to Taylor, not so much. There were a lot of times when Taylor and her ego were in a room and there wasn't space for anyone else.

India

There were things that were hard.

Tom
What kinds of things?

India
Long hours, for starters. There was filming for the show and then all the other things we were doing. Taylor with la tierra, me with modelling, Locke with his TV presenting—

Locke
And before that I was heavily involved in editing all the footage for each week's episode. That was a full-time job, and Mum didn't trust an outsider to do it.

India
It was completely relentless. Every evening, Mum would send us each a schedule for the next day. I was lucky if I got a toilet break some days.

Whatever we were doing, Mum always had another plan and goal, like launching another product or trying to break into America. There was always more to do. It was never enough.

Tom
For your mum?

India
And Taylor. She always moaned that we messed around and didn't take it as seriously as Mum did.

Locke
We had to have a laugh, though. The show wasn't like other jobs. It was our whole lives. There was very little downtime, especially in the early days.

Tom

And before the early days, before the show, what was life like? I want to understand how a seemingly normal family made the step into reality TV. I'm guessing *Living with the Lancasters* was Lynn's suggestion?

Locke

First of all, we were never normal. Second of all, Mum never suggested anything. She told us what was happening, and it was a case of get on board and support the family or get on board and support the family. As for being surprised when Mum suggested the show – no, I don't remember being shocked. It was just the next thing. Were you, India?

India

No.

I really think that Mum always saw herself as famous, even before she was. Or maybe not famous in the beginning but elevated from others. She loved Dad like crazy but I'm sure a part of the appeal was his footballing career. She was always encouraging him to do more TV stuff. It was like a mission. A mission to fame. When Dad died, she turned that mission on to Taylor.

The end goal was always her own show. 'The Lynn Lancaster Show', she called it. It was supposed to be this trendy-mum, *Desperate Housewives* thing about managing a famous daughter. She touted it to all the producers. All those contacts she'd cultivated over years and years of parties and sucking up. She'd always say to us, 'Nothing is for nothing', whenever we were kids and would complain about another dinner we had to sit through with people we didn't know.

Locke

Oh yeah. Mum would be like, 'Either sit with us nicely or go to bed with a pill.'

Tom
A pill?

Locke
A sleeping tablet. Well, half a Zalpodine. Mum would make us have one if we were being disruptive to her socializing.

Tom
I'm sorry. Can you say that again? About the sleeping pills.

India
Mum would make us take a small dose of sleeping tablet when she wanted us upstairs and out of the way during her social events.

Tom
Your mum gave you Zalpodine – a prescription sleeping tablet – when you were children? The same drug that was found in lethal doses in her body during a post-mortem?

[Pause]

India
Yes. It was just a bit of one, but it made me so groggy the next day that I happily sat through all the boring dinners.

Tom
And how old were you during this time? I'm trying to understand at what age exactly your mum was giving you prescription sleeping tablets.

Locke
Oh, like seven or something. I don't remember getting them that often, but I remember you were threatened a lot, weren't you, India?

Especially the year you got that Dictaphone and followed everyone around recording their conversations. You were what, eight then?

India
I'd totally forgotten about that. I'd spend hours in my room writing up what I'd heard in a notebook.

Locke
Which you'd hide in your wardrobe and me and Taylor could never find it to see what you'd written about us.

Tom
Can we go back a step, please? You're both talking very casually about this, but can we be clear – your mum drugged you with one of the strongest prescription sleeping tablets available when you were children. That is not normal behaviour. How often—

India
Look, we weren't toddlers, and Mum was always careful to only give us a little bit of a dose. And you're right. We are talking about it casually, and we probably shouldn't. I don't know about Locke, but I think I'm still in some kind of shock about Mum's death. There is so much to wrap my head around and—

Locke
And that story is the tip of the iceberg, mate.

India
Locke's right. It's just one of dozens of examples of how we weren't a normal family, even before the fame.

At all the parties and dinners Mum threw, she wasn't just having a good time. She was networking. Even then, six years or so before

Taylor's song hit the charts, Mum was talking about being famous and how to make that happen.

Tom
And Lynn did make it happen by launching a reality show in 2007. A year after Taylor's single reached number one. What was that time like?

India
It wasn't easy. For about a month in 2007, Mum bounced from one production company meeting to another, but they all said no in the end. They didn't see the appeal, the vision that she saw for a show that followed around a forty-something woman and her kids. There was no comparison. People always liken us to the Kardashians, but their show didn't actually start until October 2007. We started in April.

Mum called a family meeting at the end of January. She said, 'Those imbeciles don't have a clue what people want. So I'm going to do it myself.'

YouTube hadn't been around that long. Maybe six months or something. Way before 'YouTuber' was even a word, and way before people saw the potential to create a whole TV series on there. I'll say that for Mum, she was pretty revolutionary.

It all happened pretty quickly after that. Mum hired a marketing and PR firm to handle the launch, and they had quite a bit of input into what the focus of the show would be. It went from *The Lynn Lancaster Show* to *Living with the Lancasters* and suddenly it wasn't about Lynn and Taylor any more, it was about all of us.

Locke
People assumed from the get-go that we were this filthy-rich family and that's the story we were selling, but the hilarious thing was that

Mum blew a ton of money getting Taylor's single to number one and then setting up the show. No exaggeration – we were flat broke by the time it aired. She'd already mortgaged the house to put a budget together for Taylor's song. Any royalties were going straight into paying the debt we owed.

I remember Mum was getting calls from the school every week because she hadn't paid the fees for so long.

We were pretending to be rich like that for years. We'd go on these shopping sprees – mostly Taylor – and she'd buy dozens of outfits and dresses and shoes, but the next day, when the camera wasn't filming, Mum would return them all.

Things didn't pick up until the endorsement deals started coming in series three, but even then it was slow. Mum didn't give us any kind of allowance, or salary I suppose you'd call it, until her diet pill – Slenderelle – took off, which was in 2011, four years after the show launched.

I think people will be surprised how little we had. Even when the money started coming in, most of it went to Taylor and it went on keeping the rich story going – the right car, the right clothes, the right everything.

India
To be fair, Taylor was the one doing a lot of the work.

Locke
And we weren't? Do you have any idea how many hours I spent every week editing the show?

India
I know, Locke. I'm not trying to be mean. I'm saying it how it was. You make it out like she was a princess who didn't lift a finger, and we were her slaves. That's not true.

Locke
Isn't it?

Tom
Was there ever a point when either of you felt you'd had enough of the show? When you considered leaving and doing something else?

India
Of course we thought about it, but only in that faraway daydream kind of thinking. It was never an option. Never.

Locke
Mum wouldn't have let us. One of her favourite things to say was 'over my dead body'. Like, 'Over my dead body will they run that magazine without Taylor's face on the cover.' 'Over my dead body will anyone tear us down.'

[Pause]

I guess that's what it actually took.
    Can we take a break? I need some air.

Living with the Lancasters
Series 4, episode 4 (2010)

PUBLISHED TO YOUTUBE: SUNDAY, 24 JANUARY 2010

Lynn Lancaster, confessional

For years, people thought of me as a wife to a footballer, a mum and a socialite. As if my life only began when I said 'I do' to Ed. In actual fact, I have a degree in business and was an events coordinator for a global hotel chain.

That's where I met Ed. I was staying in the Manchester hotel. It was around May time, but I was already knee-deep in organizing the Christmas functions they'd be offering. I was only twenty-one and studying on the side.

A group of footballers came into the bar and I recognized Ed straight away, although I pretended I didn't. I just ignored them all. I refused to even look in their direction. They were used to having every wannabe WAG in a ten-mile radius throw themselves at their feet and I wasn't going to be one of them. I was better than that.

They were a noisy group, drinking hard. At one point Ed came over to the table where I was working and apologized if they were being too loud.

He ended up joining me for a drink and the rest is history. We were married that same autumn. I finished my degree the following year and then Taylor arrived.

We both wanted a big family. My childhood had been lonely as an only child. Ed had had a brother growing up but sadly he died in a car accident when Ed was ten. That loss really affected him. And his desire for a big family, I think, was in part to fill some of the hole left by his grief.

Ed was such a charmer. Cheeky but also sweet. When he was talking to you it felt like you were the only thing that mattered to him in the world. He made everyone feel like that. It didn't wear off either, once we were married.

EXTRACT FROM EVIDENCE COLLECTED
BY THE METROPOLITAN POLICE FROM THE
LANCASTER PROPERTY ON 22 NOVEMBER 2023

Item No: 2

Description: Notebook titled 'Detective's Notes 2 by India Lancaster, age 9'

Friday, 21 June 2002

Overheard conversation (recorded and transcribed):

Me: When will you be home?

Dad: I'll be home in time to collect you from school on Monday like always.

Me: Can I come with you?

Dad: Do you play golf?

Me: I play crazy golf. I got a hole in one last time.

Dad: That's not quite the same thing. Sorry, pickle, this is a golf weekend for golfers.

Notes
  – Dad has not packed his favourite golf trousers or his golf shoes

Suspicion
  – Dad is not playing golf this weekend

I have tied black thread around the zips of the pocket on his golf bag where Dad keeps his golf balls and tees. If the thread is broken then he opened the bag and played golf. If it is not broken then he didn't play golf.

Monday, 24 June 2002

The thread is still on the golf bag. Dad is not playing golf.

<u>Mystery</u>

What is he doing with his friends if he's not playing golf?

Why is he lying?

2022 trending video: #LWTLFavMoments

@GreggyLeggy95

Easy. Episode twelve in series thirteen. There was a photoshoot at the house for something for Taylor, and Locke got chatting to the hairdresser upstairs and they ended up sleeping together in the bathroom. We obviously didn't get to see it on camera, but we see her pull Locke behind the door. He gave the camera a wink, and then it cut to Taylor stomping around the house looking for the hairdresser to redo her curls or something.

Her face when she stormed into that bathroom. I was like, 'Why didn't they lock the door?'

So funny. Taylor hit the roof.

@JosieMMason

I loved Locke. And I mean loved. Huge crush. The way he would turn to look at the camera and wink, it melted me every time. I always thought it was a shame Taylor and India got so much of the attention. I was so glad when he finally got the presenting role on the *Xtra Factor*. Although he should've got that quiz show, too. I don't know how Locke didn't kill Taylor for that one.

He finally gets his shot at doing what he wants to do instead of following his sisters around all the time, and Taylor has to sabotage it by answering his phone when he's in the shower and then not giving him the message about the audition. So unfair! It wasn't like she wanted the job for herself. She just didn't want Locke to get it. Taylor doesn't mind her family being famous, just as long as they aren't more famous than her.

Lynn should've stepped in and helped then. She's always interfering in their lives. She could easily have phoned the quiz producer and sweet-talked him into giving Locke another try but she didn't. We didn't see it, but I think Taylor asked her not to. And I think Lynn agreed because them two are always as thick as thieves.

@JackBurns_FilmBlogger

Not my favourite episode but how funny was it when the Lancasters started endorsing products in series three? Out of nowhere every scene had them holding these cans of fizzy drink none of us had ever heard of. It was so blatant it was funny. You'd think it would put us off but we were lapping up the crazy by then.

And then came their own products. Yes, I'm talking about la tierra. But before that, who remembers the time Lynn launched her own diet pill in series five? That was so funny! Not the pills and what happened. Don't send the trolls after me. What was funny was the way she did it.

The whole family got involved. We saw shots of stomachs poked out, all of them weighing themselves, constant junk food eating. And then bam, along came Slenderelle and the whole family was skinny again in a week.

It was so cringe. And it shouldn't have worked but it did. The Slenderelle website sold out in minutes. No health warnings. No facts or science. Just the Lancasters telling people to buy it. I've no idea how they got away with it.

@VanessaMcMahon_Heartdoc

Are you looking for Slenderelle? Stop! It's alarming to see how the LWTLFavMoments hashtag has reignited an interest in Slenderelle. With people asking how they can get some. So I want to tell you my experience of Slenderelle as Head of Cardiology for Guy's Hospital.

Slenderelle was a caffeine-based product claiming to aid weight loss. Did it work? I don't know. That's not my field, although I believe the links between caffeine and long-term weight loss are rather tenuous.

Regardless of its effectiveness, Slenderelle was an incredibly dangerous product. Caffeine stimulates the receptors in the cells in your heart, causing it to beat faster. And in very high doses, as seen in Slenderelle, it raises blood pressure and can lead to atrial fibrillation and, in extreme cases, kidney failure.

No approval required from any official regulatory body.

Women and men were taking two, three times the stated dose. By the late summer, those with undiagnosed heart conditions found themselves in A&E and then on my ward. They were, quite frankly, lucky to be alive.

Thankfully, Slenderelle is no longer on the market, but don't go searching for similar products. If you want to lose weight, speak to your doctor.

Tom Isaac Investigates: What really happened to Bradley Wilcox?
Episode 8: The shocking childhoods of the Lancaster children! (cont.)

PUBLISHED ON YOUTUBE AND SPOTIFY:
FRIDAY, 13 OCTOBER 2023

Voice of Jerry Olaski, JO Music Productions
I first met Ed and Lynn at a dinner hosted by a mutual friend in 1999. We hit it off straight away. They were a really fun couple. And sweet together, too. They'd do this thing where they'd leave little notes for each other under the pillow or in the fridge. Or Lynn would hide one in Ed's golf bag. *I love you*, or something else mushy.

My wife and I have been married thirty-four years. We love each other but we've never been like that.

We saw the Lancasters quite a lot. Ed and I played golf together once a month or so. We were good friends. He was a real character. Always turning up to the golf course in some outlandish clothes – neon-green gingham or pink zig-zags.

[Laughing]

He said he knew it annoyed the old boys who acted like they owned the place, and he was right, it did. Ed and I always had a laugh. He took his golfing a lot more seriously than me. Every few months he'd go to Portugal or Spain with some other golfing friends and they'd play pretty much non-stop. I'm not sure why, but I never got an invite. Maybe it was a work thing to do with his football agent stuff.

After Ed's funeral, we lost touch with Lynn and the kids. I felt bad about that at the time and so when Lynn called me a year or so later to talk about Taylor, I was happy to help. Typical Lynn, she launched straight in with this nutty idea. She said, 'I want Taylor to have a number-one hit. I want to know how we do that. Let's have lunch.'

I laughed my head off. Like it was that easy. But we had lunch the following week and I laid it out in simple terms – all the issues they'd face. I thought Lynn would give up. I basically told her it was impossible. But she shook her head and made a ton of notes like she was in class. I remember over that lunch saying something like, 'I didn't know Taylor was interested in becoming a singer.' I'll never forget Lynn's reply. She said: 'Taylor doesn't know it yet either.'

A week later, Lynn was phoning again to book some studio time for Taylor. Lynn was the most determined and stubborn woman I've ever met, and I've worked in the music industry my whole life. What came next for that family didn't surprise me at all. Lynn loved her kids and she wanted to give them everything.

LOCATION: LIVING ROOM (LOCATION UNDISCLOSED)
INTERVIEW BETWEEN TOM ISAAC, LOCKE LANCASTER AND INDIA LANCASTER

Tom
I'd love to know how much of the show was real and how much was fake. This is a question that has been asked repeatedly by fans and the press many times over the last sixteen years and you have always maintained that everything in the show was completely real.

Locke
Yeah, that was the story.

Tom
What do you mean by 'story'?

Locke

Mum always told us to stick with the story. She said it pretty much every day. The story was that *Living with the Lancasters* was a no-holds-barred, totally real, reality show. So that's what we stuck to telling people.

Like I said, we were flat broke when the show started, but the story was that we were wealthy.

Tom

So the show was fake?

Locke

Not all of it. You couldn't film for that many hours a day and always be in character. In the beginning it really was a reality show, despite the extra sass and retakes and some careful editing. But in the last five or six years we've had a concept writer develop episode ideas and write prompts. It wasn't scripted, but there were definite things we were supposed to say. We got the prompts in the evening alongside the next day's schedule.

I don't know if people will find that surprising. The show ran for so long. It was hard to keep it fresh. That's one of the reasons we started digging out old family videos from when we were kids. The fans lapped them up.

Tom

So what started as a reality TV show with a few retakes and some careful edits developed into something with specific storylines and scene prompts. With this in mind, I'm dying to know – Taylor and Craig's wedding in 2018, series twelve?

Locke

[Laughing]

Completely fake.

India

Hang on, Locke. Craig and Taylor were actually in a relationship for a while but—

Locke

From the second the proposal was out, we all knew what was going to happen on the wedding day.

Tom

Even Craig?

Locke

I . . . don't actually know what Taylor told him.

Tom

And the family fights? All those screaming matches between the three of you and your mum?

India

There were a few times when it was real, like when it was between Taylor and Locke. But most of the time Mum would sit down with the concept writer and they'd look at the schedule and cook up some . . . tension and stuff, I guess. Like, for this one modelling shoot, we made out that Mum got lost and we ended up stuck in traffic and only made it in time for me to run in front of the camera without going to hair and make-up.

That was totally cooked up. We knew the shoot was going to be a 'just out of bed' messy style and that's why the story worked. Me and Mum fuming at each other in standstill traffic, going the wrong way down a one-way street, then sprinting down corridors into this studio. It was more entertaining than watching me arrive twenty minutes early and spending two hours in make-up, which is what actually happened. But it was stressful acting out scenes every day on top of a long day of modelling.

Tom
You both describe Lynn as the one making all the decisions. You said earlier, Locke, and I'm quoting you here because this has really stuck in my head: 'It was a case of get on board and support the family or get on board and support the family.'

I can only imagine, then, that there must have been times when you didn't agree. You said before that leaving was never an option, but did you ever question Lynn's plans? Because it doesn't sound like the three of you ever did, which I could understand if you were small children, but by the time the show started, Taylor was twenty, Locke, you were seventeen, and granted you were only fourteen, India, but I remember being pretty vocal with my mum at that age about a lot of things. So did you ever question her or just flat out refuse to do something she wanted?

Locke
Tom, sorry, dude, but you just don't get what she was like. We loved her.

India
What Locke means is that you're right, we weren't little kids when Mum was telling us to do things we didn't always agree with, but we were little kids once. We've grown up with it always being that way. Mum had a plan or an idea or whatever, and we always went along with it. Dad did too. She had this way when we were little of making out like . . . like if we didn't want to do it then we were basically

saying we didn't love her. She could be manipulative. Like the affirmation notes she'd leave around the house would be stuff like: 'Your loved ones will understand what you're doing one day.' Or 'Have patience with those that don't trust in the plan.'

But everything she did, she did for the family, for us.

Locke

Yeah, what India said, plus Taylor was always the first to leap in and say yes to anything Mum suggested. So then it was, 'Taylor loves me enough to say yes. Taylor gets what I'm saying, don't you, sweetheart? You're Mummy's best friend, Taylor, aren't you?'

India

You sound just like her.

[Pause]

God, sometimes I can't believe she's really gone.

She wasn't like other mums. She didn't bake us cookies when we were younger or play board games with us, but she was a lot of fun. Everything was a party. She really, really cared about our lives and our futures. She wanted us to be on top of the world always. It was just . . . Mum's version of the world didn't always tally with ours. Like the nose job when I was thirteen. Did I want one? No. Did I tell her that? No.

We grew up never saying no and that's how it's always been. Trying to change that would've been like trying to speak another language without any lessons.

Tom

I'm sorry. What? India, are you saying that you had cosmetic surgery when you were thirteen years old? That your mum forced you to have an operation you didn't need or want?

Locke

I'd forgotten about that. Are you sure you didn't break it?

India

That was just the story – that I went to go outside and thought the glass door was open but it wasn't and I ran straight into the glass and broke my nose. This was in January 2007 when I was thirteen. I turned fourteen in the March and we started filming *Living with the Lancasters* in April.

I feel a bit weird talking about this. We've kept it quiet for so long. I probably shouldn't have said anything. I just meant it as an example of her world versus our world – my world. She believed one hundred per cent that I needed a nose job in order to be happy and to become a model, which is always what she saw me doing.

She told me she loved me a lot and made out like it was a massive sacrifice she was making for me. She said something like, 'We don't really have the money for it, but I'm going to borrow some for you because I want you to have the best life and for all your dreams to come true.'

I didn't actually think there was anything wrong with my nose until she said it, and then I couldn't stop staring at it in the mirror.

I think I probably wanted to suggest we leave it a few years, until we had the money and I was older, but I think Mum sensed my hesitation because she said, 'Once the show starts and we're all famous, it will be too late to get it done because everyone will know you've had it done and you'll always be the girl with the big nose.'

I'm sure she told me it didn't hurt, which was a lie because it really did hurt, and even now I get sinus problems when I get ill.

Tom

When you look back at that time, at that operation you didn't want, do you feel angry or upset?

[Pause]

India

You used the word 'forced', but it really didn't feel like that. Everything with Mum happened in this whirlwind. When I think about it, I think it's just something that happened. I mean, I sometimes wonder how she did it. I don't think it's legal for a thirteen-year-old to have cosmetic surgery, but Mum could sweet-talk anyone into getting her way. And to be fair, Mum was right. I've had a hugely successful modelling career just like she always planned.

Tom

I feel slightly traumatized. I can't believe it.

India

I can look back now as an adult and see that it was totally nuts, but at the time it was just the next thing to do, the next step. Mum was very into grooming. We'd have a waxing lady come to the house and we'd all get our eyebrows done together.

Now our waxing lady does our Botox and fillers. It was just what we did. It was normal. Even a nose job at thirteen felt normal.

Taylor had it just as bad, to be honest. OK, she didn't have surgery, but she had to get up at crazy o'clock to work out for at least two hours a day. Even when she was ill. You were lucky, Locke.

Locke

Lucky Mum only had time to focus on Taylor's career and yours, you mean? Lucky Taylor's epic mood swings distracted Mum from ever making the calls that would help my career? Yep, really lucky. But I was the lazy and annoying brother, so I didn't get a look-in.

That was my role. The story we were spinning. I had to sit back and watch Taylor and you land all these deals, doing all these amazing things, because Mum only had tunnel vision for you two. You guys couldn't sneeze without Mum wiping your noses.

I had things I wanted to do too, you know? I thought about modelling and stuff, but Mum wanted me at home. She thought it would split the show too much for all three of us to be off doing our own things.

It was only after Taylor's wedding that Mum finally realized that maybe Taylor was doing too much and that it was time for me to establish myself. It was hard for Taylor to go places without being mobbed, to be honest. It was always a mix of diehard fans and people who hated her guts – the haters, she calls them. After the wedding stuff, there were more haters than fans, and Mum decided Taylor should lie low for a while, which quite frankly was the least she could do.

Of course, Taylor wasn't happy about it. I'd spent years standing back, letting her have her time in the spotlight, never screaming and shouting about how unfair it was. The minute it was my turn, she totally kicked off. She tried to ruin it for me too. She was constantly taking my phone and trying to mess up my meetings.

But within, like, a week I had three offers for TV presenting and a DJ slot on Radio 1. I really like presenting, man. I know I'm good at it. I'd still be doing it now but when the Bradley stuff all came out and Mum started getting a lot of heat, it made it hard for me, too.

And personally, I think the nose job thing is way worse than anything Taylor had to do. I've never really thought about it before but you were just a kid. Plus, Taylor wanted it all. She always has. She's a piece of work and I'm starting to see that my mum was too, with what she put us through, so maybe they both got what they deserved.

Tom
So if they were both really driven, and as you say, both would do anything to get what they wanted, what happened if they disagreed on what that thing was?

Locke
I think we've found out.

India
Locke, you can't say that.

Locke
What? We said we'd be honest, and I am.

They rarely disagreed – Mum and Taylor – but this year that changed.

Tom
Why did it change?

Locke
I'm sure you can imagine. We were facing a lot of criticism in the media and on Twitter over Bradley's disappearance.

Taylor felt that Mum should step away from the brands and the show because the criticism was directed at her and we were all getting the backlash. I think there was a bit of payback after the wedding episode backfired and Mum said the same thing to Taylor.

But Mum was having none of it, and was all, 'Stick to the story and people will move on.'

Tom
There isn't a nice way to phrase this question or soften it, but I really need to ask, do you believe Taylor killed your mum?

Locke
I do. I think Taylor could see that a whole lot of shit was about to come Mum's way and that Mum was going to drag Taylor down with her. Maybe she felt she had to choose family or fame, and

Taylor being Taylor not only chose herself, but thought she'd get away with it. Either that or she finally cracked.

Tom
What about you, India? Do you agree with Locke? Do you think Taylor killed your mum?

India
She's my sister. I don't know how to answer that question.

LOCATION: TOM'S STUDY

Tom
So ... how interesting was that interview? It was actually fun at times listening to the way they talk about the show with each other. But despite the sometimes light-heartedness, it was hard not to sense the tension crackling beneath the surface. Like when India mentioned that this is their last time sitting in front of a camera, and Locke shot her a look of disbelief.

What about the serious resentment Locke clearly holds for Taylor? I don't know about anyone else, but I did not get that impression on the show. Obviously there were fights, but they always ended each episode laughing about it.

One thing is for sure – there is a lot more to Lynn Lancaster.

The Lynn we saw on the show was a tenacious, hard-working businesswoman, and a mother who wanted the world for her kids. But as we scratch the surface, it seems we're learning about a darker side to the woman who created one of the nation's biggest-selling brands.

And yet, before it was *Living with the Lancasters*, the show was called *The Lynn Lancaster Show*. It was all going to be about Lynn. It seems she really did have tunnel vision when it came to becoming famous.

Voice of Locke Lancaster
Mum never suggested anything. She told us what was happening, and it was a case of get on board and support the family or get on board and support the family.

Tom
Some of the revelations from today's interview are completely shocking! What kind of woman – what kind of mother – makes her thirteen-year-old child have a nose job? Not to mention drugging her children as young as seven with prescription sleeping pills if they misbehaved or if she just wanted them out the way for her social events. And not only that, but Zalpodine – the same drug found in near-lethal doses in Lynn's body the night she died. Yet another element to Lynn's death that doesn't feel like a coincidence.

I think we . . .

[Pause]

I think we need to dig . . .

[Pause]

Into what kind of woman Lynn was.

[Pause]

Sorry, guys, I've just seen something in the background. I just need to check it's not . . . Oh my God. It's—

[Shouting] Mumsie?

[Shouting] Mumsie?

Laura Isaac
What is it? Are you all right?

Tom
Look at this. There's a dead rose on my bookshelf. It just caught my eye as I was recording. Did you put it there?

Laura
No, of course not. It looks just like those ones that were left on the doorstep with that awful note. How did it get here? Has someone broken into the house?

Tom
I don't know.

Laura
Oh no. I've just remembered, I left the back door unlocked yesterday. I took Snowy out and forgot to lock it and when I came back it was open a fraction. I thought the wind had blown it open. I'm so sorry, Tom.

Tom
It's not your fault. Can you give the police a call? I just need to finish this.

Laura
Of course.

[Pause]

Tom
I can't believe someone has been in my home. Someone left this rose for me to find. There's no note, but clearly they wanted me to know they could get to me. I feel like this is another threat, another warning to back off. I must be getting close to something.

Tom Isaac Investigates: What really happened to Bradley Wilcox?
Episode 8: The shocking childhoods of the Lancaster children!

PUBLISHED ON YOUTUBE AND SPOTIFY:
FRIDAY, 13 OCTOBER 2023

88,134 COMMENTS

Ernie Martin
Scary stuff! Hope you're OK, Tom! I guess we can rule Lynn out as the person behind it.

Wendy Clarke
Lynn drugged her children and forced India to have a nose job!! Unbelievable! That is blatant child abuse. I never thought I'd say this, but I feel really sorry for all of them. Hope you're OK, Tom.

> **Ernie Martin**
> Feel sorry for them? Don't be daft! None of them have worked a day in their life.
>
> **TI_BiggestFan**
> You can see the stress has taken its toll on them two. They've really lost their shine.
>
> **KMoorcroft58**
> I thought India looked really skinny.

Katy Shepard

What about Locke's whole 'Taylor and Lynn getting what they deserve'?! I think Locke killed Lynn and framed Taylor.

> **TrueCrime_Junkie1001**
>
> Tom, are you sure of Locke's alibi? Can you look into this pls?

LWTL_No1Fan

BTW, my brother-in-law looked up the flight manifests for August 2003. A private jet left Blackbushe airfield at 7 a.m. on the morning after the party with one passenger on board. Destination was Scotland!

> **Katy Shepard**
>
> 1 passenger??? Has to be Bradley! I knew he was still alive and out there somewhere. How can we track where he went next? Maybe he killed Lynn and has been threatening Tom!

> **SyfyGeek90**
>
> Cassie said Bradley would not have run away! This is a waste of time. We need to focus on the Lancasters! Taylor was alone in the house the night Lynn died. Tom, when are you going to ask India and Locke about Bradley?

To: CraigKnowles@Kerboodi.com
From: Tom@TomIsaacInvestigates.com
Subject: Docuseries into Lancasters
Date: 14.10.23

Hi Craig,
My name is Tom Isaac. I'm an investigative journalist with my own YouTube channel. I'm doing an investigation into the Lancasters and would love to chat about your wedding to Taylor in 2018. Would you have five minutes to answer some questions?
   Thanks so much.
   Best wishes,
   Tom

Living with the Lancasters
Series 4, episode 6 (2010)

PUBLISHED TO YOUTUBE: SUNDAY, 7 FEBRUARY 2010

Lynn Lancaster, confessional

Life was very normal for us before Taylor's success. Any parent with three kids knows how hectic life is. There's always somewhere to be, something that needs doing for one of them.

In the very early days, Ed was living in Manchester for most of the week for training and matches. We talked about setting up a life up there together, but we knew he'd be retiring and we both wanted to live in London and didn't want to uproot the kids at a later stage.

It was hard without him around. I didn't have a nanny. I didn't want someone else raising our children. And by the time India was born in ninety-three, Ed was retiring from professional football.

Everything was different for all of us after that. Having Ed home all the time was wonderful. I felt like I could breathe properly for the first time in years. It was probably around then that I started to think about what I wanted to do with my life. I was a wife and a mother but I was only twenty-nine and I had big ambitions. I wasn't sure what I was going to do at that point, but I knew I wanted it to be a family business of some kind. Even when the kids were really little, I knew I didn't want to be one of those parents who only sees their adult kids at Christmas and the occasional weekend.

EXTRACT FROM EVIDENCE COLLECTED
BY THE METROPOLITAN POLICE FROM THE
LANCASTER PROPERTY ON 22 NOVEMBER 2023

Item No: 3

Description: Notebook titled 'Detective's Notes 3 by India Lancaster, age 10'

Sunday, 30 March 2003

Overheard conversation (recorded and transcribed):

Mum: I know she's young but she's got my dark hair and it really shows, don't you think?

Waxing lady: I see what you mean. I can do a tiny bit just here and here.

Me: Is this going to hurt?

Mum: Only for a second.

Me: I like my eyebrows as they are.

Waxing lady: Don't worry, sweetheart. I'm going to make them look even better. Sit down for me.

<u>Notes</u>

Waxing hurts for more than a second. I <u>do not</u> like my new eyebrows. They look like Taylor's.

Overheard conversation (recorded and transcribed):

Me: Daddy, why doesn't Uncle Jerry go on your golf weekends? He plays golf.

Dad: Uncle Jerry works in music, sweetheart. My golf weekends are for my football friends.

Me: Like the footballers who you work for to get better deals?

Dad: No. They're my clients. My golf weekends are for my old friends and other agents like me. It's networking.

Me: What's networking?

Dad: It's where we all talk about what we're doing and we see if we can help each other.

Suspicions

Dad is NOT playing golf on his golf weekends.

I still don't know what he is doing. I looked in his suitcase after he packed it last week and it had in it his favourite shirt, swim shorts, T-shirts and trousers. No golf clothes, but no clues.

EXTRACT FROM INTERVIEWS RECORDED
BY THE METROPOLITAN POLICE
BETWEEN 10–12 OCTOBER 2023

Location: Twickenham Police Station

Cassie Wilcox
Look, I didn't plan to go anywhere near the Lancasters' house. I was just driving around and sort of unconsciously found myself there. I didn't want to mention it because I knew it would look bad. I parked up and sat in my car for a bit and then I drove home. I swear. That's it.

I still don't understand why you're asking me about this. You've arrested Taylor. She killed Lynn, not me.

2022 trending video: #LWTLFavMoments

@MagsMentoring_LifeCoach

Favourite episode – blimey. The wedding, I guess. And that whole build-up to it. All those times Taylor went into her bedroom to cry, and then telling the camera that it was just nerves and that she was happy really. Yeah right! We had a Lancaster Wedding party night. We got our friends over to watch the episode. Taylor looked stunning, didn't she? Maybe a bit trampy, but that's her style. When she stood at the end of the aisle, I swear we all shouted at the screen to run. The cheers when the episode ended were pretty loud.

[Laughing]

Craig was never right for her.

@JackBurns_FilmBlogger

The wedding. That was one of the craziest things they did. Taylor met Craig Knowles during Chris Evans's breakfast radio show in the spring of 2018. Craig was there promoting his stint on some dance show and Taylor was talking about her latest fashion line.

It was the usual celebrity whirlwind romance. Walks in the park, holding hands over dinner, sunbathing together on a yacht in the Med.

Three months after that first meeting, Craig threw an elaborate proposal. Candles, rose petals and let's not forget the intimacy of an entire camera crew there to capture the moment he dropped down to one knee. It was over the top and reeked of fake and we lapped it up.

Six months after they met – it was the wedding, which took place in a huge white marquee in the Lancasters' garden. The whole episode was nail-biting even though we knew by the time the show aired that the wedding was off. When Taylor finally appeared it was obvious she'd been crying, and then it all kicked off.

@TaniaEdwards1

I used to love the drama, but I stopped watching it after the wedding in series twelve. I mean, come on! That was so fake and they didn't even try to hide it. Look at the timings. Lynn's Insta post declaring the wedding was off happened before Taylor walked down the aisle and apparently realized she couldn't go through with it.

A load of my friends stopped watching then too, but I know a ton of people who saw all the backlash and started watching the show. They don't care it's all fake.

To: CraigKnowles@Kerboodi.com
From: Tom@TomIsaacInvestigates.com
Subject: Docuseries into Lancasters
Date: 19.10.23

Hi Craig,
Sorry for bothering you again. I just wondered if you received my previous email and whether you had five minutes to chat about your experience of spending time with the Lancasters in 2018?
   Thanks so much!
   Best wishes,
   Tom

To: Tom@TomIsaacInvestigates.com
From: CraigKnowles@Kerboodi.com
Subject: RE: Docuseries into Lancasters
Date: 19.10.23

Yes, I got your email. Lynn is an absolute piece of work. I'm glad she's dead. That family made my life a living hell after I went public on Twitter about the show. They make everyone who steps into their house sign a non-disclosure agreement, which I broke. I had to declare bankruptcy after all the legal stuff they threw at me. I'm not the only one who's been burned by them. If I was you, I'd stay well away from that family!

Please don't contact me again. I don't give you permission to share this email on your show or talk about its contents with anyone.

C

Tom Isaac Investigates: What really happened to Bradley Wilcox?

Episode 9: Who is the real Taylor Lancaster?

PUBLISHED ON YOUTUBE AND SPOTIFY:
FRIDAY, 20 OCTOBER 2023

Voice of Jerry Olaski, JO Music Productions
I never thought Lynn could pull off a number-one hit, but she did, with my help. Lynn and I signed a contract in that first recording session to produce and distribute Taylor's single. We split everything fifty-fifty – that's me and Lynn. Taylor signed a separate contract for Lynn to act in Taylor's best interests, giving Lynn total control over the song and any financial gain. I've seen similar contracts with children and teens. Taylor was over eighteen at that point, but she obviously trusted her mum to share the profits.

'Girls Girls Girls' was my most successful song ever. It made Lynn and me a lot of money.

Voice of Locke Lancaster, taken from *Living with the Lancasters* confessional, series 6, episode 6 (2012)
Do I think Taylor needs to calm down sometimes? Yes. Do I think she's got anger management issues? Totally, yes. We didn't call her Tantrum Taylor growing up for nothing.

[Laughing]

I'm not sure I should have said that. She will literally kill me when she watches this back. Do I hate her guts for being a spoilt brat? No way. She's my sister. And when I go downstairs again in ten minutes, she'll have cooled off and we'll be fine again.

We're a close family. And part of that is because we have to be. Who else would want to be part of this unless it's to use us to become famous? We're all we've got. It's a madhouse, but I love it and I love them.

LOCATION: HM PRISON BRONZEFIELD, PRIVATE INTERVIEW SUITE
INTERVIEW BETWEEN TAYLOR LANCASTER AND TOM ISAAC

Tom

Welcome to *Tom Isaac Investigates*, episode nine. I'm in an interview room at HM Prison Bronzefield in Ashford, Surrey, only a thirty-minute drive from the lavish Lancaster mansion in Hampton Wick.

When I arrived forty-five minutes ago, I was expecting a looming, dirty brick building with barbed wire and guard towers – very *Shawshank Redemption*. But the buildings are new-looking, light beige and only two storeys high. From the outside, it could be a school or a business centre. I certainly would never have guessed that inside these walls are some of the most dangerous and deadly women in the country.

But then the minute you step through the doors and join the slow queue for security, you realize this place is seriously secure.

As you can see, the room we're in is tiny. Javi has set up the camera behind me to capture Taylor's face. There are no windows, which I hate. Especially in a place like this. But it's clean and comfortable, despite having the same plastic chairs we all remember from school. Did we ever discover what these rectangular holes in the back were for?

I'm babbling. Sorry. I'm pretty nervous now and feeling all the pressure. This is Taylor Lancaster, one of the most famous women in Britain and someone I've watched pretty much every Sunday night for over a decade. I need to build a rapport with her in these interviews and get answers for Cassie and Bradley, and I only have three one-hour interviews scheduled over the coming weeks, so I have a lot to cram in.

I'm in a unique position. I have an opportunity in front of me that no one else has. Like India and Locke, Taylor is only speaking to me, something her legal team aren't pleased with considering she's awaiting trial for murder. I've had to fill in a hundred forms and do a lot of begging to get the special permission to not just talk to Taylor privately like this, but to record our interviews as well. This is not an everyday occurrence, and it's down to me now to get the truth.

I obviously want to ask Taylor about Bradley and her mum and her life growing up, but I also want to ask more about the inner workings of the show, and especially Taylor's wedding, one of the most viewed and most controversial episodes of *Living with the Lancasters*.

Their astronomical success was all down to the outlandish antics of the family, and yet we've heard from Locke and India that a lot of that was contrived or completely fake. Will Taylor be as open with us about the 'stick to the story' motto her mum had?

Looking on social media, it seems like the nation is torn right down the middle over whether Taylor is innocent or guilty, and hearing Locke and India talk has really got me thinking about motive. We know Taylor and Lynn were arguing on the day Lynn died. And that Taylor wanted her mum to step away from the brands after la tierra was withdrawn from UK retailers. Just listen to this confessional from Taylor, recorded three years ago.

Voice of Taylor Lancaster, taken from *Living with the Lancasters* confessional, series 14, episode 10 (2020)
La tierra is my baby. My world. I'm so proud of it. It means everything to me. I will never let anything happen to it or let anyone stand in my way of making it every bit as successful as I know it's going to be.

Tom
Was Taylor's desire to protect her brand and fame the motive for killing her mother? Was—

[Door opening]

Taylor
Hi Tom, great to see you again. What's it been? Four years?

Tom
I think seven, actually.

Taylor
Wow. Time flies.

Tom
It does. Thanks for agreeing to talk to me.

Taylor
I managed to squeeze you in between my very busy schedule of doing nothing and doing nothing.

[Laughing]

Come on, let's sit. I gather we don't have a lot of time. You'd better fire away.

Tom
Thanks. As I explained in my letter, I'm doing a YouTube docuseries on Bradley Wilcox and also on your mum and what happened. And—

Taylor
I didn't kill her. This whole thing is totes ridic. I'm innocent. I've done nothing wrong. You'll see.

Tom
Of course. Totally.

I'm also looking back at *Living with the Lancasters* and its popularity, so I'd love to understand what life was like for you growing up and what it's like for you right now too. It's impossible to imagine what you're going through. Just a few short months ago, you were one of the highest-paid celebrities in the country and running a leading fashion label. You'd branched into activewear and an underwear collection for men and women, and you were doing nightclub appearances, TV and radio interviews, and regularly appearing on the cover of national magazines. Not to mention starring alongside your family in Britain's most popular reality TV show.

And now you're in prison with no access to social media or the outside world. So the first question I want to ask is, how are you, Taylor? How are you coping with this dramatic change?

Taylor
Like, oh my God, can you believe I didn't get bail? Like, in what world am I a flight risk? I still can't believe it. And it makes me . . . either really angry or really upset, and sometimes both at the same time.

[Raised voice] I am not going to run away!

I want to clear my name and prove my innocence so I can get my life back.

[Pause]

This place . . . it's awful, Tom. It's vicious and nobody cares about anything. I can be . . . walking down a corridor and someone will just punch me for no reason.

The price of fame in a place like this is that I'm a target. People want to get to know me. They think it's cool to have a famous friend. They think I can pull strings for them. If I could pull strings, I wouldn't be in here in the first place. But with that attention comes jealousy and nastiness. It's like I wake up and I don't recognize my life any more.

The food is awful. Not that I've had much appetite. Lynn would've been so pleased with my weight right now. The best diet ever, guys – just get arrested and spend a few weeks in prison.

[Laughing]

Tom

You say you want to clear your name to get your life back. Do you think that's possible? I mean, if you were released from prison right now, do you think you could return to the same lifestyle and career?

Taylor

Oh yeah, of course. I have to believe it, right?

Tom

I can see hope would be important in a place like this.

I want to focus today's interview on getting to know the real Taylor Lancaster and how you became one of the nation's most famous women.

Your father, Edward Lancaster, was a well-known Premier League football player who, at the height of his career in the early nineties, played as a striker for Manchester United as well as for England, scoring the winning goal in the 1992 Euros against France. He's still ranked today in the top twenty all-time Premiership goal-scorers.

After retirement, he became a football agent and was a regular feature on sports news as he sought to improve youth football. What was it like growing up with a celebrity parent?

Taylor

Sorry, I'm smiling because my dad would've laughed if you'd called him a celebrity. He never saw himself that way, and we definitely weren't in the spotlight at all back then.

Dad retired from football in the summer of 1993. I was seven, so that made Locke three, and India was about six months old, I think. We went from having a dad who was only home one night a week to having a dad that was there 24/7, making us pancakes for breakfast every morning and driving us to school.

We had a great childhood but we weren't famous. Dad was never a Ronaldo or a Beckham. If we were at a restaurant, someone might come over to shake his hand and say hi, but it was nothing to what came later for us as a family, with the show and la tierra. Honestly, growing up, we were a totally normal family.

Tom
And that all changed in the summer of 2006, at the age of twenty, when you released the song, 'Girls Girls Girls'. It stormed the charts, staying at number one for six weeks and becoming an iconic tune that is still played regularly on radio stations during the summer months. Considering this success, I think many people would've expected you to continue a career in the music industry, or at the very least release another song. Why didn't you?

Taylor
Because I can't sing. Seriously, I have zero talent when it comes to singing. The lyrics for that song are: 'Girls, girls, girls, we love the summer. The summer. The summer.' It's ridic. Ed Sheeran, George Ezra, Lady Gaga. They are talented singers and songwriters. I was neither.

And I never wanted to be. My passion has always been for fashion. Ever since Lynn took me shopping on Bond Street when I was six, it's been about the clothes for me. I was obsessed with trying on everything in Lynn's wardrobe and clomping around the house in her heels.

The funny thing is, that song might have been number one or whatever but it wasn't even supposed to be released. Lynn had this friend, Jerry, who owned a music studio. As a birthday present, Lynn hired the studio for me to have a recording session. It was just a fun thing to do on a Saturday afternoon.

I honestly had no idea that they'd do anything with it, let alone that it would be so successful. For about three months I went up and down the country singing that one song. Shopping centres during the day, then nightclubs in the evening. Plus a load of TV appearances. It was a bit mad when I think about it. I didn't want to be a singer.

Tom
Talk me through the months that followed the single release. *Living with the Lancasters* aired for the first time on Sunday the eighth of April 2007, just nine months after your single came out. Were plans already in motion for the show when you recorded 'Girls Girls Girls'?

Taylor
Oh God, all Lynn talked about was doing a reality show. She saw the song as a chance to put us on the map. We really weren't known before that. Dad might have been a footballer but he wasn't famous enough outside of football for anyone to care about what his family were doing. He wasn't someone who craved the limelight in the way Lynn did.

What I'm saying is that until my song was released, we were nobodies. Lynn knew that she couldn't start a reality show and make it a success without a kick-starter into fame and she got that from my song, which was her plan.

A lot of money went into promoting 'Girls Girls Girls'. A lot of money. People talk about snowball effects – things just taking off – and yeah, 'Girls Girls Girls' was a massive snowball, but someone had to climb the mountain first and make that snowball, and start it rolling, and that meant a lot of investment in advertising.

I often wonder where we'd be if the song had flopped. It really should've done when you think about it. What the hell did Lynn know about promoting music? As soon as it hit the charts, plans for *Living with the Lancasters* were put in motion.

Tom
What did you think of the reality TV show idea? Were you on board?

Taylor

Oh yeah. I could totally see what Lynn was planning. I knew it would be fun.

When we were growing up, Lynn was obsessed with *The Real World* on MTV and then *The Osbournes*. It was totally different to anything else out there. Having a camera catching every little thing. Warts and all. Lynn was mad for all of it.

I think Locke and India were maybe less keen than I was about the show. Definitely India, anyway. She was so much younger though and really into studying. A total swot. She had this idea that she was going to be a scientist, but when she was really young, she wanted to be a detective. She'd walk round the house recording all of our conversations on a tape player and then would write in a little black leather notebook she kept hidden in her wardrobe. It drove me and Locke crazy. We were always trying to find it so we could read what she'd written, but we never did.

It took India a few years to realize that *Living with the Lancasters* was a stepping stone. No, that's not right. It was a platform. A way to build and promote our products. In series one and two, the episodes were only ten minutes long, but we'd do three, sometimes four episodes a week. By series four when we had a lot more endorsements coming in and YouTube changed their limits on how long a video could be, the episodes were an hour. Which basically meant we had an hour-long advert for whatever we were selling that week or month.

I make it sound like we had Nike ringing us up and offering us deals and we didn't. Not for a long time. Anytime we weren't filming, Lynn was on the phone to the marketing departments of every company she could think of, trying to sell the show and what it could do for their products. Eventually, Chase drinks took a chance in series three.

It was exciting in those early years. I was doing club appearances. I was singing 'Girls Girls Girls'. I was cutting ribbons at the openings of new stores. I did a bit of modelling too. There was always something going on. Lynn said yes to everything. Literally everything. It got full-on and I'd get stressed and argue with Lynn or Locke and India. There was always some kind of disagreement rumbling, but that's the drama everyone loved.

[Laughing]

Sometimes the family drama was so much fun and sometimes I wanted to kill them.

[Pause]

That was a joke, obviously.

Tom
Right. Of course.

I'm a huge fan of the show and I'd love to get a sense of what life was like for you while filming. How much of what we saw in the final episode that aired every Sunday was real?

Taylor
Oh my God, Tom, it was all totally real. Everything you saw was how it happened and how it would've happened if the camera was on or not. The only edits were boring bits.

Like there was this one time a few years in where Locke ate my lunch. I was ordering these really delish salad boxes from a store in London. They came fresh every two days. I was obsessed with them. And he ate the last one. And worse than that – he only had a few mouthfuls and then threw the rest in the bin. I was furious. Proper hangry.

After a shouting match, Locke went outside to sunbathe and I locked all the doors and hid the keys. He was out there all evening and all night, banging on the back door so hard we thought he'd break it. Lynn was yelling at me to let him in, but I refused. In the end, India threw his duvet out the window for him and it landed in the pool.

It was so funny.

Anyway, the haters went nuts. It was all over socials that we'd faked it. Like there was no way I'd have done that to Locke. But honestly, it was totally normal for us and completely real. If it wasn't me shouting about something then it was Lynn. She always had big ideas for what we'd do next. Things on the show or with la tierra, but she wasn't particularly patient, and she'd hit the roof if she felt like someone or something was standing in her way.

Tom
It certainly sounds like right from the very beginning Lynn had a clear vision of a future for you in particular, as well as the Lancaster family. You said you were behind the show, but did you always agree with these plans? Was there ever a time when you thought to yourself, *I don't want to do that?*

Taylor
Never. I completely trusted Lynn. She only ever wanted what was best for us.

Tom
Even your wedding in 2018?

Taylor
I . . .

[Pause]

Actually, could someone get me a glass of water super quick please, Tom?

Tom
Sure. Of course.

Tom Isaac Investigates: What really happened to Bradley Wilcox?

Episode 9: Who is the real Taylor Lancaster? (cont.)

PUBLISHED ON YOUTUBE AND SPOTIFY:
FRIDAY, 20 OCTOBER 2023

Craig Knowles video posted to Twitter, 20 August 2018
So me and Taylor are no more. Be still my broken heart. I'm just kidding. It's all good. In fact, it's better than good. You want to know why? The whole wedding was a set-up for the show. I was just playing the part. Might as well have been *EastEnders* to be honest. Do I get an Oscar for my shocked face?

[Laughing]

LOCATION: HM PRISON BRONZEFIELD,
PRIVATE INTERVIEW SUITE
INTERVIEW BETWEEN TAYLOR LANCASTER
AND TOM ISAAC

Tom
Let's take a step back from the wedding for a moment. By 2012, series six of *Living with the Lancasters* was in full swing and had a growing fan base. You were a recognized celebrity, regularly appearing in weekly magazines and tabloids.

And you'd launched la tierra, your gorgeous clothing label, which first sold through ASOS and then through many department stores. In September of that year you had another big break when you were invited on to *Richard Park Live* on Saturday-night TV to promote the label and the show. I hope it's OK, but I'm going to show you part of that interview.

EXTRACT FROM *RICHARD PARK LIVE*, 14 SEPTEMBER 2012

Richard: Tell us about your secret boyfriend, Taylor.

Taylor: I don't have one. Right now I'm focusing on launching our new clothing range. It's called la tierra, which means 'earth' in Spanish. My grandmother on my mother's side was Spanish, so it was important to me that we recognize my heritage in my fashion label, and my family, who mean the world to me.

Richard: Yes, it's a great line, and I think you're wearing one of the la tierra dresses now, is that right? Why don't you stand up and give us a twirl.

Taylor: Oh . . . OK.

Richard: Gorgeous. Absolutely stunning. Let's get a round of applause for how stunning Taylor looks.

[Audience applause]

It really shows off your . . . assets. Talking of assets, I know I'm not the only man in the studio tonight who's wondering, are they real?

[Audience laughing]

We all saw your mother's, er . . . enhancements. Have you done the same?

Taylor: Um . . . the thing about la tierra is that it's for all body types. I'm curvy but my sister, India, has a completely different frame, and the clothes look just as good on her. That was really important to me – to make clothes that make women of all body types feel a million bucks.

Richard: So, the boob job?

Taylor: You want to know if my boobs are fake? Are you really asking me that?

Richard: I guess we are.

[Audience laughing]

Taylor: Can we talk about my fashion label instead?

Richard: Sure, sure. We will. Once you answer the question.

Taylor: Fine. They're real.

Tom
It's hard not to cringe listening to that interview. I can feel your discomfort, Taylor, at the direct, sexist and completely inappropriate questions. How do you feel watching that back now?

Taylor
Pretty crap. I'd like to think I'd handle it differently now, but I don't know if I would. I wish I'd walked out, to be honest.

Tom
Why didn't you?

Taylor
And have a story spun that I couldn't hack live TV? That I refused to answer questions? No way. Besides, Lynn was just off camera gesturing at me to laugh and play along. It might have been best for me to storm off but it wasn't best for the brands.

Tom
I think I'm getting to understand Lynn a little better, and if I'm honest I'm surprised she didn't walk on to the set and give Richard Park a telling-off. She was your mum, after all.

Taylor
The only person Lynn was angry with about that interview was me. She felt I should have played along more with Richard. There was a playful tone to his questions. I should've given a bit of banter. A 'I'll show you mine if you show me yours' kind of game, but I was honestly just too stunned and I came across like a deer in headlights. I thought I was there to talk about my new fashion line, something I was totes proud of. And I was just so excited to be on live Saturday-night TV.

Afterwards, I felt like they'd only had me on to poke fun at me and be mean. But Lynn was adamant that any publicity was good publicity and told me not to worry. It wasn't the last time I faced sexist and out-of-order questions from interviewers.

Tom
It's interesting that you talk about there being a difference sometimes between what's right for you and what's right for the bigger picture – the *Living with the Lancasters* brand. Were there other times you had to make that choice?

Taylor
Probably. We all made sacrifices for the show. Like Locke wanted to do TV presenting way before he actually did, and India wanted to go to university but chose modelling instead.

Tom
And was one of those sacrifices your relationship with Craig Knowles?

Taylor
God, I've never thought of it like that before.

Tom

If we can go to 2018 now and your wedding to Craig. Over the sixteen years *Living with the Lancasters* ran for, I think many would put that wedding as one of the most memorable moments for many reasons. I hope it's OK if I play a clip from that episode for you now. It's the moment you walked down the aisle under a thousand glittering fairy lights strung around a marquee and reached Craig.

EXTRACT FROM *LIVING WITH THE LANCASTERS*, SERIES 12, EPISODE 32 (2018)

Taylor: Sorry, everyone. I just need a second. Craig, can I talk to you over here?

Craig: Now? We're about to get married. Everyone's waiting.

Taylor: Please. It's important.

[Pause]

Taylor: [low voice] I can't do it. I'm sorry. I don't think we should get married. It's all happened too fast.

Craig: What the hell? You're seriously doing this now? Taylor, I love you. Whatever your mum is saying—

Taylor: This is about us. I'm sorry.

Craig: If you do this, if you embarrass me like this, I will make it my mission to end you.

Taylor: I know you're hurting right now. I'm so sorry. I'm really sorry but I can't marry you.

Tom

I remember gasping at the screen the moment you told Craig you couldn't marry him. It was an emotional scene. I really felt your pain and the agony of making that difficult decision, especially in front of the cameras.

It seemed to me, and to many of the fans watching, that this was a genuine moment of indecision on your part. But then on the Monday after the show aired, Craig released a video on Twitter claiming the entire wedding and your relationship was fake and that he knew all about the plan to call off the wedding right from the start.

As I'm sure you recall, this caused a lot of backlash and criticism from the fans and the media.

Taylor
It's still really hurtful that Craig said those things. Of course our relationship was real.

Look, he was really cut up with how the relationship ended, and I understood that. He wanted to hurt me and he wanted to hurt the show and he did both those things in one swoop while also saving face because suddenly he wasn't the man jilted at the altar any more.

I actually think it's really sad that he can say all that stuff and people just believe him over me, even after watching our relationship. His claims were really damaging to me and to our family and it was a complete lie. Craig and I fell in love. It's right there on the show. You can't fake that stuff. Or at least, I can't. Craig is the actor, so maybe it was all fake to him, but it wasn't to me.

His proposal was one of the happiest days of my life. I was madly in love with him, but the pressure on our relationship with the show and planning the wedding and my commitments to la tierra and the new underwear line we were launching . . . It was just too much for us. I started to have doubts but I felt like I was on a one-way train and I couldn't get off. I kept telling myself that I'd feel differently when the wedding was over and we were married. But then I stepped down that aisle and I just froze. I looked into Craig's eyes and I just knew that we weren't right for each other. It was heart-breaking to do that to him. I loved him but I wasn't *in love* with him.

Tom

So despite the doubts, you didn't know that you wouldn't marry Craig until the moment you walked into the marquee? Would you be surprised to know that Locke remembers it differently?

Taylor

Locke doesn't know anything. He never has. He's lazy and self-absorbed and always just along for the ride.

Tom

But it wasn't just Craig's claims that caused people to believe the wedding was fake. There was the Instagram post from Lynn's account which announced that the wedding had been called off and encouraged viewers to tune in to Sunday's episode of *Living with the Lancasters* to find out what had happened.

That Instagram post went live at 15.01, but it was another five minutes before you would step into the marquee. If that's the case, if you didn't know until you looked at Craig that you were going to call off the wedding, then how did Lynn know five minutes earlier?

Taylor

I . . . well . . . it's just that . . . that was a mistake. It's just . . . OK, like, so I sort of knew like five minutes before I went into the marquee that I wasn't going to be able to go through with it. Totally, that was the max amount of time that I knew. Lynn said I needed to go into the marquee and tell him. It was important for the show for people to see it. Lynn asked her PR person to put the post up when it was over and I guess the PR person got the timing wrong or something.

But it doesn't change the fact that I was heartbroken and really sad. And I promise our relationship wasn't a stunt for the show. I'd never have done that.

Tom
So you've just been sticking with the story this whole time?

Taylor
Who told you about that? Was it Locke?

[Pause]

Look, this is really hard to talk about. I genuinely cared for Craig, and I'm sorry I wasn't completely honest about it. Sometimes it's hard to separate what actually happened and what we told everyone over and over.

[Door opening]

Voice of prison officer
Time's up.

Taylor
Hang on one sec. Tom, can I say something into the camera?

Tom
Sure.

Taylor

[Pause]

Hey guys, I just want to say . . . don't believe the haters. You know me. You know I wouldn't do what they're saying. Hashtag-Taylor-Is-Innocent. I love you all.

LOCATION: KENSINGTON GARDENS

Tom

What an interview! We've just got home after sitting in loads of traffic. I'm so tired. All this driving! For a born and bred Londoner who likes to hop on the tube, it's wiping me out. But Snowy was desperate for a walk and how can I ever say no to my gorgeous girl who is currently having a lovely sniff in the bushes just ahead of me. Javi has come for some fresh air too and so he's filming, which is way better than me holding the camera in front of my face. No one wants to see a close-up of these tired eyes.

Meeting Taylor was not what I expected. She wasn't a broken woman struggling to cope in prison. She didn't seem riddled with guilt – a hand-wringing Lady Macbeth. There were moments of emotion, talking about prison life and Craig, but for the most part she appeared completely removed from the gravity of her situation, as though this is just the next crazy plot twist on their reality show.

We're hearing a lot about what kind of woman and mother Lynn was, and . . .

[Pause]

Sorry, I've just lost sight of Snowy. I'll have to edit this bit out.

[Shouting] Snowy?

[Shouting] Snowy?

I can't find Snowy. Javi, can you see her?

Javi

No. Is she over there with that other dog?

Tom
No. She doesn't like other dogs and she never runs off. She's too nervous.

[Shouting] Snowy, here, girl. Come here.

Oh God, someone must have . . .

[Shouting] Snowy.

[Heavy breathing]

I can't see her anywhere.

[Pause]

Javi
Look! Over there by the gates.

Tom
Oh God, someone is holding her.

[Heavy breathing]

[Shouting] Hey, that's my dog!

Unknown man
Oh, hi. Great. I was just looking for the owner. Here you go.

Tom
Oh Snowy, come to Daddy. That's it. I've got you.
  Thank you so much. Where was she?

Unknown man
Out on the road, cowering by a car. She kept trying to run in front of the traffic to get into the park. I only just managed to grab her.

Tom

That doesn't make any sense. She never leaves my side and is too nervous of cars and dogs to run out of the gates by herself.

Unknown man

I'm glad she's safe. I'd better get going.

Tom

Hang on. There's something around her neck. A scarf. Is it yours?

Unknown man

No. She had it on her when I found her.

Tom

What the hell? Javi, look at this. She's got a red scarf around her neck. It's silk and looks expensive.

[Pause]

Oh my God, it's la tierra.

Javi

No way.

Tom

This is . . . this is another threat, isn't it? Someone has snatched Snowy in broad daylight and dumped her outside the park, and they tied this scarf around her neck so I'd know it wasn't an accident.

My poor baby girl. Are you OK, Snowy?

Javi

What are you going to do?

Tom

I don't know yet. But something.

Tom Isaac Investigates: What really happened to Bradley Wilcox?
Episode 9: Who is the real Taylor Lancaster?

PUBLISHED ON YOUTUBE AND SPOTIFY:
FRIDAY, 20 OCTOBER 2023

95,116 COMMENTS

Wendy Clarke
So glad Snowy is OK!! How scary!

TI_BiggestFan
Please be careful, Tom!

LWTL_No1Fan
Wow! So scary. I can't believe I'm actually saying this but I believe Taylor over Craig. No one can fake a relationship for six months like they did.

> **SyfyGeek90**
> She just admitted to lying about jilting Craig at the altar and now you believe her?

> **Ernie Martin**
> Who cares about this stupid wedding? You aren't asking the right questions. Did you kill your mum? What happened to Bradley? Let me in there and I'll get the truth out of her.

> **SyfyGeek90**
> Agree! That whole interview was Taylor acting a part – the naive and innocent woman! No one should believe a word that comes out of her mouth! How can she say that their show was

completely real when we all know the wedding was a sham? Tom, I hope you're not buying this!

TrueCrime_Junkie1001

'Growing up we were a totally normal family' – yeah, totally normal to live in a mansion with a pool and be driven to private school in Daddy's sports car. Another example of just how removed Taylor is from any kind of reality.

SyfyGeek90

Tom, have you thought about going to the Lancaster home to look around? If India and Locke aren't there then it's empty right now. It would be good to get a sense of where it all happened – Bradley's last known whereabouts and Lynn's death!

> **LWTL_No1Fan**
> YES YES YES!

EXTRACT FROM INTERVIEWS RECORDED
BY THE METROPOLITAN POLICE
BETWEEN 13–22 SEPTEMBER 2023

Location: Twickenham Police Station

Taylor Lancaster: I've told you all of this already. It was a quiet night for us. We'd been at a meeting with our European distributor for la tierra in the afternoon. Sundays were usually catch-up days on admin and stuff, but Lynn wanted to meet with the supplier that day. She did that sometimes – booked meetings on weekends – to test their commitment.

We'd had an invite to a drinks event in the evening but . . . we decided not to go. We were facing a lot of negativity from the press and it was exhausting trying to keep smiling and pretending I couldn't hear the whispers going on around me and listening to the faux-concern from those wanting juicy gossip. And Lynn had an interview with a YouTuber wannabe journalist first thing Monday so we decided to have an evening at home.

We got home about seven and I made a cup of herbal tea and went up to bed. It was nice to have an evening to myself, to be honest. I read for a bit and did some stuff on social media. By nine thirty I was asleep.

I don't know what Lynn did. She probably worked in her study for a few hours and then had a glass of wine and watched TV while doing some admin stuff. Lynn wasn't a great sleeper. She would often stay up until midnight, tinkering with adverts and scheduling social media posts.

It's entirely possible she invited a friend over after I'd gone upstairs. It's no secret Lynn loved company, but the other side of that love was a hate for being alone. Some nights she'd wake one of us up to ask us something that could easily have waited until morning or rope us in with packing goody bags just so she had someone to hang out with. On the odd occasion she'd wake us all up.

She didn't get me up that night and I sleep with earplugs, so if she'd had a wild party with fifty people going on downstairs, I wouldn't have known.

And just to say on the whole 'I was the only one there that night' thing, it doesn't mean someone else couldn't have come in. Not only could Lynn have invited anyone over, but, like, twenty people had keys to our house and knew the access codes to the security system. The cleaners, the PR team, all the crew. Mum gave keys to everyone.

Why are you making this massive deal about how I was the only one there and no one is talking about the fact that the security system was turned off that night? Like, why would I do that? I was already in the house! It has to be someone coming in who didn't want to be seen.

And there's a side gate to the house. You know that, right? We used it all the time. Just because none of the paps caught anyone on the driveway, it doesn't mean someone else wasn't there.

Living with the Lancasters
Series 4, episode 9 (2010)

PUBLISHED TO YOUTUBE: SUNDAY, 28 FEBRUARY 2010

Lynn Lancaster, confessional
The original plan was that Ed would retire and take over raising the kids and I'd start my own business. But like I said before, having children changed my perspective. I still wanted to do something amazing with my life, but I wanted it to involve my family, which Ed was fully supportive of.

So while we were figuring out what my dream looked like, Ed became a football agent. He'd been in the industry for so long, he knew practically everyone anyway. He was always so passionate about helping talented young footballers. You wouldn't believe the kind of shady deals that used to go on back then. They probably still do.

I worked as Ed's assistant for the entire time he was agenting. Making calls to the boys, arranging meetings. It was so inspiring to see how Ed was helping them.

He had a dream to clean up the industry and put more rules in place to protect young footballers. Don't forget, a lot of these lads had spent so many hours playing football, they weren't always very well educated. They'd have signed anything from anyone if they were promised a shot at playing in the Premier League. It made them incredibly vulnerable and Ed wanted to protect them.

And he did that. Right up until the day he died.

Living with the Lancasters
Series 4, episode 9 (2010)

PUBLISHED TO YOUTUBE: SUNDAY, 7 MARCH 2010

Lynn Lancaster, confessional

So I've had a lot of comments from last week asking for me to talk about Ed's death and what happened. It isn't easy. He died so young, making me a widow at forty.

It was so stupid and pointless – Ed's death, I mean. If only we'd been in the house, we could've stopped it.

So it was February and I was taking the kids shopping. There was a new boutique opening on Bond Street and I'd been invited. I was planning to take just Taylor, but then Ed threw his back out. It was an old football injury that flared up now and again if he played too much golf. He had to lie on the floor for hours at a time and eventually it eased up. He was always grumpy when his back was like that.

He hadn't slept the night before because of the pain, so I took Locke and India with me too so he'd get some peace and quiet.

When we got home that evening, he was dead. The coroner said he'd taken a massive dose of painkillers and mixed it with sleeping pills. It was a stupid accident. I think he just got really frustrated and was thinking about wanting to sleep.

It was the most devastating moment of my entire life. And for the children too. I knew the grief we were all feeling could destroy us. For so many years it felt like our lives had revolved completely around Ed. He was the sun and we were the planets.

I knew that as a family we needed a focus. Something to work towards. Ed and I had been talking about a reality show around him being a football agent, but Ed had a lot of reservations about the impact and intrusion on the kids.

I understood and shared some of those reservations, but when he died, I had to channel my grief into something. I had to make sure the kids all had a focus. And that became making *Living with the Lancasters* happen.

EXTRACT FROM EVIDENCE COLLECTED
BY THE METROPOLITAN POLICE FROM THE
LANCASTER PROPERTY ON 22 NOVEMBER 2023

Item No: 3

Description: Notebook titled 'Detective's Notes 3 by India Lancaster, age 10'

Tuesday, 29 July 2003

Overheard conversation (recorded and transcribed):

Dad: It's my party, not a work event. Why are we inviting my clients?

Mum: It's a nice thing to do. Besides, you have a good relationship with your lads. Let's show that off.

Dad: Fine. But if I get pinned into a corner talking Premier League scouts all night, you'd better come and rescue me.

Mum: I will, darling. You know I will. Besides, Dale is still causing problems. It will be a good opportunity for him to remember how lucky he is to have you as his agent.

Dad: Good point. You're not just a pretty face, are you, Mrs Lancaster?

Mum: Oh Ed, you goof.

Text messages, 21 October 2023

Tom
Hey Locke,

Quick question (and it's totally fine if the answer is no) – a few TIs watching the show have suggested I do an episode walking through the house. Would it be too weird for you to go back?

Locke
You can have the keys to the house, mate. I'll post them up to you special delivery.

No way I'm going back but knock yourself out!

Living with the Lancasters
Series 4, episode 11 (2010)

PUBLISHED TO YOUTUBE: SUNDAY, 14 MARCH 2010

Lynn Lancaster, confessional

I know what people think of me. They think I'm controlling. But that's rubbish. There's a huge difference between controlling and being in control, and I am always in control. I have to be.

Look around you. All this – everything we've built – is because of me, because I have been three steps ahead of everyone else. I've made the difficult decisions. I've worked relentlessly to make sure we always come out on top.

Let me tell you something – if I was a man, they'd call me business-minded. But I'm a woman so obviously that makes me a control freak and a bitch, too. Well, this bitch is always going to come out on top.

Tom Isaac Investigates: What really happened to Bradley Wilcox?
Episode 10: We find the shocking truth!

PUBLISHED ON YOUTUBE AND SPOTIFY:
TUESDAY, 24 OCTOBER 2023

Voice of Tom Isaac
The following episode contains scenes which some viewers and listeners may find disturbing.

LOCATION: TOM'S STUDY

Tom
Hi everyone, welcome to *Tom Isaac Investigates: What really happened to Bradley Wilcox?*

So first of all, it's not Friday. My regular viewers will know that this is the first time ever that I've released an episode early. Javi and I have been working non-stop to get this footage edited and as polished as we can, but it's been a rush. It's currently the early hours of Tuesday morning, we're exhausted and still in shock, so please forgive some of the places where the sound is a bit muffled.

As you're about to find out, we finally have answers on what really happened to Bradley Wilcox. It's already hit the online media and socials, and will be in the papers this morning. My phone hasn't stopped ringing and there are photographers outside my house. I thought it wasn't right to wait until Friday. It feels super important to get the truth out there right now.

I don't know what else to say, except that I've put a warning at the start and an age rating on this episode. It's going to get . . . well, it's brutal, but I've always said we would find the truth, and this is it.

LOCATION: OUTSIDE THE LANCASTER FAMILY HOME, HAMPTON WICK, LONDON

Tom

I'm standing on the front steps of the Lancaster house. I keep expecting Taylor and Lynn to throw open the front door and start bickering over Taylor's choice of shoes or something.

It's one of those perfect winter days where the sun is a pale buttery yellow and the sky is streaked with the criss-cross of plane contrails.

Before we dive in, I just want to say thank you for all the lovely messages of support for Snowy. It means a lot. I'm not sleeping great and still keep thinking about that moment I realized she was gone, but Snowy is completely safe now. She's gone on a little holiday with Mumsie for a few weeks while I find out who is behind the threats. I'm missing them both like crazy, but while I'm prepared to put myself at risk, I won't do it to those I love.

So why are we here? What do we hope to find? I don't think this episode is about answers. It's more about perspective. This house is at the very centre of our investigation. It's the last place anyone saw Bradley Wilcox. It's the place Lynn Lancaster was killed only six weeks ago. It's the set of *Living with the Lancasters* and was the centre of a multimillion-pound empire.

And I have the keys and permission from Locke to look around.

[Jangling keys]

But I'm not doing this alone. First of all, this place gives me the total creeps. I'm getting shivers down my spine big time. Like, I know there's nothing to be scared of. It's not like Lynn's murderer is going to be lurking behind a doorway, ready to jump out at us. And I know her body isn't still in there, but there is no way I'm going into this house without a wingman.

Javi has the camera as always and Cassie should be here any

second. I've visited this house a handful of times as a kid, but Cassie spent most of her childhood here and knows the layout better than me. Plus, it was the last place her brother was seen, so it's going to be emotional for her to be back here.

I've also asked Badru to be here. Badru will not only have insights into Bradley's investigation, which started with a party in this house, but as a retired detective who still regularly assists in active investigations, he may see things that we would otherwise miss.

Oh look, here they come.

Cassie

Sorry we're late. I actually got here an hour early because I've been awake since 4 a.m. Actually, that's a lie. I've not slept at all. Four a.m. was when I gave up trying. So I met Badru for a coffee and we lost track of time. Sorry, I'm seriously nervous.

Tom

Oh God, you're giving me all the anxiety. Deep breaths, darling. We've got this.

Before we go in, I'd like to ask you both, what do you think we're going to find today? What is making you nervous, Cassie?

Cassie

I feel like . . . this is it. This is my last chance to get answers. I'm certain the truth about Bradley is in this house . . .

[Pause]

I've thought about Bradley every day for the past twenty years. When that video came out in February, I thought we'd finally learn what happened to him that night, but it's been months and nothing has happened. You're the only one doing anything, Tom.

Badru
Cassie, we've talked about his. The chances of finding anything that can contribute to the investigation into Bradley's disappearance are very small. The house would have been searched after Lynn's death.

Tom
Badru, did the police ever do a proper search of the house back in 2003?

Badru
No. As you know, our entire investigation was focused on Bradley disappearing between Richmond and East Twickenham. We had no reason or cause to search the house. We still have no solid evidence that anything untoward happened to Bradley at the party.

Cassie
I don't see how you can still think that. After Dale's interview and Lynn's death. Not to mention the video, which really looks to me like it shows Lynn spiking a drink she gives to Bradley. And now Tom is getting threats. There is something to find here. I know it.

Tom
Do you need a moment? We've got all day, we don't—

Cassie
No. Let's do it. I'm ready.

Tom
When were you last here, Cassie?

[Pause]

Cassie
I was here the afternoon after Ed's party when I came to look for Bradley. And then once more a few months after Bradley disappeared. By that point, I was starting to question what Lynn and Taylor had said to me about Bradley leaving, and I wanted to ask Taylor about the text message Bradley sent me. We'd been best friends for most of our lives, and I thought if there was anything she wouldn't tell the police, then maybe she'd tell me.

But she was really cold with me. Kept me standing right here on the doorstep. She told me she didn't have a clue what the text message meant, and that Bradley had been drinking at the party and was probably drunk when he sent it, which didn't sound like Bradley at all.

It was clear I was never going to get any more out of the Lancasters, and I've not spoken to her since.

[Dogs barking]

Tom
What's that? Javi, are you getting this? A van has just turned into the driveway and is heading this way. I can hear dogs inside.

Cassie
They're with me.

Tom
What do you mean? Why have you brought dogs with you?

Cassie
I . . . didn't want to say anything in case you said I couldn't do it or we should ask for permission—

Tom
Permission for what? What's going on?

Cassie
Don't freak out, but I've hired cadaver dogs. Trained dogs that can smell human remains.

Tom
What?

Cassie
I'm sorry. I know I should've told you, but I couldn't risk you saying no.

Tom
And you can just hire them?

Cassie
Yes. Badru gave me the name of a company who could help.

Tom
Badru, you knew about this? And you're OK with it? Surely it's breaking some kind of law? This feels like something the police should be doing, not us.

Badru
Technically, you have permission from a member of the Lancaster family to look around, and at this stage, that's all we're doing. But I would suggest calling one of the family and letting them know. Just to cover our backs in the unlikely event that we find something.

Tom
Yes . . . I think I should. Looking around a house and searching for human remains doesn't feel like the same thing. Give me a minute, Javi.

[Recording paused]

[Recording started]

Tom

OK, I've spoken to Locke and he's said he's happy for us to proceed. His exact words were, 'Do what you like.' But I have to ask, Cassie, are you sure you want to do this?

Cassie

One hundred per cent. I haven't seen my brother for twenty years. Taylor – all the Lancasters – totally shut me out after that party. They were like family to me, but after the party, I stopped existing to them. It hurt. Not as much as losing Bradley, but it still hurt. Why would they do that unless they had something to hide?

I've been searching for answers for more years than I got to spend with Bradley. The party video showed he was never in that taxi. What if he never left at all? What if something happened to him at the party and they covered it up? It's really the only scenario that makes sense to me, and if he's still here then I want to know.

And yeah, you're right, this is something the police should be doing – should have done years ago, in fact – but they haven't and I don't think they ever will. Sorry, Badru.

Badru

It's OK, Cassie. I can understand your frustration. I'm as desperate as you are to find answers.

Tom

I can't believe we're doing this.

Javi, make sure you capture this. There are two people in khaki uniforms heading this way with two very big brown and black German Shepherds. Those dogs are keen, aren't they?

[Dogs barking]

Cassie

Tom, this is Phil Parker and Angi Platt, and their dogs, Rocket and Bruno.

Tom

Hi, welcome to *Tom Isaac Investigates*.

I've only just found out about this so bear with me.

I'm Tom. The tall bearded Frenchman behind the camera is Javi, and this is Badru, a retired police officer. And I guess you know Cassie.

Phil

Nice to meet you all.

Tom

What happens now?

Phil

Very simple. We unleash Rocket and Bruno and they'll have a good run around the property and alert us to human remains.

Tom

Even very old remains?

Angi

Absolutely. Even remains that are a few decades old, which I believe is what we're looking for today, can easily be detected by cadaver dogs. They can detect remains up to fifteen feet underground and have a ninety-five per cent accuracy.

Tom

They're really barking. Does that mean they can smell something now?

Angi
No. The barking means they're excited to start. If they sniff out human remains then we'll see them lie down in that area and stop barking, and that's when we get the shovels out and dig.

Phil
I know we went through this over the phone, Cassie, but I want to make it clear that it's important to understand that even if the dogs do lie down, it could be from ancient remains, which is why we dig first before alerting the authorities.

[Barking noises]

Tom
I'll open the front door and walk through the house to the back door so they have access to the gardens. Once it's open, I'll shout out and you can take off their leads. Javi, you come with me so we're ready to follow the dogs wherever they go.

[Pause]

Tom
[Shouting] The back door is open.

Gosh, they're off quick. They've run straight through the house and out the back door. Come on, Javi, we need to follow them.

[Heavy breathing]

This is completely insane. God, I think I'm going to have a heart attack. Look, there's the pool where Lynn was found. The dogs aren't stopping. Where have they gone?

Cassie
They're in the trees.

Tom

For those listening on the podcast, Cassie, Badru and I have just run from the back door that leads out of the kitchen, past the pool and the patio. There's a tennis court to the left and flower beds and shrubs to the right. In front of us is a huge lawn that slopes down towards a small woodland area at the back of the property. I can't see the dogs any more.

[Heavy breathing]

Angi and Phil are just ahead of us. The dogs have entered the copse. Can you hear that?

[Pause]

The dogs have stopped barking. Have they found something?

We're entering the woods and we're slowing down. The dogs are in here somewhere. Everyone is walking now. I've gone cold all over. Total goosebumps. This feels—

Cassie

There they are. They're lying down. Tom, the dogs are lying down. There's something here.

[Crying]

I knew it.

Tom

Oh. My. God.

Badru

Cassie, it could be something else. Remember what Phil said. It could be ancient remains or an error. It might not be Bradley.

Cassie
I know. I just . . . I've waited so long for answers and this could be it.

Angi
Cassie, as you can see, Rocket and Bruno have found this spot underneath an oak tree. Phil is heading back to the van now to get some shovels.

Badru
Why don't you go inside and take a seat, Cassie? There's no reason to watch this.

Cassie
No! I'm staying. I have to see. I have to know.

Badru
It's going to be a little while. Let's pause filming and get some water. Just take a five-minute breather. I can come and get you if there's anything to see. What do you think, Tom?

Tom
Yes, let's do that.

Badru
I'm also going to put a call in to DS Ewings, the lead investigator on Bradley's case, to give her a heads-up on what's going on here.

Angi
Please, all of you – I know this is a highly emotional moment – but even though it's unlikely, there are rare occasions when the dogs get it wrong. Let us do our thing now and we'll let you know as soon as we find something.

Tom Isaac Investigates: What really happened to Bradley Wilcox?

Episode 10: We find the shocking truth! (cont.)

PUBLISHED ON YOUTUBE AND SPOTIFY:
TUESDAY, 24 OCTOBER 2023

LOCATION: GARDEN OF LANCASTER FAMILY HOME, HAMPTON WICK, LONDON

Tom
I'm standing in the grounds of the Lancaster property. We're in a wooded area at the bottom of the garden where an hour ago two cadaver dogs identified an area that potentially contains human remains. The cadaver dogs' owners, Phil and Angi, have been digging for a while now and the hole has got pretty deep. We are all feeling incredibly tense as we wait for—

Phil
I've got something.

Tom
They've stopped digging. They've found something.

Badru
I can't tell you to stop until we have something confirmed, but please be careful how much you disturb.

Cassie
What can you see? Tell me.

Phil
We've dug approximately four foot down and we've found some blue tarpaulin.

Tom
Javi, get as close as you can. I'm right beside you, Cassie, I'm here. Hold my hand.

[Pause]

Cassie
What's happening? What is it? I can't look.

[Crying]

Someone please tell me what's going on.

Angi
OK, Cassie, I can talk through what I'm doing. We've found a long sheet of blue tarpaulin. I'm just uncovering it now. I want to disturb as little as possible so I'm moving slowly.

[Pause]

I'm pulling the tarpaulin back. I can see a lot of dirt and . . . a skull and a body. I can confirm we've found a body.

Badru
That's it. Angi, Phil, thank you. But I now need you to step away from the grave. I'm calling the police. Cassie, Tom and Javi, please stand well back now.

Cassie
Is it Bradley?

Phil

I'm afraid we can't answer that.

Cassie

But is it . . . is it recent? It's not like an ancient burial site?

Phil

No. It's not ancient remains. The body is wrapped in blue polyethylene which suggests the burial took place within the last seventy years.

Tom

Oh my God.

Angi

Cassie, do you remember if Bradley was wearing a watch the night he disappeared?

Cassie

Yes. It was a silver Seiko diving watch. It has a silver surround and a black strap. It was a gift for his eighteenth from my parents. He never took it off.

Angi

As Phil said, we can't give you a definitive answer, but I can tell you that I can see a watch that matches that description.

Cassie

No. Oh no.

[Crying]

Oh Bradley. I knew it, Tom. I knew he was here. But I . . .

[Inaudible]

Tom
You still hoped he wasn't. I know. Come on, let's go inside. You need to sit down.

Badru
That's a good idea. The police are on their way.

LOCATION: KITCHEN OF LANCASTER PROPERTY

Tom
It's late afternoon. The police have been here for hours. They've exhumed the body and taken it away. Cassie is devastated, which is completely understandable, and Javi has driven her home. Badru is still here somewhere talking to DS Ewings.

We won't have a formal identification on the remains found earlier in the Lancaster family's garden until a post-mortem examination, but considering that a silver Seiko diving watch identical to Bradley's has been found with the remains, I feel like it has to be him.

I'm completely exhausted, but wired, too. Everything feels very raw. My heart is broken for Cassie. She arranged for the cadaver dogs to come, and I think a big part of her was expecting this, but there's a difference between expecting something to happen and it actually happening.

She's been looking for her brother for twenty years and we've finally found him. The search is over. I said at the start of this docuseries that I would find out what really happened to Bradley Wilcox and I have done, and it's heart-breaking and awful, but we have the truth.

There's still a lot we don't know. We don't know how Bradley died. His body will be examined by a pathologist, which will hopefully lead to answers. But it might not. He is just . . . well, he's just a skeleton now.

We don't know if his death was an accident or foul play, but we do know that whatever happened here, someone in the Lancaster family was involved in covering up his death. Someone dug a very deep hole and buried Bradley's body. Someone has been lying. And do you know what I think . . . watching the effort it took Phil and Angi to dig that hole, it's made me think that getting Bradley's body from the house to the woods, then burying him – it's not something you could easily do on your own, and not something that would go unnoticed by everyone else living in the house.

Lynn and Edward Lancaster may both be dead, but there are three other Lancasters who aren't. One of them must have seen something, or know something. We're going to find out.

Tom Isaac Investigates: What really happened to Bradley Wilcox?
Episode 10: We find the shocking truth!

PUBLISHED ON YOUTUBE AND SPOTIFY:
TUESDAY, 24 OCTOBER 2023

119,875 COMMENTS

JulieAlexander_1
RIP Bradley #JusticeForBradley

TI_BiggestFan
I hope you're OK, Tom. That must have been really hard for you and Cassie. RIP Bradley!

LWTL_No1Fan
I'm not surprised at all. Well done @SyfyGeek90 for suggesting Tom go to the house!

Katy Shepard
OMG this was the most exciting episode I've ever watched of anything ever!!!!!

> **TrueCrime_Junkie1001**
> You realize this is real, right? That Cassie just found out her missing brother is dead and is devastated? But great that you were entertained!

Wendy Clarke
Condolences to the Wilcox family. RIP Bradley #JusticeForBradley

NOVEMBER 2023

TRANSCRIPT FROM SKY NEWS LIVE
WITH PATRICK MONAGHAN AND
AMBER CARNEY, 1 NOVEMBER 2023

Patrick: In today's top story, human remains found last week in the grounds of the home of reality TV family the Lancasters have now been formally identified using dental records as teenager Bradley Wilcox, who went missing following a party at the Lancaster house in August 2003.

Amber Carney is here to tell us more.

Amber: Thank you, Patrick. This is certainly a tragic story that has gripped the nation. As you know, Bradley's remains were discovered by his sister Cassie, as part of a search during *Tom Isaac Investigates* – a YouTube documentary series on her brother's disappearance.

I sat down with Cassie Wilcox this morning.

[Pre-recorded interview]

Amber: Cassie, thank you for joining me. Tell me what it was like finding your brother after all this time.

Cassie: It was the worst moment of my life. I feel like I've been held prisoner for twenty years by the not knowing. It's devastating that he died that night. But we could've grieved back then. We could've moved on with our lives eventually.

Amber: What do you hope will happen now in your brother's investigation?

Cassie: I'm furious that the truth about my brother was hidden from us. Someone in the Lancaster family, someone at that party, must know what happened that night. My hope is that the police will finally take this seriously, and that Tom Isaac's investigation will give us the answers we need, and we'll finally get justice for Bradley.

[Sky News live]

Patrick: Amber, has there been a comment from any of the three Lancaster siblings yet?

Amber: From Locke and India, no. They are both still in hiding, although we can assume they've been questioned by police.

We have been given a statement from Taylor Lancaster's legal team which says: 'My client is devastated by this development. Her heartfelt condolences go out to Bradley's sister, Cassie. Taylor is cooperating fully with the police investigation into Bradley's death.'

Patrick: Thank you, Amber. We're just getting reports in that the post-mortem on the remains of Bradley Wilcox has been inconclusive. A coroner has ruled 'No Cause of Death' for the teenager who went missing on the second of August 2003. This news will be another blow for the police investigation following months of delays and the death of key witness, Lynn Lancaster.

EXTRACT FROM EVIDENCE COLLECTED
BY THE METROPOLITAN POLICE FROM THE
LANCASTER PROPERTY ON 22 NOVEMBER 2023

Item No: 3

Description: Notebook titled 'Detective's Notes 3 by India Lancaster, age 10'

Saturday, 2 August 2003

Overheard conversation (recorded and transcribed):

Dad: Taylor, go and change. That dress is far too short.

Mum: Leave her, Ed, she looks stunning. She's not a child any more.

Dad: That's what worries me. You were the one who invited my footie lads.

Taylor: Tell them not to talk to me. I hate footballers.

Dad: Thanks a bunch. On second thoughts, keep thinking that.

Mum: I wouldn't worry, love. Taylor only has eyes for Bradley and he wouldn't hurt a fly.

Locke: Mum, Dad, can I come down and be at the party for an hour at the start?

Dad: Maybe.

Mum: Ed, we agreed.

Dad: You're right. Sorry, Locke. Your mum and I did discuss it, and you're just a bit too young. This is an adult party and your mum and I will be busy with our friends.

Mum: I'll be having my fortieth birthday party next year. Maybe you can come to that one for a little bit.

Locke: Whatever.

Questions

Is Taylor an adult now? (She's bossy enough as it is.)

Why does Dad not want Taylor to like his football clients?

Tom Isaac Investigates: What really happened to Bradley Wilcox?
Episode 11: Taylor speaks out!

PUBLISHED ON YOUTUBE AND SPOTIFY:
FRIDAY, 3 NOVEMBER 2023

Voice of Jerry Olaski, JO Music Productions

My wife and I went to a lot of their parties, and yes, before you ask, we were at Ed's fortieth. Although don't ask me what I remember. We were all drinking heavily and it was twenty years ago. All I can say is that it was a good night. A real laugh.

I do remember Ed disappeared for a bit at one point. I assumed all the people got a bit much for him. You could tell the party was all Lynn's doing. But he came back after a bit and got everyone dancing to these proper eighties bangers. ABBA and whatnot.

You know what, I think it might have been me who recorded that video. The one of Ed dancing. I have a hazy memory of picking up a camera because Ed looked like a right clown. I had no idea what was going on at the other end of the room or how important that video would turn out to be.

LOCATION: TOM'S STUDY

Tom

This is episode eleven of *Tom Isaac Investigates: What really happened to Bradley Wilcox?* So much has happened. I've had another tidal wave of new followers. Thank you! Since the horrific moment we found Bradley's remains in our last episode, you'll have seen in the news that the coroner has ruled 'No Cause of Death'. It would have been such a relief to learn how Bradley died, to get those final answers, but the reality is that with the level of decomposition – twenty years in the ground – it's almost impossible unless a murder weapon is found with the body, or there is significant damage to the bones of the skeleton or skull.

But do not think that this ruling tells us nothing. We now know that there was no skeletal damage. No head wound, no sign of violence at all.

What did happen that night? Why was no ambulance ever called? Why did no one at the party report anything out of the ordinary? What led a pretty normal family with no criminal history to bury a body in their garden and carry on with their lives as though nothing had happened? If that is what happened, of course. We still have a lot to uncover in this investigation.

And also, a big question we need to answer – who in the Lancaster family was involved?

Voice of Cassie Wilcox
Lynn answered the door in full tidy-up mode, which to Lynn meant getting a cleaning team in and telling them what to do while she drank coffee.

Tom
Lynn was the last person we know of to speak to Bradley. With everything we now know about her and this family, it seems likely she was involved in Bradley's death. But Lynn doesn't strike me as the type of person to dig a grave herself. So should we assume then that Ed dug the grave and was complicit in the cover-up?

Ed has so far not featured much in this docuseries. For the main reason that he never lied to the police in 2003 about seeing Bradley leave. Ed also died in 2004, just six months after Bradley, following an accidental overdose, so he wasn't around for any of what followed or the rise of his family's fame. But I think we should start to work on the assumption that whatever happened that night, Ed was involved in covering up Bradley's death.

And what about Taylor? Now the only member of the Lancaster family still alive who was at the party that night, and someone who we know lied to the police. I'm leaving shortly for my second interview with Taylor where I will be asking tough questions.

LOCATION: HM PRISON BRONZEFIELD,
PRIVATE INTERVIEW SUITE
INTERVIEW BETWEEN TOM ISAAC
AND TAYLOR LANCASTER

Taylor
Before you say anything, can I just say how totally shocked and heartbroken I am about Bradley. I seriously cannot believe he's dead . . . and . . .

[Pause]

Sorry. I'm still so upset. I can't believe he was in our garden the entire time. It's so tragic. Poor Cassie.

Tom
Have the police questioned you about Bradley's death?

Taylor
Yes, but I wasn't any help. It's all just so awful.

Tom
We know from a text Bradley sent at 11 p.m. on the night of the party that he wanted to leave. My theory is that he saw something he shouldn't have done, and that Lynn convinced him to stay in some kind of damage-control situation, and that was the conversation captured on the video released in February.

Taylor
What do you think he saw?

Tom
I don't know. By all accounts it was a wild party. I'm wondering if he saw someone – Lynn perhaps – in a compromising position with another guest. But I wasn't there and you were. You invited Bradley to the party. What happened that night?

Taylor
I really wish I could tell you something useful. Bradley and I spent time together early on in the evening, but I didn't see him after, like, ten. I went upstairs for ages and didn't come down until the fireworks.

Tom
You didn't see him after 10 p.m.? You told the detectives investigating Bradley's disappearance that you saw him get into a taxi at 11.45 p.m.

Taylor
I meant I didn't hang out with him after ten. I didn't speak to him. I didn't mean I didn't—

Tom
We know Bradley didn't get in the taxi that night. Why did you lie to the police?

Taylor
[Inaudible]

Tom
Sorry, what was that?

Taylor
All right. God!

[Sigh]

Look, Lynn told me to say it, OK? I know it was wrong. Honestly, Tom, I've felt truly awful about it every day for twenty years. Mum told me she'd seen him leave. She said it would help Bradley's case if there was another witness who saw the same because then the police would be focused on exactly where he'd gone missing rather than on questioning us. I did what I was told, and even though I regretted it afterwards, I couldn't unsay it or take it back without getting in trouble, and getting Lynn in trouble, too.

I was just a stupid kid.

Tom
I think a lot of people would say that you were seventeen, and that's old enough to know right from wrong.

Taylor
I know, but I honestly didn't see the harm in just repeating what Lynn saw. I wish I could tell you more.

Tom
Sorry, Taylor, but I'm finding it hard to believe that you don't know more about Bradley's death. It happened in your house. He was there because of you. You lied to the police about seeing him leave that night. And you're still lying twenty years later.

Burying a body takes hours of digging. What do you remember the morning after the party? Where were you? What did you see?

Taylor
I was . . . I was trying to sleep off a hangover.

Tom
Right. Of course you were.

I think we should probably stop here. This is our second of only three interviews together, and I want to carry on talking to you, but you're wasting my time. We're not getting anywhere, are we?

Javi, stop the—

Taylor
Wait. Don't go. I can't go back to my cell yet. Being trapped in this place . . .

[Pause]

Look, I'm sorry I can't help more with Bradley, but I can tell you anything you want to know about Lynn's death. I thought you were investigating that too? That's what you said. That's why I agreed to this. Despite what you think, I'm innocent. I didn't kill Lynn, and I need your help to prove it.

Tom? Please don't give up on me. My life is completely ruined. I'm stuck in prison, for God's sake. I have nothing left. La tierra is dead. I'm heartbroken. And I'm pretty sure the world hates me and a jury are going to convict me of something I didn't do.

[Crying]

Please help me.

Tom
I do want to help you, Taylor. I've made my whole life about finding the truth, the answers others have missed. But what's the point of asking questions if you're not going to be honest? I have other leads and other interviews I could be doing.

This investigation isn't just about you and your life. Cassie needs the truth. Locke and India are in hiding. I'm receiving threats. My family is in danger. I will find the truth, with or without you.

Taylor
I am telling you the truth. I swear. Please. Ask me anything about Lynn's death.

Tom
Did you kill your mother?

Taylor
No.

Tom
What about the call to the police the morning you found her? There has been a lot of speculation across social media about the fact that the police were not your first call, or even your second. You called India and then Locke before calling the police. I'm going to play your call to emergency services for you now.

AUDIO RECORDING OF EMERGENCY SERVICES CALL
CENTRE, WATERLOO ROAD, LONDON

(11 September 2023, 5.15 a.m.)
Leaked online 15 September 2023

Operator: Emergency. Which service please?
Caller: I don't know. I don't know. Who do I need for a dead body?
Operator: Transferring you to the ambulance service now.
Caller: I don't need an ambulance. I need the police.

Taylor
I don't even remember making that call. I was in shock. I just kept thinking of all the stuff I was supposed to be doing that day and how I'd have to cancel it all and what a mess my schedule was going to be.

I couldn't even process that Lynn wasn't there any more. If I'd been screaming or crying when I made that call, I'd still be here. They'd just have spun it all another way. I'd have been faking it or emotional because I was feeling guilty. There is no way to win.

Tom
Let's talk about the cause of death. A near-fatal dose of Zalpodine prescription tablets was found in Lynn's system. There's no record of Lynn having a prescription for these tablets, but there is a record for these tablets in your name. Can you explain why you had them? And if you didn't give them to Lynn, then who else had access to them?

Taylor
They're not mine, Tom. I never spoke to a doctor or asked for a prescription for them. I've never had trouble sleeping, and even if I had, I wouldn't, not in a million years, have taken Zalpodine. I hate that stuff. My dad took it when he threw his back out. He took a bunch of painkillers and some sleeping tablets and accidentally overdosed.

Like, why would I ever take it? I hate it. It's . . .

[Pause]

Tom
It's what?

Taylor
Nothing. Just, if I'd have seen Zalpodine in the house, I'd have thrown it away.

And here's something else. Something you probably don't know. Those prescriptions that I supposedly asked for from the doctor were all dated from January and done through a phone consultation with a private GP.

Tom
January 2023?

Taylor
Yes. Eight months before Lynn's death. Anyone could've called and pretended to be me. They only ask for an address and a date of birth. The whole world knows that.

And the security cameras were all switched off at the house that night. Did you know that? Why would I have turned them off when I was already in the house? The police have made this big thing about how I was the only one there that night, and how because the press were outside and they didn't see anyone come up the drive, it means no one else could've been involved. But there's a side gate. You turn down the road before the house and keep going and it's on the left. So anyone could've come in that way and not been seen.

Tom
If you didn't kill Lynn then who do you think did? What do you think happened that night?

Taylor
I think someone came into the house and killed her and framed me.

Tom
What about the death threats you made? You have said on countless occasions on the show – both to your mum, and in the confessional – that you'll kill her one day and—

Taylor
[Loud exhale]

Oh my God. Seriously? That's a catchphrase. Everyone knows that. 'I'm going to kill Mum' is the same as 'That's ridic', or 'To die for'.

Lynn wanted us saying the catchphrases as much as we could. It was part of the brand. No one actually thinks I meant it, do they?

[Pause]

I don't know what I'm supposed to do without her. I'm telling you the truth.

[Door opening]

Voice of prison officer
Time's up.

Taylor
Please believe me, Tom. I didn't get those sleeping tablets. I swear.
OK, OK, I'm coming.

LOCATION: TOM'S STUDY

Tom
I've just got home to a cold and empty house. I'm really missing Mumsie and Snowy but I'm glad they're safe. As I got out of my car, it really felt like someone was watching me. Maybe I'm just being paranoid. Finding Bradley's body has really hit home to me that this is real. That probably sounds stupid. It's not like I ever thought it was a game before. But I'm completely obsessed with finding the answers, and I'm a bit scared too.

Not just of the threats and how close poor Snowy came to being seriously hurt, but of finding out the truth. Or not finding out the truth, actually. Everything is unravelling so fast and I'm scared I'm going to miss something or be the reason Cassie doesn't get the answers she deserves and needs, and that we never get justice for Bradley or find out who killed Lynn. These are human beings and they're dead. And rightly, or wrongly, I feel that their deaths are for me to solve.

At the heart of this docuseries is Lynn Lancaster, but sitting right beside her is Zalpodine, a sleeping tablet that has featured throughout the Lancasters' lives: as a means to keep them quiet as children, as a drug that played a part in the deaths of both parents, and, considering Lynn's use of it to calm her own children down, I'm going to speculate here that it was Zalpodine Lynn mixed into Bradley's drink the night he died.

So here's what I'm thinking. If someone knew about Bradley's death or guessed that he died the night of the party, and they also knew about Lynn's use of Zalpodine, then wouldn't it have been poetic justice that her murder involved the same drug? And in that case, Taylor is still my number-one suspect for Lynn's death.

There is something else about the sleeping tablets that is niggling in the back of my mind. It's bound to come to me in the middle of the night, but right now we need to consider who else knew about Lynn's love for Zalpodine.

If Taylor is innocent, then who wanted Lynn dead and Taylor framed for her murder?

Tom Isaac Investigates: What really happened to Bradley Wilcox?
Episode 11: Taylor speaks out!

PUBLISHED ON YOUTUBE AND SPOTIFY:
FRIDAY, 3 NOVEMBER 2023

151,212 COMMENTS

TI_BiggestFan
How can she say she's so sorry about Bradley and still be lying about the night of the party. I really don't like her.

> **Wendy Clarke**
> If Taylor is guilty then I think there is a bigger question here surrounding victims of abuse.

> **KMoorcroft58**
> What do you mean? Who has been abused?

> **Wendy Clarke**
> Taylor has been abused by her mum for years. They all have. Listen to the words she uses when she talks about Lynn. I worked for a domestic abuse charity and we saw this kind of coercive control a lot. It's very damaging. If I was her defence lawyer, I'd be focusing on this.

> **Ernie Martin**
> Taylor was a grown woman. She could do what she liked. People need to stop making Lynn out to be a monster. All the kids keep saying how much they loved and needed her so she can't have been that bad.

Wendy Clarke

You clearly don't understand abuse if you think adults can't be victims, and that victims can't love their abuser at the same time as wanting to be free from them.

TrueCrime_Junkie1001

If we consider Tom's theory that someone knew about Lynn's use of Zalpodine and wanted to use it in her murder, then who could that be?

- Taylor
- Locke
- India
- And what about Cassie? She was always at the house when they were younger!

SyfyGeek90

Anyone else think that Taylor's wording at the start of the interview was totally off? 'I can't believe he was in our garden the entire time. It's so tragic.' She made it sound like Bradley fell down a well and no one thought to look. Like it was an accident and not a murder someone in her own family (including her probably) covered up . . .

TRANSCRIPT FROM SKY NEWS LIVE
WITH PATRICK MONAGHAN AND
AMBER CARNEY, 7 NOVEMBER 2023

Patrick: You're watching Sky News on Tuesday the seventh of November. It's time for an update on the Lancaster story with our celebrity reporter, Amber Carney.

Amber: Once again, it's Taylor Lancaster making headlines this week. We've seen: 'NO GOING HOME FOR TAYLOR' and 'CHRISTMAS BEHIND BARS' following the news that a bail appeal by Taylor's legal team failed to secure her release from prison, where she is currently awaiting trial for the murder of her mother, Lynn Lancaster.

Interestingly, in a closing statement, the Honourable Malcolm Pritchett cited public unrest and Taylor's own safety as two of the reasons why bail was denied. But with the recent discovery of Bradley Wilcox's body in the grounds of the Lancaster home, it's possible more legal trouble could be on the way for Taylor Lancaster.

And Taylor isn't the only one facing jail time in this case. Dale Peterson, a key witness in the original investigation into Bradley Wilcox's disappearance, recently retracted his witness statement, and has been charged by the Metropolitan Police with perverting the course of justice. He's now facing a large fine or even prison time.

Patrick: I understand Taylor's case has also made a splash in the US again?

Amber: Yes, it has. Things got a little crazy on Tuesday when former US president Donald Trump tweeted his support for Taylor.

This prompted a significant rise in viewing figures for *Living with the Lancasters* from the US, and we also saw the Bradley Wilcox case mentioned on America's top morning show, NBC's *Today*, so this story is clearly making waves both here and across the pond.

And in related news this week, the *Daily Express* reported that Cassie Wilcox has signed a six-figure book deal with a major publisher. The memoir, which is expected to be published in the summer of 2024, will tell the story of Bradley's disappearance, the police investigation and Tom Isaac's docuseries that led to the discovery of Bradley's remains twenty years on. The Lancaster family are also expected to feature heavily, and it will no doubt be an emotional and heart-breaking read.

2022 trending video: #LWTLFavMoments

@SophieDavidson_PT

My favourite episode of *Living with the Lancasters* was when Taylor totally girl-bossed that other designer at the Paris fashion show. I don't know why everyone hates her. That whole 90s Paris Hilton princess doesn't get her nails dirty thing was just an act. She's a super-smart businesswoman.

Tom Isaac Investigates: What really happened to Bradley Wilcox?
Episode 12: Who killed Lynn Lancaster?

PUBLISHED ON YOUTUBE AND SPOTIFY:
FRIDAY, 10 NOVEMBER 2023

Lynn Lancaster, talking on *Loose Women* (August 2021)
I love my kids. What mother doesn't? There is nothing I wouldn't do for them. Nothing! I'm their mum, their manager, their cleaner, their personal trainer, their social secretary. People always ask me, what about my life?

[Laughing]

They are my life and they always will be. No matter how old they get, no matter where they go, I will always be there to guide them.

Extract from *Living with the Lancasters*, series 17, episode 1 (2023)
Taylor Lancaster, confessional
Happy New Yeeaaaarrr! Call me nuts, but I love January. I love the feeling of starting over you get. Especially this January. It's 2023, baby.

I have so many things going on this year. I'm so busy, it's ridic. I have a whole new activewear line coming out for la tierra, and I have two words for you – leopard print. You are going to love it. We also have a whole new men's underwear range hitting the shops this summer. It's to die for.

But the biggest news from me is . . . I have decided that this . . . is . . . *the* year I will find love. There, I said it. I've decided. I'm going to make it happen. I'm going to put myself out there. I can't wait!

LOCATION: TOM'S STUDY

Tom

Welcome back to *Tom Isaac Investigates*. We're now fifteen weeks into this docuseries.

Nine weeks since Lynn's death.

Three weeks since we found Bradley's remains.

We are moving closer to the truth on both investigations. And talking of investigations, Badru Zubira will no longer be part of this series. He's been asked to join the team investigating Bradley's death as a consultant, which I'm really pleased about because Badru, like me, isn't going to stop until he gets answers.

I chose those particular interview snippets for the start of this episode for two reasons. Firstly, listening to Taylor talking in the first confessional of this year, she doesn't sound like someone who is anything but excited about the year ahead and her plans for her business. And yet, behind the scenes, the police believe she spoke to a private GP and was given a Zalpodine prescription, with a plan to kill her mum.

Today, I'm interviewing Locke and India Lancaster for the first time since we found Bradley's remains. I obviously have questions for them about the party and the following day and what they might have seen, but . . .

[Pause]

I'm not going to ask them about Bradley today. I know what you're thinking. I mean, hello, after finding Bradley's body, surely we have to ask Locke and India about what they know. And we will. Just not in this episode. After Taylor's interview, I'm feeling super frustrated with asking questions and getting nowhere. Besides, we know Lynn had forbidden the two younger children from going downstairs during the party, so yes, I want to talk to them, and yes, they might have seen something odd in the days following the party, but right now I want to continue the focus on Lynn.

LOCATION: LIVING ROOM (UNDISCLOSED LOCATION)
INTERVIEW BETWEEN TOM ISAAC, LOCKE LANCASTER AND INDIA LANCASTER

Tom
Here we are, back in the living room of Locke and India's temporary home. There's a fire crackling in the log burner beside me. It's warm and cosy in here and we've all got our WC2 coffees. Remember to check out the discount code in the show notes from those lovely people at WC2 Coffee.

Thanks so much for talking to me again today, guys.

India
Of course. And I'm really glad you're here. It's been really hard watching the news about Bradley. How is Cassie doing? And how are you, Tom? That must have been tough. I feel so sorry about it all. Like I said in our first interview, I wish we had done more to help his investigation sooner, although now I understand why Mum never let us talk about Bradley. She clearly didn't want any interest in his case for fear the truth would come out.

Tom
Thanks, India. Cassie is doing OK. She's grieving and it's hard for her right now.

Locke
She didn't waste any time getting a book deal, I notice.

India

Locke, for God's sake. As if we have any right to comment. Besides, you know as well as I do that these deals take months to sort out. It's probably been in the works since the video was first released.

Locke

Yeah, sorry. I'm stir-crazy today and it's making me into a bit of a dick. I'm as shocked and gutted about Bradley as India is. It's all we've been talking about. It's just . . . it's unbelievable, man.

Tom

There's a lot we still don't know about Bradley's death. But I'd like to save those questions for next time, and instead talk about your mother's death. I know it will be hard. Is that OK?

Locke

Right. OK, then. Wasn't expecting that.

India

It's fine. Ask what you want to ask.

Tom

I guess my first question is, where were you the night of Sunday the tenth of September? You both have alibis, but why weren't you home that evening?

Locke

I usually stayed at my girlfriend's on Sundays. She lives in North London.

Tom

And your girlfriend is TV presenter Kelly Lacey, your co-host on the *Xtra Factor*?

Locke

Yeah. We've been seeing each other for a while now.

[Pause]

It's all good. Really good.

India

And I was staying over at a friend's flat in Richmond. Sorry. Actually, that's not true. That was the story. I rent a lovely apartment in Richmond. It's my happy place. Where I feel most myself.

I stay there once or sometimes twice a week if it fits in with filming for the show. It was somewhere to go when everything at the house got too intense. That's where I was that Sunday night. There are electronic doors on all the floors that you have to tap a key fob on to go in and out of. The police were able to check the computers and confirm I didn't leave the building until after I got the call in the morning from Taylor.

Tom

You're thirty years old, India. I don't think anyone would think it strange for you to move out. Why did you need to lie about it on the show? Surely you weren't expected to live with your mum for ever?

Locke

I think that's exactly what Mum expected. Right, India?

India

You have to remember, Tom, that the show – the brand – was all about how we were one big, messy, in-each-other's-faces family. That's what *Living with the Lancasters* meant. It's in the title. If I moved out, I wouldn't be *Living with the Lancasters* any more. And no way was Mum going to ruin the brand by allowing that.

But I wanted a little space now and again. A little something that was mine. So we kept the flat on the QT. It was just easier.

Tom
I get that. So what happened that morning?

India
I got a call from Taylor at 5 a.m. It wasn't unusual for us to be calling each other at that time. I thought it was going to be Taylor having another panic about . . .

[Pause]

She was worried about Mum being interviewed by you. Anyway, I answered and she said, 'Mum's dead.'
I was like, 'What? What happened?'
Taylor just said, 'She's in the pool. She's in the pool.'
I asked if the police were there and Taylor said she hadn't called them yet and I asked why not. She said, 'Because I'm calling you.' I told her to hang up and call the police. I arrived at the same time as the first two officers.

I was in such a rush to get home and be with Taylor that I don't think I really registered that Mum was dead until I got to the house and saw her in the pool. I wanted to jump in and get her out but one of the officers told me that it was better that the police did it.

Tom
Your mum was still in the pool when you arrived? Taylor hadn't tried to get her out?

India
No. I asked Taylor why not, and she said she couldn't touch a dead body.

Locke

Man, that's messed-up. But at least you answered the phone straight away. I didn't. I saw Taylor calling me and thought the last thing I needed was to start my day listening to her freak out about something we had zero control over. I let it go to voicemail a couple of times but when she kept calling, I figured something was wrong.

So I didn't get to the house until after India and the police.

Tom

Your mum's death was initially treated as not suspicious. There was immediate speculation online that it was suicide, which, as an outsider looking in, made sense when you consider the pressure Lynn was under in connection with the Bradley Wilcox investigation.

We don't yet know all the details of Bradley's death, but it is safe to assume that Lynn had something to hide and perhaps saw killing herself as a way out. But then a week later the police publicly announced that they were treating your mum's death as suspicious.

What was that space of time like for you both? What were your first thoughts on learning your mum was dead?

Locke

See, this is where me and India fall out, because I was pretty convinced straight away that something wasn't right. Sure, total nobodies on Twitter are going to have their theories about what happened, but I knew that there was no way, literally no way in hell, Mum would've killed herself. She was too invested in everything we were doing and the show. And she wouldn't have done it in a pool either because she hated swimming.

It's everything we've been talking about with what kind of person Mum was. She would never leave us to our own devices. No way.

But India thinks differently so I guess one of us is wrong.

India

I'm not saying someone didn't kill her. Of course that's a possibility. A horrible one, though. I just think that in the run-up to her death she was super stressed. I mean, her normal stress levels were way high anyway with how much she was trying to juggle, but this was stratospheric.

It's really hard to describe what this year has been like for her and for all of us. It's like we've been living in a pressure cooker and pretending that everything is normal when it wasn't, when we all knew we could explode at any moment. We couldn't say or do anything without the narrative turning to Bradley and that was hard for Mum because, like Locke said, she wanted to be in control of it all. But this was something she couldn't control.

Tom

In my last interview with Taylor, she told me something I hadn't realized. We all know that the Zalpodine found in your mum's system came from a prescription in Taylor's name, but what I hadn't realized is that the prescription was filled in January this year.

It's been bugging me.

Locke

What has?

Tom

I think it's the fact that it was January. Did Taylor ever mention having trouble sleeping back then?

Locke

Not to me, man, but I'm the last person she'd tell. Look, I see where you're going with this, and what you need to remember is that Taylor was all about the long game, just like Mum. It would be exactly like her to start planning a murder eight months in advance.

India
Locke, don't say that.

Tom
What about you, India? Do you remember Taylor having trouble sleeping or getting a prescription for sleeping tablets?

India
No, sorry.

Locke
What does it matter when she got the prescription?

Tom
It's just ... it doesn't matter. Thanks for your time today, guys. It feels like we're finally getting closer to the truth.

LOCATION: TOM'S CAR (LOCATION UNDISCLOSED)

Tom
Sorry about the abrupt end to that interview. I've just left Locke and India's house and I'm sitting in my car, but I can't drive away without saying this. I've finally figured out what's bugging me about the Zalpodine prescription. I didn't want to tell Locke or India until I've had some time to process it and what it means, but hear me out.

Taylor got the prescription in January, right?

As Locke just said, it was a whole eight months before Lynn's death. He thinks Taylor was all about the long game, like Lynn, but here's the thing – Taylor's motive for killing her mother is what? That Lynn was dragging down la tierra and ruining Taylor's fame because of how tangled up she'd become in Bradley's disappearance.

But January was a month *before* Locke shared the old video from the party showing Bradley in the background.

So if we assume it's true that Taylor hated taking sleeping tablets because one: her mum forced her to take them as a kid when she misbehaved; and two: her dad died of an accidental overdose involving the same sleeping tablets, then Taylor would only have got the prescription in January knowing she was going to use them to kill Lynn. But if that's the case, then what was the motive? Life was great for the Lancasters in January, especially Taylor, who'd finally bounced back from the wedding hate.

And if she did have a motive that we're not seeing, then why wait eight whole months to kill her mum? One thing is for sure – Locke is adamant that Taylor is guilty, and the more convinced he is, the less convinced I am.

Tom Isaac Investigates: What really happened to Bradley Wilcox?
Episode 12: Who killed Lynn Lancaster?

PUBLISHED ON YOUTUBE AND SPOTIFY:
FRIDAY, 10 NOVEMBER 2023

174,543 COMMENTS

SyfyGeek90
Here's what I think – Taylor didn't get in the pool to try and save her mum. Why not? Because she knew she was dead. And the only way to really know someone is dead in that situation is if Taylor had something to do with it.

> **JulieAlexander_1**
> Taylor totally did it!

Ernie Martin
Is Tom being paid to endorse that coffee he keeps banging on about? Come to think of it, wasn't there a health bar he was constantly eating in the last series as well?

> **LWTL_No1Fan**
> It's influencer marketing. Companies pay Tom to talk about them. It's how he makes his money.
>
> **TI_BiggestFan**
> He's not like the Lancasters, if that's what you're getting at.

SyfyGeek90
Tom, when are you going to ask Locke and India what they know about Bradley's death?

Wendy Clarke

I would like to know this too. However interesting this is, I'm concerned that we're moving away from #JusticeForBradley.

SyfyGeek90

It's up to us to keep digging! Who can help and how? Can we chat privately, Wendy?

Wendy Clarke

Yes. DM me on Instagram. I'm @Wendy_Clarke89

EXTRACT FROM EVIDENCE COLLECTED
BY THE METROPOLITAN POLICE FROM THE
LANCASTER PROPERTY ON 22 NOVEMBER 2023

Item No: 3

Description: Notebook titled 'Detective's Notes 3 by India Lancaster, age 10'

Saturday, 2 August 2003

Overheard conversation (recorded and transcribed):

Locke: Have you been downstairs?

Me: No.

Locke: India, Mum will kill you if she sees you.

Me: I just went to watch the guests arriving. Mum said be upstairs at 7 p.m. Some people arrived early and I wanted to see what they were wearing. No one saw me.

Locke: Good. Come on. We're having a movie night, remember? And stop recording on that thing. It's annoying.

Overheard conversation (recorded and transcribed):

Me: Can we watch another film?

Locke: No. Go to bed. It's late.

Me: But the music is too loud. I won't be able to sleep.

Locke: I can't help you with that. Go to bed.

Me: Why are you so grumpy?

Locke: I'm not.

[Pause]

Locke: Fine. Go get ready for bed and we'll watch one more film, but it's my choice.

Tom Isaac Investigates: What really happened to Bradley Wilcox?
Episode 13: New evidence in Bradley's case

PUBLISHED ON YOUTUBE AND SPOTIFY:
FRIDAY, 17 NOVEMBER 2023

Voice of Olivia Hatton-Smith, body language expert
I've watched hundreds of hours of *Living with the Lancasters* for this docuseries, focusing mainly on the confessionals. These video diaries are where we see the truest glimpses of the Lancaster family's personalities. I can say confidently that all three of Lynn's children had anger issues.

In the earlier years of the show, India showed micro-aggressions towards her mother and Taylor. Interestingly, though, she showed no such aggression towards Locke.

Then, from series six in 2012, India's aggression disappears. Whereas Locke started the show very open and relaxed, we see tension creeping in as the years pass. There are many instances of passive aggression directed at Taylor and Lynn, which Locke tries to mask with laughter.

Taylor is slightly different. We see a lot of her outbursts outside of the confessional. But when she's sat on the pink sofa, her tone is always light; her words appear carefully chosen. It's her body language in the confessionals which is most telling. Her facial muscles are often pinched, her shoulders tense. She touches her tongue against her teeth often. These are all signs that she is feeling angry or frustrated.

In my expert opinion, Taylor, Locke and India have all displayed signs at one time or another of wishing not just their mother, but each other, ill will.

Voice of Kelly Lacey, co-presenter of the *Xtra Factor*

I don't mind talking to you. Maybe Locke will finally get the message. I've been trying to break up with him for weeks but he won't listen. He calls me up late at night and keeps talking about this future time when everything is back to normal. He doesn't get it. There is no 'normal' for him.

I really like Locke, but we weren't serious, and I have to think about my career. There's a long queue of white guys who look just like Locke who want my job, and a lot of TV producers who would prefer it if my face wasn't on their screens, so I have to be extra careful. I can't be tainted with all this shit.

Locke's a nice guy and I wish him well, but we're over and we have been for months. If you're going to see him, you can return the la tierra top he sent me for my birthday last week. Wearing it would be like wearing a T-shirt with 'Team Lancaster' written across the front.

Sorry, you want to talk about the night his mum got killed, right? Yes, Locke stayed at mine that night. I've got a house in Angel. I'm not sure I can say I'm his alibi. We went to bed at ten and I fell asleep. I woke up at some point in the middle of the night – I'm not sure when – and Locke wasn't in bed, but that wasn't unusual. He's a bit of an insomniac. He rarely falls asleep before 3 a.m. and a lot of times he gets up and goes for a walk.

I asked him about it the next day and he said he was watching TV, which I'm sure he was. But he could've been anywhere really, couldn't he? I've never felt comfortable with people, with the police, thinking I'm his alibi. His phone was in my flat the whole time. You can see that on one of those app things. That's a better alibi than me.

Locke didn't talk about his family much when he was with me and we never talked about me meeting them. The way I saw it, Locke shut that side of his life off when he was with me. He'd always get pretty moody when his mum or sisters called him, and he never answered if it was Taylor, but all families have weird dynamics. I can't stand half of mine.

What was the other thing you asked? Oh right, my car. Yes, I've got one. It's a black Audi A1 that barely makes it off the drive from one week to the next. Locke drove it sometimes if we went away for the weekend.

LOCATION: TOM'S STUDY

Tom
Welcome to *Tom Isaac Investigates*.

You've just been listening to Olivia Hatton-Smith's conclusion that all three Lancaster siblings showed some serious anger towards their mum and towards each other. To be fair, I can't imagine a scenario where working together day after day, living together, being filmed constantly, wouldn't cause some anger during the sixteen years the show ran for, but it's worth keeping in mind, especially with Locke's girlfriend – or ex-girlfriend now – telling us she couldn't account for Locke's whereabouts on the night Lynn was murdered.

Did Locke sneak out of Kelly's flat, borrow her car, drive home and kill his mother? He'd been suspended from the *Xtra Factor*. His career as a presenter looked over before it had properly begun. He must have been upset. Angry even. Maybe he was also thinking about how much Lynn had held him back over the years. That tunnel vision focused on Taylor and India, but never on him.

Is it motive enough for murder? Maybe. We're going to find out!

[Phone ringing]

Ah crumbs.
Hello? . . . Yes, this is Tom.

[Pause]

Wendy? Er . . . of course. Wendy Clarke, one of my lovely TIs. I'm actually in my study recording right now. Let me put you on speaker.

Wendy
Tom? Are you there?

Tom
Yes. Hi Wendy. You're on speaker.

Wendy
Oh. Hello. Er . . . I found your number on your website and I was calling because I was messaging with another TI and we were talking about what we could do to help Bradley's investigation while you were . . . er . . . interviewing Locke and India about Lynn's death, and the other TI – SyfyGeek90 – suggested we look more closely at the video of Bradley at the party and, well, my brother is a restoration expert for the British Museum, specializing in photographs and videos. I sent him the video and . . . he's found something.

Tom
He has? Oh my God. What?

Wendy
I don't know. He just told me to come to his office and I thought . . . I wondered if you wanted to come with me today about lunchtime? It's fine if you're too busy. I can—

Tom
No, I mean yes. I'm not too busy. Of course I want to come. I can move things around. I have my next interview scheduled with Locke and India this afternoon so I won't be able to stay for long.

LOCATION: THE BRITISH MUSEUM,
BASEMENT ROOM
INTERVIEW BETWEEN TOM ISAAC
AND HAL CLARKE

Tom

I'm filming this part of the episode from the basement that runs beneath the hallowed halls of the British Museum. This place is so cool. The corridor behind me is extremely narrow and on both walls are huge dark wood cabinets with glass fronts, which look like relics in themselves. The cabinets are filled with old pieces of electrical equipment, like this camera with a veil thingy from the late 1800s. There's also a gramophone and a lot of stuff in this cabinet which looks more like it's from a science fiction film.

This whole basement is amazing. Just around that corner is a stuffed polar bear which made me scream out loud – dramatic, I know. I'm glad Javi didn't have the camera recording for that bit.

Now, if we walk carefully between these cabinets and around the corner, we see the basement opens into what looks like an ubermodern editing suite, which makes my little office in Mumsie's house look completely Amateurville. I'm counting four screens, two laptops and a desktop. Plus a lot of other equipment I've never seen before.

In a moment I'm going to introduce you all to Hal Clarke, a restoration expert who specializes in video and photography for the British Museum. He's also the brother of Wendy Clarke, one of my TIs, who is here too, but has asked not to be on camera.

I just want to say that I'm completely in the dark right now. I have no idea what I'm about to be told and whether it will help us uncover what happened to Bradley that night.

Hal has been analysing the 2003 party video shared on *Living with the Lancasters* back in February. The video has been shared millions of times across social media. We've all watched it. I've even had body language expert Olivia Hatton-Smith analyse it frame-by-frame and we've all speculated over whether Lynn drops something into Bradley's drink or not. So, what exactly did TIs Wendy Clarke and SyfyGeek90 hope to find that we'd all missed? And were they right? Let's find out.

Hal, thanks for taking the time to talk to me.

Hal
No problem. It's great to meet you. My sister never stops talking about you. She's completely obsessed with your show.

Wendy [Background voice]
I am not.

Hal
You're not what I was expecting, actually.

Tom

[Laughing]

I never am. It's my secret weapon. The people who remember me from my boy-band days expect me to still have blonde highlights and walk around in a white tracksuit. Or they think I'm some public-school pretty boy. Either way, it makes them drop their guard, and tell me more than they want to. Most of the time, anyway.

Hal

[Laughing]

I won't make that mistake then.

So, you want me to show you what I've found on the video Wendy asked me to look at?

Tom
That would be great.

Hal
If you look at screen one, what I'm going to show you is the video from Edward Lancaster's fortieth birthday. I found this particular clip on the Sky News website. Obviously, the rest of the episode was cut, leaving us this short clip.

I've done a Google search and checked social media and as far as I can see this edited version by Sky News is the one that has been used and shared across social media.

Tom
I can one hundred per cent agree with that. It's the same clip I've used in my docuseries showing Ed Lancaster dancing, and Lynn and Bradley talking in the background.

Hal
I started by slowing it down and zooming in on Lynn and Bradley, but I'm not a wizard and the quality of the video just wasn't good enough to yield any insights.

And when I realized this, I thought to myself, 'Hal, go back to the original.' Because it's always better to work with them. It's one of the first things we're taught about restoration.

We don't actually have a hard copy of the video, because the police probably have that, but we do have a more original version than this edited clip. We have the video used in the *Living with the Lancasters* episode. So I went back to that episode and I found that the video clip we've just been watching had five seconds cut off the end. Those last five seconds look like a blur, so I can see why it was cut short.

Here, let me show you.

So, this is the original video. It's exactly the same as what we just watched.

And this is the final five seconds shown in the episode.

Tom

OK, I see it, but it's just someone putting the camera down and then turning it off, right? All I see is a stream of blurred colours where the camera is being moved too quickly.

Hal

Exactly, which is why I suspect it was cut. But this gave me something to work with. I won't go into the technical details, but if you imagine that the normal speed of the video is one, if I slow it down to half the speed, it will be 0.5. And I've slowed these final five seconds down to 0.1, so we're watching what looks like a series of still shots. And at the same time, if I zoom in to this area here where Lynn and Bradley are talking, we see something.

Tom

I'm still not sure . . .

[Pause]

What? Sorry. Can you play that again? Can I lean closer to the screen?

Hal

Knock yourself out, just don't touch it.

Tom

Oh my God.

[Pause]

Tom
Javi, did you get that?

Javi
Can you play it again, mate?

Hal
Sure. I can send this to you to keep. Here, I'll put it on a loop so you can see it over and over.

Tom
For those listening on the podcast, what we're watching is a very, very slowed-down version of what was a blur of nothing, and it's now showing us the final seconds of Bradley and Lynn's conversation, and if we look right here—

Hal
Don't touch the screen.

Tom
Sorry.

What we're seeing in this section of the screen right here is the edge of the staircase, and just in the final seconds before the video cuts out, we see a pair of feet appear on those stairs, literally right above where Bradley and Lynn are talking. Whoever was standing there probably heard some, if not all, of what was said between Bradley and Lynn. And better than that, I know exactly who that person is. This changes everything.

Tom Isaac Investigates: What really happened to Bradley Wilcox?

Episode 13: New evidence in Bradley's case (cont.)

PUBLISHED ON YOUTUBE AND SPOTIFY:
FRIDAY, 17 NOVEMBER 2023

Voice of Taylor Lancaster
This whole thing is totes ridic. I'm innocent. I've done nothing wrong. You'll see.

Voice of Locke Lancaster
We want the truth as much as you do – about Mum and about Bradley.

Voice of India Lancaster
If this is the last time we ever sit in front of a camera then I want it to be honest.

LOCATION: TOM'S CAR (LOCATION UNDISCLOSED)

Tom
Javi and I are sitting in my car outside Locke and India's secret location. It's pouring with rain so we can't see a thing out of the windows, but just in case, Javi is keeping the camera zoomed in on my face, because despite everything I don't want to give anything away about where I am. Sorry, I know a close-up of my face is not a pretty sight. This series has got really under my skin. I'm not sleeping well.

[Pause]

I haven't called Cassie. I know I need to tell her about this development, and it's making me feel slightly sick that I haven't yet, but I also know that she'll insist on being here and I don't think Locke or India will talk to me with Cassie in the room. I have spent weeks building a relationship with them. I thought they'd been honest with me. It felt like they were opening up. Now I'm not so sure.

LOCATION: LIVING ROOM (LOCATION UNDISCLOSED)
INTERVIEW BETWEEN TOM ISAAC, LOCKE LANCASTER AND INDIA LANCASTER

Tom

I'm back in the living room at Locke and India Lancaster's temporary home just as I was five weeks ago when I first sat down to talk to them. On the surface, everything feels the same, but we've come a long way. We've talked about your childhoods, the show, your careers and more recent events with the death of your mum. Today, I want to take our journey back to 2003 and talk about Bradley and your dad's fortieth birthday party, because the more I dig, the more convinced I am that these two tragic deaths – Bradley and Lynn – twenty years apart, are connected. And I believe the truth about one will lead to the truth about the other.

Locke

I totally get that, Tom. But surely you should be speaking to Taylor about this, not us. She's the link, right? Bradley was at the party because of her, and she's the one who's about to stand trial for killing our mum.

Tom

Absolutely, but if you could help me build a picture of that time in 2003 it would give me some important background. Locke, you were thirteen and India, you were ten. Where were you doing during the party? Did you get to attend any of it?

Locke
Nope. Like we said, Mum liked us sitting nicely around a dinner table but kids totally ruined the vibe at parties. We were banished upstairs to have a movie night. Mum basically said to me, 'Only come downstairs if the house is on fire, and make sure your sister goes to bed at ten.' We watched a couple of Adam Sandler films and then I told India to go to bed. I stayed up to watch an action film. I think it was an old Arnie classic. I was pretty obsessed with them.

India
But I couldn't sleep because the music was really loud so I went back into Locke's room and watched it too. It was *Total Recall*. I remember because I was petrified of the aliens.

Locke
Oh yeah.

[Laughing]

I figured no one was going to come up and check that India was in bed, and I was right. As long as we didn't go downstairs, Mum didn't care what we did.

India
After the film finished, Locke sent me to my room. It took ages to get to sleep because I was so scared. So I went into my secret hideout—

Tom
Your hideout in your wardrobe, right?

India
Yes.

When I got up the next day, Taylor was crying in the kitchen and Dad was being sick in the downstairs toilet.

Tom
Sorry, can I just stop you there. Taylor was downstairs the morning after the party?

India
As I remember it, yes. But I was only ten and it was twenty years ago.

Mum made me a bowl of cereal and sent me back to my bedroom, telling me to stay in there until she came to get me. She said there was loads of broken glass around the house and I needed to wait until the cleaners had been, which I didn't think was fair considering I'd been upstairs all night too.

Locke
I don't remember that.

India
That's because you always stayed in bed until lunchtime.

Locke
Because I have insomnia and have never been able to sleep before 2 a.m. my whole life.

India
Mum was lying anyway, because she came and got me a few hours later, and when I went downstairs the cleaners hadn't arrived.

Tom

So in the morning after your dad's fortieth birthday party, you – India – were told not to leave your bedroom. Why do you think your mum said that?

[Pause]

India

You're the investigator, Tom. I was a ten-year-old girl. Why do you think she wanted me out of the way?

Tom

I think they – your mum and dad – needed to bury Bradley's body in the garden.

India

I think that too.

Locke

Oh man. That's messed-up. I still can't believe his body has been in our garden for twenty years. You guys think Taylor knew?

India

She wasn't sent to her room, was she?

Locke

But the wedding? How could she have a wedding in the same place she knew a body had been buried? Who does that?

Tom

I'd like to be really clear on this next question, so bear with me for a moment. We know with absolute certainty that Bradley Wilcox attended a party at your home on the second of August 2003 and died that night. He was then buried in your garden. Are you both telling me that you knew nothing about his death? That at no point over the course of the days that followed, or any day in all the years since, you didn't catch even a whisper of conversation about Bradley's death or a hint that members of your family were involved?

Locke
Tom, think about it. If I thought there was anything to hide, would I have given you my keys to the house? If I knew that a body was buried in our garden, what would I have to gain by letting you find it? If there was any shred of hope that we might come back from this, it's gone now. This has ruined us.

Tom
What do you remember about the time immediately after Bradley's disappearance?

Locke
It was a really difficult time for our family. I'm not saying it was anything like what Cassie's been through. I feel really sorry for her, but everything changed for us that day too.

Tom
In what way?

Locke
Things were different after the party. Obviously, I can look back now and think, yeah, they covered up the death of a teenage boy and their behaviour makes total sense, but at the time it felt like Mum and Dad were going through a really rough patch.

You'd walk into a room and it felt like they'd just argued about something, except they hadn't because when we argue in our family, everyone always shouts. There was no shouting at all. My parents were barely talking.

Taylor was always in a massive mood as well. At the time, I put it down to worrying about Bradley and Mum saying she couldn't see Cassie any more, which I thought was stupid because they were always falling out over stuff.

Tom
Cassie and Taylor used to fall out? I remember them always being together in school.

Locke
Oh, they argued a lot, especially as they got older. Cassie could be pretty mean to Taylor. She called her a spoilt princess a lot and would ignore her sometimes for no reason, or make her give her stuff. She made Taylor lie to all of our friends and say Cassie was her neighbour. Normal teenage stuff, I guess. But I always thought Taylor was better off without Cassie in her life. And at the time, I thought Mum told Taylor she couldn't hang out with Cassie any more because she thought Cassie was bullying Taylor a bit and was worried it would get worse after Bradley disappeared.

Hand on heart, at the time, I never thought or suspected for a single second that Taylor or Mum lied about him leaving that night. I just thought Mum and Dad were arguing more than normal. I didn't connect it to the party or Bradley.

And this is going to sound really weird, but things only got better after Dad died. For Mum, I think, anyway. I was so upset and hurt and angry with Dad for being stupid enough to take too many painkillers.

Tom
It must have been hard losing your dad so young.

Locke
Yeah. It wasn't even the first time he'd thrown his back out. Anytime he played too much golf, it went.

[Pause]

I think there's a big part of me that still feels angry towards him for not being more careful. But Mum wasn't angry at all. I can't really describe it.

[Pause]

Sorry, this is heavy. What I'm saying is, she didn't even seem sad that he died, man.
   I really hate her. I'm glad she's dead.

India
Locke, you don't—

Locke
It's true. I don't think I realized until we started to talk to you, Tom, how bad she was. Living with her control, day in, day out. I couldn't see it, but I am glad she's dead and so are you, India. Think of all the things she made us do. How we could never say no.

India
I know, but she was still our mum. She loved us in her own way.

Locke
Loved you and Taylor, maybe.

[Pause]

Look, this is heavy. I'm going to grab some air.

[Door slamming]

India

Sorry about Locke. He'll be fine in a bit. He sees himself as totally clued-up. He thinks he understands everything, but Taylor isn't the only one with a temper and a filter for how she sees things.

Tom

I guess we all have our own way of seeing the world.

[Pause]

Do you mind if I show you something on my iPad? It's the video from the night of your dad's party. It's the reason I'm here, actually.

India

Sure.

Tom

One of my TIs had the video analysed and we've found something new that I'd like to show you while Locke is out of the room.

Here are Lynn and Bradley. We've all seen this bit before but see here – it was just a blur until we slowed down the video and zoomed in on the stairs behind Lynn and Bradley. Then we saw what looks like a pair of feet and . . . here . . . what looks like a fragment of pink that I think is a nightdress or a dressing gown. And the only way that makes sense to me is if those feet belong to you.

[Pause]

India

Oh.

Tom

Is it you, India? Were you there that night on the stairs while that video was being recorded?

India
Oh God.

[Crying]

I . . .

Tom
Were you on the stairs directly above Bradley and your mum at twelve fifteen on the night of your dad's birthday party?

India
I'm sorry.

Tom
What are you sorry for? Lying or being caught lying?

India
I didn't lie. I just . . . I just missed a bit out. I didn't tell you that I went downstairs.

[Crying]

I'm sorry. It's not easy, you know?

Tom
What isn't?

India
Being one way your entire life and then finding out it isn't normal and trying to change. We had to stick to the story. Always. Whatever it was, that's what we had to say.

I ran into a door and broke my nose.

I wanted to be a model more than anything in the world. More than studying, and university and a life in academia. There's ... there's other stuff too that I've not told you. But I had to stick to the story.

Tom
Lynn is dead. The show is over. There is no story any more. Nothing to stick to. So you can tell me what you remember from the night Bradley died, can't you? All of it this time.

India

[Nodding]

[Sniffing]

Like I said, I got scared by the film and I couldn't sleep. I went to my secret den in my wardrobe but I still couldn't sleep. I wanted Dad to tell me a story and make it all OK. But I knew I wasn't allowed to go down to the party. I couldn't stay in my room because I was too scared, but I couldn't go downstairs either. So I sat at the top of the stairs out of sight for a while and peeked through the banisters, watching everyone dance. I thought Dad might look up and see me, but he didn't. No one did. I liked watching, though. There wasn't anything to be scared of with everyone having so much fun.

[Crying]

Tom
Did you hear your mum talking to Bradley? Do you remember?

India

[Pause]

Yes. I was hidden out of sight, ready to sprint back to my room at any second in case Mum came up, but she didn't and I started shuffling down one step and then another. I just wanted to be part of Dad's big celebration. So I kept shuffling down until I could see better. The lights upstairs were off and the stairs were in darkness so I was pretty hidden.

It was fun at first. I remember thinking how bad Dad was at dancing and that Taylor would be dead embarrassed if she saw him.

There was a little makeshift drinks trolley in the corner of the room and I liked listening to people talk as they made their drinks. It was really late so maybe the waiting staff had gone home.

Then Mum walked across the room, heading straight for the stairs and I froze. I thought she'd seen me. But then she started making a drink and I knew I should move and go back to bed before I got in trouble, but I thought she'd hear me if I tried. So I stayed still.

She was making a drink for Bradley. I remember wondering if it was some kind of cocktail because it was taking her ages to make it and she was stirring it lots, like she did when she gave us the sleeping tablets in a cup of milk.

I could tell she was angry about something. When you grow up in the family I grew up in, you know when someone is upset or mad. I thought it was me. I thought she'd seen me and was making me the drink, but then she turned to Bradley and told him to calm down. She said something like, 'Bradley, you don't need to look so concerned. This is all a big misunderstanding.'

But Bradley kept saying that he didn't think it was and he wanted to talk to someone about it. Then Mum gave him the drink. He didn't want to take it. He kept telling her he didn't drink but ... Mum could talk anyone into anything, and he took the drink and he drank it. Then Mum led him into the snug – the little TV room just off the main hall – and came out a few minutes later.

Everyone was going outside by then because it was time for the fireworks. I could hear them all chatting and laughing on the terrace.

Tom
And what did you do?

India

I went to see Bradley.

Tom

You went into the snug?

India

I wanted to watch the fireworks and I knew I'd be able to see them from the den window. I thought Bradley might be doing that too. I knew I had to be quick and quiet so I crept downstairs and tiptoed across the hall and pushed open the door.

There was a lamp on in the corner and I could see Bradley on the sofa, asleep. I went over to him and gave him a little shake because I thought he'd want to watch the fireworks. He mumbled something but didn't wake up so I turned off the lamp and left him to sleep and went to watch the fireworks from my bedroom window instead.

Tom

And you never told anyone this?

India

No. On the Monday after the party, two police officers came to the house and questioned Mum, Dad and Taylor about what happened to Bradley that night.

Tom

What did your dad tell the police? Do you know?

India

He told them that he'd been too drunk to remember any of the guests that night, let alone an eighteen-year-old friend of his daughter. To be fair, I think that was probably true. You can see from the video how drunk he was when he was dancing.

I wanted to tell the police officers that I saw Bradley asleep in the den way after Mum said he'd left. I tried to tell Mum and Dad when it was just us, but Mum said, 'That was a dream, India. If you tell anyone, you'll look like a silly attention-seeking little girl, and Mummy and Daddy will be very angry with you. You don't want to upset us, do you?'

Even Dad told me to go to my room, which wasn't like him. He was usually a total softy.

I'm really sorry, Tom.

[Pause]

[Crying]

I should have told you this earlier when you first asked. I really have tried to be honest with you. I should have told the police back in February. I know that. I know it was wrong. I really have tried to be honest but . . . it's like you said – I've spent over half of my life on the show. Half of my life living . . . living a lie. Being a liar.

Tom
And after you went to your room that night, did you see Bradley again?

India
No, I didn't.

Tom
You are now the last known person to have seen Bradley alive. And you were there the next morning when you saw Taylor crying in the kitchen.

What do you think happened to Bradley in that time?

India
He died. That's obvious, isn't it? He died and my parents buried him in the garden. Locke was right about our parents. They weren't the

same after that night and I think it's because of what happened to Bradley. What they did.

I don't know how Bradley died. That's the missing piece now, I get it. You should ask Taylor, though. Lay it all out for her, trip her up or whatever it is you do with your nicely-nicely way of asking questions. Taylor was upset for weeks after that night. She cried all the time. She was involved, whatever it was.

Tom

I think I'm starting to finally understand your family dynamic and I have a pretty good idea of the answer to this, but I have to ask – you grew up in this family, you know them all better than anyone else. Why do you think your parents, and possibly Taylor too, covered up Bradley's death instead of calling the emergency services?

India

I think . . . because it would've been this huge scandal. A teenage boy dead at Ed Lancaster's wild fortieth celebrations. You can see what the tabloids would say.

Dad had this whole hero thing going on with the media – the England star turned agent out to save youth football. In Mum's mind, it wouldn't have mattered how Bradley died. If it was an accident or not. She couldn't have the Lancaster name associated with that kind of scandal. Don't forget, she already had all these plans for us, even then.

It wouldn't have crossed her mind what his disappearance would do to Cassie and her parents. She'd have been focused on protecting the family, protecting the image and her future.

I know she said she'd tell you everything in your interview, Tom, but I'm telling you now, she wouldn't have done. She'd have stuck to the story no matter what. We all did. Even me, although I'm so sorry for it. But I had no idea back then that they'd killed him and buried him in the garden.

Tom
What did you think happened that night?

India
I . . . I'm not sure. I knew Mum and Taylor were lying, but it didn't occur to me that they'd killed him or covered up his death, if that's what you're asking. I thought about going to the police or speaking out when I was a teenager and as I got older, but I had no idea that what I saw would help find Bradley. I might have suspected something happened to him, but I didn't know for sure. And even though I wanted to say something, I couldn't, and it wasn't just because of how we'd been conditioned to stick to the story. It's because I was scared, OK?

Tom
What were you scared of?

India
What do you think? Mum.

She was not the type of person you crossed. Ever. It's not just that she would've made things difficult for me, she would've destroyed me. She knows us. Knew us better than anyone. She knew exactly what buttons to press to get us to do things and exactly what buttons to press to hurt us.

I've never told anyone this before, but . . . remember the summer after my A-levels when I wasn't in the show?

Tom
You were working abroad at a holiday camp with some friends.

India
That was the story. The truth is that I was in hospital being treated for anorexia. It was the most horrendous time of my life. I'd never

been someone who was bothered about my weight, but then the year before, in 2011, Mum said she was going to launch Slenderelle and to sell them we'd all have to put some weight on and then lose it again. She made it sound really simple. Eat loads of junk and then stop eating loads of junk and take the pills. Mum, Taylor and Locke did it no problem, but when I stopped eating the junk and lost the weight I'd gained, I . . . liked it. I liked the control it gave me over my body. And so I carried on with the pills and the dieting.

I wore oversized hoodies and no one noticed until I fainted at sixth form. Luckily, it was after my exams, when I'd gone back to collect some coursework. Because I hit my head on the side of the desk when I fell, the school called an ambulance. I was taken to hospital and it became apparent to everyone that I was—

[Pause]

This isn't something I've ever talked about. I was very ill. I stayed at the Priory for eight weeks. I wouldn't say I'm cured. I don't think you ever can be. There are days when I still struggle, but I don't starve myself any more.

At the time, Mum did what she always did when things veered off plan – she pretended it wasn't happening. In a weird way it made me realize that being part of the family, making Mum happy, was more important to me than a chemistry degree, so when I left the hospital, I withdrew my university application and I went home and I committed. To Mum and to the show.

The reason I'm telling you this now is because when I say Mum knew what buttons to press, I mean my anorexia. She'd have poked and manipulated. She'd have made me feel fat, she'd have raked up all my old feelings and I'd have got sick again and gone back to hospital. I think that's how she'd have got rid of me.

So I had to keep quiet while she was alive, and then when she died, there was so much to deal with.

I was going to tell you what I saw that night, I was just trying to find the right words to explain everything and how scared I was.

LOCATION: TOM'S CAR, LOCATION UNDISCLOSED

Tom

So India was there that night. After we thought she was upstairs asleep the entire time. I feel . . . like I'm happy we've made another breakthrough. I was right. Bradley saw something that night and Lynn didn't want him to leave the party.

But what the hell did he see?

I'm getting pretty sick of this family hiding things from me, then admitting stuff and tagging on an apology like that makes up for two decades of lies.

But I do, in part, understand India's silence. Lynn was clearly incredibly dominant and controlling. India's revelation about her eating disorder was heart-breaking but hearing her fears that Lynn would've used it against her was even worse. I can see it would've been hard to speak out against a parent in a normal family, and there was certainly nothing normal about the Lancasters.

And there's what Locke told us about Taylor's friendship with Cassie to consider as well. He painted a very different picture to the one Cassie gave. Does it matter? Is Cassie hiding things from me, too?

Tom Isaac Investigates: What really happened to Bradley Wilcox?
Episode 13: New evidence in Bradley's case (cont.)

PUBLISHED ON YOUTUBE AND SPOTIFY:
FRIDAY, 17 NOVEMBER 2023

215,721 COMMENTS

LWTL_No1Fan
I think we need to focus on Taylor. She clearly knows what happened to Bradley and was involved in covering it up because she was crying at the table the morning after the party.

> **SyfyGeek90**
> That's her motive too!! She killed Lynn to keep her involvement in Bradley's murder a secret and to save her career.

Katy Shepard
Anyone thinking Cassie killed Lynn?

> **TrueCrime_Junkie1001**
> Motive?

> **Katy Shepard**
> Revenge for Bradley. She knew Lynn was never going to tell the police or Tom the truth and so she killed her.

Ernie Martin
Why is no one saying it was India? It's always the quiet ones! She had a bad time of it growing up.

SyfyGeek90

I don't see it. India couldn't even speak out against her mum with what she knew about Bradley. She's not perfect but no way would she have been able to kill her mum. She doesn't have the temper like Taylor does.

Wendy Clarke

Agreed! But what about Locke? He has no proper alibi and he had access to his girlfriend's car.

TI_BiggestFan

You're doing so well, Tom!! Keep going!!

TrueCrime_Junkie1001

Locke killed Lynn.
Taylor killed Bradley. They're not connected.

SyfyGeek90

Tom, can you go back to the Lancasters' house? You never got to look around last time.

EXTRACT FROM EVIDENCE COLLECTED
BY THE METROPOLITAN POLICE FROM THE
LANCASTER PROPERTY ON 22 NOVEMBER 2023

Item No: 3

Description: Notebook titled 'Detective's Notes 3 by India Lancaster, age 10'

Saturday, 2 August 2003

Overheard conversation (recorded and transcribed):

Dad: Now isn't the time, Dale. This is my birthday party.

Dale: I'm sorry, Ed. I just want to talk about the contract quickly. I don't understand why I don't have any money. I'm getting paid a good salary but barely any of it is going into my account every month.

Dad: It's all in the contract. Did you read it?

Dale: Yeah, sort of.

Dad: Look, there's nothing I can do here. You signed the contract. It's airtight and that's to protect you. I'm talking to the Man City recruitment team next week and I was going to talk to them about you, about how you're way too good to be on the bench in the second tier, but if you don't trust me—

Dale: No, I do. I do. Sorry, Ed. Have a good party.

Dad: Thanks. And Dale?

Dale: Yeah?

Dad: I've got a lot of friends in this business. A lot of people who owe me favours who can help you, or quite as easily not help you. Don't challenge me again.

Dale: Sure. I'm sorry. Please forget I said anything.

Tom Isaac Investigates: What really happened to Bradley Wilcox?

Episode 14: Why was Bradley killed? We find the motive!

PUBLISHED ON YOUTUBE AND SPOTIFY:
FRIDAY, 24 NOVEMBER 2023

Tom

The following three episodes were all recorded within a frantic forty-eight-hour period and have been released together. In these episodes, we finally find the truth about Bradley and Lynn's deaths.

LOCATION: TOM'S STUDY

Tom

This is episode ... er ... fourteen. It's 2 a.m. I'm awake because someone has been ringing my doorbell off and on for the past few hours. They ring it, stand on the doorstep for a minute and then disappear, coming back about twenty minutes later and doing it again. I can see them on my phone from the doorbell camera app.

They're hooded and wearing dark clothing and have the menacing look of someone I will not be answering the door to.

Don't worry. The house is secure and I've called the police. They said they'll send a patrol car but I don't know when that will be, and obviously there is no way I'm going back to sleep now.

I've been using the time to catch up on all of your comments, and something SyfyGeek90 suggested has got me thinking. They suggested going back to the Lancaster house to look around, which we didn't do last time, and I think since I'm due to meet Cassie again anyway, we should talk at the house.

I'll call Badru in the morning and see if he wants to come too. He can't answer questions any more because he's part of the active investigation into Bradley's death, but he might be allowed to poke around with us.

[Doorbell ringing]

[Whispering] Oh God. He's back.

Look – there on the screen of my phone, a person wearing all black with a hood pulled low. They're keeping their head down so I can't see their face.

[Banging door]

Shit. I don't know what to do.

Hang on, they're leaving. Oh, a police car has just driven by. Thank goodness.

LOCATION: OUTSIDE LANCASTER HOME, HAMPTON WICK, WEST LONDON
INTERVIEW BETWEEN TOM ISAAC, CASSIE WILCOX, BADRU ZUBIRA AND DALE PETERSON

Tom
I'm standing on the pavement outside the Lancaster home. Across the street we can see the press barrier is still up but there's no one here right now. I'm with Badru and Cassie and the whole street feels eerily quiet. Maybe that's because it's freezing cold today and I'm completely exhausted. I got no sleep last night. The police took a statement and have the doorbell footage but I don't think there is much they can do. These threats aren't going to end until I solve this case, which is why this morning I asked Locke if he'd mind if we looked around the house again, and he gave us permission.

Cassie
I'm sorry about the threats, Tom. I should never have got you involved. If you want to—

Tom
Hey, it's not your fault. And it shows we're getting close. I'm not going to give up now. Although I'm glad Badru is with us today too.

Badru
Considering what you found the last time you were here, it seems prudent to have a member of the investigation here too.

Tom
I know you can't tell us anything in an official capacity, but have the police made any progress?

Badru
I am very limited in what I can tell you.

Bradley's investigation has moved from a missing persons case to a murder investigation. We are continuing to re-interview guests who were at the party and establish a new timeline of events.

Tom
Both of you are obviously up to date on what's been happening with my docuseries, and Cassie, we're going to talk soon, but before that, I got a call this morning from Dale Peterson, who wants to meet, although he wouldn't say why on the phone. I told him I would be here at the Lancaster home, and he offered to come. He's just pulling up now.

[Pause]

[Car door opening and closing]

Tom

Hi, Dale. Thanks for driving over here this morning.

Dale

Sure, no problem.

Tom

This is Cassie, Bradley's sister. And Badru Zubira, the retired detective who is now—

Dale

Yeah, we met last week.

Badru

Good to see you again. I do need to make you aware that my presence here today means that anything you say—

Dale

Yeah, don't worry. I get it. It's on camera anyway. I'm already facing prison, aren't I? Can't get any worse for me.

Tom

How are you doing, Dale? I saw in the papers that you've been charged with perverting the course of justice.

Dale

Yeah. I want to plead guilty, just so you know. I shouldn't have lied that night, but my solicitor says we should go to trial to explain everything properly. Get a sympathetic jury and all that. Lot of hate for the Lancasters out there.

[Sighs]

But I've not got it in me. Maybe I wanna set an example for my boy.

Tom

I can see that. Why did you want to talk to me today?

Dale

I've been thinking a lot about Ed's party and I remembered something else. Something that happened earlier in the evening. I didn't make the connection to what happened later to Bradley at the time, and it might still be nothing, but I thought you'd want to know.

Cassie

What—?

Tom

Why don't you tell us what you remember?

Dale

So, you know how I said Ed was my agent and that's why I was at the party? Well, Ed had this image, yeah, of being this football legend. This good guy, but he wasn't. He was ripping his clients off. Exploiting us, like.

Tom

Financially?

Dale

Yes. I didn't realize at first. No one likes to admit they've made a bad decision, and this was Ed Lancaster – he played for England and was a top Premier League goalscorer, and he was on the TV all the time talking about looking after young footballers. He was the best agent out there. Or so I thought when I was fifteen and he was interested in me.

I was an idiot!

Tom

Can you talk me through how you met Ed?

Dale

Like I said, I was fifteen. I'd had some trials for the youth teams at some of the top clubs but I'd signed for Crystal Palace the year before. They weren't the biggest club maybe, but they had a top youth set-up and pathway to the first team, you know? Anyway, things were looking really good for me. I thought I'd go all the way.

Then Ed turns up at one of my training sessions, and he's a famous footballer and always on the TV, and my dad can't believe it. Me and my dad signed a contract sitting in the back of his Merc that afternoon.

It was all good at first. I stayed on the youth teams for a while and then Ed got me a professional contract at Crystal Palace, but I wasn't making any money. Ed set it up so the club paid him and then he'd take his cut and pay me the rest. And his cut was a lot. I wasn't making anything like the money the other players were making.

I tried talking to Ed and Lynn about it, but they both harped on about doing what was best for me and trusting them. They told me they were investing my money for me, but I just wanted to earn what my teammates were getting. I think maybe it affected my training, and that's why I wasn't getting my shot. I kept trying to talk to Ed and Lynn about where exactly my money was being invested and when I'd get to see it, but they always fobbed me off. That was the other thing I wanted to talk to Ed about at the party.

So, after a few drinks, I decided I had to corner Ed. He wasn't happy and pretty much threatened to end my career. He kept saying I'd signed a contract and there was nothing he or I could do about it. I was upset and really angry, and I went into the garden for a bit to calm down.

Cassie

Did you see something happen to Bradley?

Dale
No. Nothing like that. I sat on a bench by myself and then after a bit someone came up and asked if I'd seen Taylor. I hadn't. He asked if I was all right and sat down and I sort of offloaded on him. Had this massive rant about Ed and the contract I was stuck in and how unfair it was.

The bloke was really nice. He told me that no contract was unbreakable and that he was sure if I took it to a solicitor they could give me some advice and I could find a different agent. I told him it was pointless though because Ed was friends with everyone. Ed had these meetings in Portugal where he took all the football managers, scouts, coaches, all the people who could make or break your career. I heard it was limitless booze and women all weekend. Everyone came away loving Ed.

So even if I could get out of the contract with him and maybe move clubs, it wouldn't matter because my career would be over. Ed would make sure of that.

The bloke was really nice about it. Thought it sounded well dodgy, and said he knew Ed and would talk to him.

Then he got up to leave and I went and found my friends.

Tom
And the bloke, you think this could have been Bradley?

Dale
Yeah, I do. It was dark and I was fuming so I wasn't really paying attention, but when I saw Bradley's photo on the news the following week, I thought he looked familiar.

Cassie
It's exactly the kind of thing Bradley would do – ask someone if they're all right. He hated injustice. It's why he wanted to study law.

Oh my God. That's what happened, isn't it? He went to confront

Ed. Then Ed and Lynn killed him to stop him telling anyone that Ed was scamming his clients.

Ed had this massive image of being this great guy, and it's the perfect cover if you think about it. Footballers desperate for a shot at the big time sign with him in a flash, and the whole time he's screwing them over and keeping the money for himself.

Badru
Dale, have you told any of this to DS Ewings?

Dale
Not yet. I'm going there next. I just wanted to tell Tom first. No offence, but if anyone is going to find out what happened here, it's probably him.

I just want to say . . . I'm sorry, Cassie. I shouldn't have let Lynn convince me to lie and I should've twigged sooner that Bradley going to talk to Ed might've been connected to him going missing. If I was in any way responsible for his death, then I'm sorry.

Tom
You couldn't have known what would happen to Bradley and you couldn't have stopped it, Dale. Only Ed and Lynn could've done that. But you're helping us get answers and justice for Bradley now.

Cassie, are you ready to go inside? If you need a minute, that's OK.

Cassie
I'm ready.

Tom Isaac Investigates: What really happened to Bradley Wilcox?

Episode 14: Why was Bradley killed? We find the motive! (cont.)

PUBLISHED ON YOUTUBE AND SPOTIFY:
FRIDAY, 24 NOVEMBER 2023

LOCATION: OUTSIDE LANCASTER HOME, HAMPTON WICK, WEST LONDON
INTERVIEW BETWEEN TOM ISAAC, CASSIE WILCOX AND BADRU ZUBIRA

[Footsteps]

[Keys jangling]

Tom
We're just stepping into the entrance hall. It feels a bit weird being back here again after the last time. I can't imagine how you must be feeling, Cassie. Does the house feel strange to you?

Cassie
It's just cold, I think. No one has had the heating on for months.

Badru
Police officers searched the house and took items into evidence in September after Lynn's death, and again last month after Bradley's remains were discovered, so it's extremely unlikely that we'll find anything today, but as a precaution can I ask you both to put these gloves on?

Tom
Sure. Of course.

Let's look in the living room first.

I've got to say, I've watched the party video so many times now I forgot the decor has changed. It's so different from how I remember it.

Cassie
This big white corner sofa used to be a gold and red tapestry-style three-piece suite, which at the time I thought was the nicest piece of furniture I'd ever seen in my life, but looking back it was very nineties. Everyone had their designated place to sit. Ed always sat in the armchair and Taylor always curled up on the left of the three-seater. India used to get really annoyed when I was there and took her spot in the middle beside Taylor.

There's less clutter than there used to be too, but I think I preferred it how it was. It looked like a home. Now, with the white walls and polished floors, it all feels a bit clinical.

Tom
I think the walls and floors might be about getting good lighting for filming, but I totally agree that it looks like a film set. Probably because that's exactly what it is.

I used to think when I watched *Living with the Lancasters* that the show was built around the family, but now I think that the family was built around the show. Does that make sense?

Cassie
Totally. Like they've been prepped their whole lives to play a part.

Tom
Exactly.

Shall we sit for a second? Is that OK? I know we're here to look around but I'd really like to talk to you about what Locke told me in our last interview relating to your friendship with Taylor.

Badru

I've got some emails to reply to. I'll be in the kitchen. Let me know when you're ready to look around.

[Pause]

Cassie

Locke is right. I was a total bitch in the last few years of my friendship with Taylor. I did pick on her and make her give me her clothes that she didn't wear and ignore her sometimes. Obviously, it was all jealousy. Ed and Lynn were always so nice to me. No one in the family ever made me feel poor, but I knew I was. I used to get so angry that everything came so easily to Taylor.

She had the acting classes and got the lead roles in the school play. She had no idea how lucky she was, and I wanted it all. I didn't realize how lucky I was to have a great brother and two parents who loved me until it all got snatched away.

I was a horrible person, but the day Bradley didn't come home changed me. I should've told you what I was really like in our first interview. And I should've told you that Taylor and I were best friends but that we fell out all the time. I didn't want you or anyone watching to think less of me. I didn't want you to think I wasn't worthy of help.

Tom

Oh, Cassie, of course I still would've helped you.

Cassie

[Crying]

Well, I know that now because you're lovely.

Tom
Shall we look around?

Cassie
No, wait. There's something else I have to say. The police questioned me about Lynn's death. They found out that I was here the night Lynn died.

Tom
You were here when Lynn was murdered?

Cassie
Not in the house, but parked on the road. It's difficult to explain. It's not the first time I've driven here at night. I've done it for years. Ever since I moved back to London to look after Dad. I think at one point early on, I wanted to confront Lynn about what happened to Bradley, but I could never get up the courage to knock on the door.

I've driven here and sat in my car a hundred times over the years. I think it was also to be close to the last place Bradley was seen. I don't know. But I never got out of my car. I never actually spoke to Lynn. Probably because I knew she'd never tell me anything.

It's messed up. I'm messed up.

Tom
You're not messed up, you're human.

Cassie
[Sighs]

That's what my therapist says. I was talking to her on the phone while I was parked here the night Lynn died. It must have been about eleven. She records all of our sessions and so the police were able to confirm that I was talking to her here and during my drive home.

There's no way I could've broken into the house and confronted Lynn while on the phone and you can hear me walking into my house while I'm talking.

They've got me on traffic cameras coming home around midnight too, which was before the time they think Lynn died.

Tom

OK, I get that you weren't involved in Lynn's death, but you do realize you could've seen something that night?

Cassie

The police already asked me, but I didn't see anything.

Do you think there was something to see? You think Taylor is innocent?

Tom

I really don't know. I'm keeping an open mind. That's my job. Can you tell me everything you remember from the night of Lynn's death? Did you see a black car, for instance?

Cassie

No, not that I remember. It was really quiet. The press were all standing on the pavement outside the house so I parked quite a way off. I don't remember seeing any cars. There were a few dog walkers and a runner. That's it. Nothing suspicious. No one turning into the Lancaster driveway.

Tom

So maybe that rules out Locke. Come on. Are you ready to look around?

Cassie

Yes, I'm ready.

Tom
Over here.

Badru, we're ready to start snooping.

Badru
That's the official term for it now, is it?

Tom
For sure.

So that's where India sat that night, sneakily watching the party, and if we walk down here, we find the snug.

[Door opening]

Which I didn't even know about. I can't remember ever seeing it on any of the episodes of the show. In fact, does this room feel different to you than the rest of the downstairs?

Cassie
What do you mean?

Tom
We've got the gorgeous tiles, that beautiful open-plan kitchen and all the white in the living room. We both just said that it feels like a set, and then we have this. A poky room with pine bookshelves and a sofa that's as old as I am. A red patterned rug on a carpeted floor. Look at those tassels on the rug. It's so nineties, just like you said about the old living room.

And check out the dust in here. Even after the months of sitting empty, the rest of the house still feels spotless.

Cassie
It's like no one has set foot in this room for years.

Badru
I know what you're thinking, but Cassie, after we found Bradley's remains, the entire house had a full forensic search, including this room, and no blood or other evidence was found.

Tom
Let's look upstairs. I want to look in India's room.

[Pause]

[Footsteps]

Tom
Here's another film-set style room for you. Dark grey walls with fairy lights around the edge and those faux-fur cushions on top of crisp white bedding. A bit like an upmarket hotel room.

Cassie
What are we looking for?

Tom
This is probably nothing, but do you remember India with a recording device as a child?

Cassie
Yes. She carried it with her everywhere and then would write up what she recorded in a notebook. It drove Lynn and Taylor crazy.

Tom
That's what Locke and Taylor said too. And India said she used to hide the notebook in her built-in wardrobe.

I'm going to open it up now. For those listening on the podcast, there is a massive wardrobe on one side of the room, but over here on the opposite side are two doors that open into a small built-in space. I'm opening it now and can see a rail of clothes – mostly dinner dresses – and shelves to the left and right.

India said she used to make a den in here on the floor with her duvet so it would make sense that her hiding place is somewhere in reach of the floor.

Cassie
Taylor was always looking for the notebooks but never found them.

[Pause]

Tom, I think we should look—

Tom
Javi, can you get a bit closer? I know there's not much space in here.

Cassie
Have you found something?

[Pause]

Tom, what is it?

Tom
I've found a loose bit of skirting board in the corner of the wardrobe. It's just wedged into place rather than stuck to the wall.

If I can just . . .

[Pause]

Yes, it's coming loose. There's some paper and— Oh my God, notebooks.

Black pocket-sized notebooks. They look pretty full. They must be India's diaries.

Badru
May I see?

Tom
Yes, of course.

Badru
I've got a lot of what look like conversation transcripts.

Cassie
Are there any from the night of the party?

Badru
I'm afraid I need to take these into evidence now.

Tom
Do you think we could get some copies first?

[Pause]

No, of course not. Stupid idea.

LOCATION: TOM'S STUDY

Tom
Today was another big discovery at the Lancaster home. We don't know yet what the diaries say and what answers they might contain, but we know from Dale that Bradley found out about Ed's financial exploitation of young footballers and probably confronted him.

And from the party video, we can guess that Lynn stepped in to smooth things out and probably spiked his drink with Zalpodine and left him sleeping in the snug.

What happened next?

How did Bradley die?

Is his death connected to Lynn's?

Is Taylor innocent?

Tomorrow, I'm going to talk to Locke, India and Taylor for the final time. I'm going to do whatever it takes to get the truth.

EXTRACT FROM EVIDENCE COLLECTED
BY THE METROPOLITAN POLICE FROM THE
LANCASTER PROPERTY ON 22 NOVEMBER 2023

Item No: 3

Description: Notebook titled 'Detective's Notes 3 by India Lancaster, age 10'

Saturday, 2 August 2003

Overheard conversation (recorded and transcribed):

Mum: Let me fix you a drink.

Bradley: That's really kind, Mrs Lancaster, but I should get going.

Mum: One more drink. Please? It's a party after all. We need to have a little talk.

Bradley: If this is about what Dale told me and what I said to Ed—

Mum: Don't worry about that now. It's late. We've all been drinking.

Bradley: I don't drink.

Mum: Really? Aren't you going to university next month? You'll need to start drinking if you want to survive that. Go on. It's just one. Then we'll have a chat and then you can go home if you want to.

Bradley: I really don't want a drink.

Mum: Bradley, you don't need to look so concerned. This is all a big misunderstanding. And when Ed has sobered up tomorrow, he'll explain everything and you'll see it's a case of crossed wires. That's all. Ed is a good guy. He's made an entire career out of making dreams come true and protecting young footballers. Surely you're not going to listen to what one stupid boy says?

Bradley: I don't think it is a misunderstanding. I think Dale, and probably other footballers, have signed contracts that give Ed a huge chunk of everything they earn, and fear for their careers is keeping them from doing anything or speaking out. I'm sure the Professional Footballers' Association—

Mum: Bradley, come on. Have this drink and then we'll talk. We're good people. You know how well we treat Cassie. She's like family to us. Here you go. Don't worry. I made it weak.

Bradley: OK.

Mum: We're good people, Bradley. You can trust us.

Tom Isaac Investigates: What really happened to Bradley Wilcox?
Episode 15: Taylor confesses!

PUBLISHED ON YOUTUBE AND SPOTIFY:
FRIDAY, 24 NOVEMBER 2023

Voice of Taylor Lancaster, taken from Instagram reel (16 February 2023)

Everyone has seen the video from my dad's party now, and I just want to say that Bradley Wilcox was my friend. I was the one who invited him to my dad's party. I feel so responsible for that. I just wanted to say that I'm as desperate to find him as Cassie is. Bradley has been missing for twenty years. He's out there somewhere. Please, if you think you may have seen him, get in touch with the police.

LOCATION: HM PRISON BRONZEFIELD,
PRIVATE INTERVIEW SUITE

Tom

In just a few minutes' time, Taylor is going to walk through that door for our final interview.

This is my last chance to get answers about Bradley and Lynn's deaths, and I have a little trick up my sleeve. If it works, we'll know everything.

It's a big 'if', though. I'm feeling a lot of pressure on top of a mountain of exhaustion. I haven't slept for two nights. I've had no more late-night visitors on my doorstep, but my head is such a mess. I feel like I'm so close—

[Door opening]

Taylor
Tom. Hi. It's good to see you. I thought you'd never come back. How are you? What's happening? It's killing me that I have no idea what's going on outside of these walls. I feel like I'm going to rot in here for ever.

Tom
There's actually been quite a big development this week. I'd love to talk to you about it if we get time before DS Ewings arrives.

Taylor
DS Ewings? Why is she coming here?

Tom
Do you remember telling me about the notebooks India recorded all of your conversations in when she was little?

Taylor
Ye-yes.

Tom
I found them. I have them here, in fact, in this evidence bag.

[Bag rustling]

Taylor
Oh my God. Where did you find them? Is there anything in them from—

Tom
The night of your dad's fortieth birthday party? Yes. It turns out little ten-year-old India couldn't sleep that night. So she crept downstairs at several points, recording some very interesting and pretty

incriminating conversations between your mum and dad, your mum and Bradley, and between you and your mum.

We know your dad was financially exploiting his football clients. We know Bradley found out at the party and confronted Ed. We know Lynn stepped in to calm things down and drugged Bradley with Zalpodine. We know everything, Taylor. DS Ewings is on her way to question you for your part in Bradley's death.

Taylor

[Crying]

Oh God.

You have to help me, Tom. I didn't mean for any of this to happen. It wasn't my fault. You see that, don't you?

Tom

The only way I can help you right now is if you tell me everything. In your own words. Explain these damning conversations India unwittingly recorded that night. Let your fans hear the truth from you.

Taylor

Yes. Yes, good idea. I . . . I don't know where to start.

Tom

Tell me about inviting Bradley to the party. You liked him?

Taylor

I really, really liked him. I thought I loved him. I don't think I've ever got over those feelings. It's why I've always struggled with relationships.

Tom

So, you wanted to be more than friends and you hoped something would happen the night of the party. Did you also arrange for

Cassie's then boyfriend to invite her to be somewhere else so that you and Bradley would be alone?

Taylor

He owed me a favour. He was a big football fan and I got my dad to get him a private tour of Old Trafford. So yeah, he invited Cassie to spend the evening with his family. She had a great night. I wasn't being mean or anything. She went to one of the nicest restaurants in London. And I got Bradley to myself.

Not that it made any difference. I looked amazing that night. I had this new dress – it was gold sequin – and I'd spent ages on my hair and make-up.

I was really nice to Bradley. I gave him a ton of compliments and I was flirty and funny. But it was getting later and later and he still hadn't kissed me, so I dragged him into the little boot room off the kitchen, kept the lights off and I kissed him.

It was perfect and I know he liked it too but then he took my arms really gently and sort of moved me away from him. Then he turned on the light and he said, 'You are so beautiful, Taylor. I'm flattered you would want to kiss me, but nothing can happen between us.' He said he wasn't looking for a relationship because he was going to university and wanted to concentrate on his studies.

I was gutted and embarrassed and really upset. I ran out of the boot room and into the garden. I think he followed me and started looking for me but I snuck back into the house, grabbed a bottle of champagne and went upstairs to my room.

I only came down again for the fireworks because I knew Lynn expected me to be there to say goodbye to the guests. She found me when I was outside and told me Bradley was sleeping over in the snug. I thought . . . I thought if he was staying then maybe he'd changed his mind and I . . . went in to see him.

He was lying on the sofa, so I walked across the room to wake him but then I smelt the vomit. It was disgusting. Even now just thinking about it, I catch a whiff of that stink.

I . . . kept going, though. I wanted to tell him to get out. I was angry that he'd rejected me and then been sick on our sofa. But when I touched him, his body didn't feel right, and I just freaked out and went to get Lynn.

Tom

Are you saying that you went into the snug after the fireworks and Bradley was dead?

Taylor

[Crying]

Yes.

Tom

Did you try giving him CPR? We know an ambulance was never called. Why not?

Taylor

I know it looks bad that I didn't try to help him. But I was a bit drunk and completely freaking out. I couldn't phone an ambulance without checking with Lynn. I think I must've instinctively known that an ambulance wouldn't save him. It was so tragic, but it was an accident.

Tom

An accident caused by Lynn giving him a spiked drink of alcohol and Zalpodine.

Taylor

She didn't want to kill him. She just wanted him to stay so she could talk to him properly in the morning and make him see sense.

Dad was acting like every other football agent out there, and Bradley was making out like it was a massive issue. Mum just wanted him to calm down.

Tom
But here's the issue I keep coming back to, Taylor. If it was an accident like you say, then why didn't anyone call the police? Whose decision was it to bury Bradley's body and cover up his death?

Taylor
We were all upset – me, Dad and Mum. Everyone had gone and we were all in the kitchen. It was, like, two or three in the morning. We were all crying. Dad had the phone in his hand the whole time, ready to call the emergency services, but Lynn said it would ruin us. She said, 'A teenage boy has died in our home. That's all anyone will ever remember. We'll never be anything. Do you want that for your kids?'

Dad was still pretty drunk but he said, 'What exactly are you suggesting?'

And Lynn kept her voice low and said, 'We can't bring him back, Ed. We can't change the outcome for Bradley or his family, but we can change it for us. We'll make it look like he disappeared or ran away on the way home from the party, that he was fine when he left us.'

They argued for ages. Hours, it felt like. Lynn was going on about damage control and Dad was talking about doing what was right for once.

[Crying]

Sorry. This is hard to talk about. I just sat and cried for Bradley and for Cassie. I knew what Lynn was saying was wrong, but I didn't know how to speak up.

I . . . I was selfish. I can see that now. Lynn had all these plans for me and I didn't want my life ruined because of something that wasn't anyone's fault.

Tom

Not anyone's fault? Taylor, your mother gave Bradley an alcoholic drink with sleeping tablets mixed into it. She drugged him. Bradley didn't drink alcohol. The one time he'd tried it, he was really sick.

Cassie told me that their mum had an intolerance for alcohol. Even a small amount made her violently ill.

What if Bradley had the same intolerance? He was alone in the snug and his body rejected the alcohol and he vomited. But because of the sleeping tablets in his system, he couldn't wake up and . . . and he drowned in his own sick. I think that's it. That has to be how Bradley died.

And none of it would've happened if Lynn hadn't given him that drink and left him alone. So I'm sorry, but I disagree. It was someone's fault. It was Lynn's fault. She is the reason Bradley is dead.

Did it even occur to you that had you gone to the police, Lynn would've been charged with manslaughter?

Taylor

Oh I . . . I hadn't thought of it like that. She said it was all about protecting Dad's image and our futures, but maybe she was thinking about herself too.

It took ages for her to convince Dad. I'd never known him to disagree with her, but eventually she got her way. It was morning by this point and Bradley was still in the snug. That's when India came downstairs and we freaked out all over again because she's always been so nosey.

Lynn made her go back to her room and Dad put Bradley in a wheelbarrow and covered him with a sheet from the garage. Mum smashed his phone up and put it in a bin bag with the cloths we used to clean the snug. She must've gone out at some point and put it in a public bin somewhere. While we cleaned, she told me the story. Bradley left the party in a taxi at eleven forty-five with some of the footballers. She knew one of them would back us up.

She made me repeat it over and over. She made me tell her about my whole day from start to finish, including the moment I saw Bradley climb into the back of the taxi.

Lynn said, 'We never ever speak of this again, Taylor. Never. Stick to the story. Always.'

It was awful. The worst time of my life. I was so upset. For Bradley and for Cassie.

I've always thought that it was because of what happened to Bradley that Lynn became so focused on me and making me famous. I think she wanted to prove that what we did was worth it. That we made something of ourselves.

[Crying]

I'm sorry. I'm so sorry, Tom.

I didn't kill Bradley, but I knew he was dead and I lied to the police and I lied to Cassie and to you, and I'm sorry. Lynn always made it sound so easy to do what she said. Stick to the plan. Stick to the story.

For what it's worth, I didn't kill her. I didn't kill my mum. You've got no reason to believe me, but it's the truth. I'm lost without her. She did everything for me. Even la tierra, that was all her, really. I'm nothing without her. I never would've killed her. You do believe me, don't you, Tom?

[Door opening]

Voice of prison officer
Time's up.

Taylor
Tom?

Tom
I don't know what to believe. No, that's not true. I believe Bradley needs justice for what happened to him and thanks to you and this interview we now have the truth.

Taylor
Me? But you said you've got the notebooks and the police are on their way?

Tom
The police have India's notebooks. That much is true. But I don't know what's in them or how much of what you've told us India captured. These notebooks here are ones I picked up from a stationery shop on the way to see you. But I'll be passing this interview to DS Ewings shortly and I'm sure she will be in touch.

Taylor
But I . . . you said . . .

Voice of prison officer
Come on now, please.

LOCATION: HM PRISON BRONZEFIELD CAR PARK

Tom
There it is – the truth. What really happened to Bradley Wilcox.

We were right. Lynn gave Bradley Zalpodine which, along with the alcohol, ultimately caused his death.

Taylor knew all along about his death and has spent twenty years lying. I'm going to call Badru in a minute. There has to be some justice for Bradley here.

Right now, Javi and I are driving down to interview Locke and India. I want to know how much they knew about Bradley.

I . . . also have a little confession, TIs. I have another piece of evidence connected to Lynn and her death. I've been desperate to tell you, but I wanted to give Bradley's case the attention and closure it deserves.

Let's finish this docuseries and find out who killed Lynn Lancaster. Spoiler alert – Taylor is innocent.

EXTRACT FROM EVIDENCE COLLECTED
BY THE METROPOLITAN POLICE FROM THE
LANCASTER PROPERTY ON 22 NOVEMBER 2023

Item No: 3

Description: Notebook titled 'Detective's Notes 3 by India Lancaster, age 10'

Wednesday, 1 October 2003

Overheard conversation (recorded and transcribed):

Dad: This has gone too far.

Mum: What has?

Dad: You know what. I'm not sleeping. We never should have—

Mum: Don't say another word. It was an accident. We do not speak about this. Don't develop a moral compass on me now, Ed. It really doesn't suit you.

Wednesday, 14 January 2004

Overheard conversation (recorded and transcribed):

Mum: What is wrong? Come to bed, it's late.

Dad: I can't sleep. I don't want to sleep either. I have nightmares about . . . the party.

Mum: You need to let this go. It's been months. No one knows a thing. We're safe.

Dad: I know. That's the problem. It's killing me that no one knows. I think I should hand myself in.

Mum: Don't be ridiculous. It's too late for that.

Dad: Hear me out. I'll say it was all me. You and the kids will be fine.

Mum: No, we won't. You'll destroy us. We will forever be the family with the father and husband in prison. I won't let you do that to us. You need to sort yourself out, Ed. Get a grip and remember the story.

Tom Isaac Investigates: What really happened to Bradley Wilcox?

Episode 16: Who killed Lynn Lancaster? The truth at last!

PUBLISHED ON YOUTUBE AND SPOTIFY:
FRIDAY, 24 NOVEMBER 2023

LOCATION: TOM'S CAR, LOCATION UNDISCLOSED

Tom

We've just pulled up outside Locke and India's house. You can hear the rain hitting the windscreen with every gust of sea air. I just knocked on the door, but Locke has asked me to wait in the car for a bit. He and India are being interviewed by the police.

I'm desperate to be in that room and hear what's being said. I'm guessing they want to verify that the notebooks I found yesterday belong to India.

There is another reason I want to be in that room right now. I have in my possession another piece of evidence, which I found behind the skirting board in India's wardrobe, right next to the notebooks. Something I didn't tell Cassie or Badru about.

I feel this knotty guilt sitting in my stomach that I should be storming into that house right now in full Poirot fashion and handing it over to the detectives. But I've kept this piece of paper I found with the notebooks to myself because I have a lot of questions that I want answered about Lynn's death, and the second this letter is in the public domain, everything changes. And I want my answers before that happens.

Oh, look, the front door has just opened. DS Ewings and a police constable in uniform are walking out towards a car. They're deep in conversation and don't look happy.

LOCATION: LIVING ROOM (LOCATION UNDISCLOSED)
INTERVIEW BETWEEN TOM ISAAC, LOCKE LANCASTER AND INDIA LANCASTER

Tom
I'm back in the living room of Locke and India's rented house for the final time. You've just had a visit from the police. Can you tell me what they asked you?

India
They asked me if the notebooks you found in the house yesterday were mine, and I confirmed that they were and that the information in them was true to the best of my knowledge. I can't remember writing all that stuff to be honest. Did you read them?

Tom
No. But I have just come from an interview with Taylor where she confessed to discovering Bradley's body, as well as telling us your mum's part in his death. Lynn spiked his drink with Zalpodine, which ultimately led to his death. And then both of your parents covered it up.

Locke
What? Dad was involved? No way.

Tom
On the night of the party, Bradley discovered that Ed was financially exploiting his clients and—

Locke
No. You're wrong there, mate. Dad was a good guy. Just look at what he was doing for youth football before he died.

India

Oh, Locke. He was not a good guy. I'm sorry to smash your rose-tinted glasses but he was ripping his clients off big time.

Locke

You knew about this? For fuck's sake. Why am I the last to know everything in this family? It's always me being pushed aside or ignored.

India

Shut up, Locke. Maybe you're pushed aside and ignored because you're incapable of thinking outside of the narrow little universe you live in, and we're all sick of pandering to your feelings of inadequacy.

Locke

[Mumbles]

Tom

How long have you known about your dad, India?

India

When I was little, I was always so curious about everything. I became obsessed with my dad's golf weekends. I used to hate it when he went away because Mum would make us do extra acting classes and then practise at home, too. Things were more fun when Dad was there.

I figured out he wasn't playing golf on his weekends away. He never got a bad back after being away, which didn't make sense because he always did if he played two days in a row at home. I wanted to uncover what he was really doing. Now, I think he was entertaining people in the football industry, bribing them and greasing the wheels and God knows what.

I was always snooping and overhearing things. I didn't understand what any of it meant. I was just a kid. We all believe our parents are good when we're little, don't we? But I think, over the years, something must've clicked into place and I began to question the story. At some point when I was a teenager, I put two and two together and realized what Dad had been up to.

Tom
I'm going to ask a difficult question now about your dad. Ed's death, just six months after his fortieth birthday, was ruled accidental. The story reported in the media at the time, the story Lynn shared on the show, is that Ed, while struggling with a back injury, took a cocktail of painkillers and sleeping pills – Zalpodine – which caused an overdose.

With everything we now know about Lynn, and about Bradley's death and that time in your parents' lives, I'd like to ask you both – do you believe your father's death was accidental? Is this just another story you've been sticking to?

Locke
Oh man, you're saying he killed himself?

India
For crying out loud, Locke. Tom is asking if we think Mum killed him.

Tom
And do you?

[Pause]

India
Yes. I do now. I've always suspected something, but now you've told me that Dad was involved in covering up Bradley's death, it makes sense that she killed him.

Locke
No way.

India
Like I said, I was the kid always hiding behind doors and listening in. Do you remember the day he died, Locke? Mum took us all shopping. It was supposed to be just her and Taylor and we were going to stay home with Dad, but she decided at the last minute to take us too, which was odd because Dad's back was playing up and we were supposed to be helping him.

It's . . . difficult, because that whole time is clouded in grief, but I think I saw Mum mixing Dad a drink before we left. Maybe it was just an act of kindness, or maybe she slipped something extra in there. Zalpodine was her go-to drug. Maybe Bradley's death was accidental, but I don't think Dad's was.

Locke
But Mum loved Dad. They were great together.

India
Wake up, Locke. Mum loved his money and she loved the lifestyle that came with his status as a Premier League footballer. You said yourself that Mum was relieved when he died. Why do you think that was?

I'll tell you, shall I? Maybe it was because Dad felt guilty about Bradley. Maybe he wanted to confess and Mum wouldn't have let that happen, so she made sure he couldn't. And then, of course, she was relieved. She'd convinced everyone that Bradley went missing on the way home and that Dad's death was an accident.

Locke
This is unbelievable. So our mum was some kind of whacky serial killer now? She killed Bradley and then Dad.

[Pause]

I need some air. I'm going for a walk on the beach.

[Door slamming]

Tom
Do you want to take a break, India?

India
No. Locke will be fine. He always takes this stuff hard. He walks around in his own little world, pretty oblivious to what's going on around him, and then gets upset when he's the last to know something. He'll be all right in a bit.

[Pause]

Remember last time you were here, you wanted to understand why I never spoke out about seeing Bradley that night? Do you get it now? This is why I could never speak out about what I saw, and why I was scared. I knew, or at least strongly suspected, that Mum was responsible for my father's death. She killed him because he didn't want to stick to the story.

My dad might've been a conman and a bit of a crook, but he wasn't a murderer, and I think knowing he played a part in covering up Bradley's death caused too much guilt for him to handle. He wanted to confess and Mum wasn't going to let that happen.

If I'd said anything, spoken up about any of it – Bradley, Dad, the abuse – I'd be dead too. I'm certain of that.

Tom
Can we talk about your notebooks a bit more, and the hiding place? When I found them, it felt like I'd found a long-forgotten treasure. But there was something else with them that makes me think the notebooks haven't been as forgotten as you'd like us to think.

India
You found the letter.

Tom
Yes.

Tom
When I found the notebooks, I was completely focused on them. They were what I was looking for. So when an envelope came out with them, I tucked it in my pocket to look at later and forgot about it until that evening.

Do you mind if I read it now?

India
Go ahead.

Tom
It's a plain white envelope addressed to 'My Darling Children'. The envelope has been opened. I assume you've read it.

India
Yes.

Tom
The letter reads:

'To my darling children, my battle with cancer has been a short one and we've all worked so hard to keep it a private one, but I can no longer fight this awful disease. So I'm making the choice to end my life on my own terms, to spare those I love the pain of my final months. I love you to the ends of the earth, my darlings. Mum.'

[Pause]

This letter, which I found hidden with your notebooks, is dated Sunday the tenth of September 2023. It's a suicide note – a goodbye letter from Lynn to you, Locke and Taylor. I'm guessing that because it was in your hiding place, in your room, that you found it.

India
Yes.

Tom
I'd like to understand where you found it. And why you hid it. Because if this letter is real then Taylor, your sister, has been in prison for the last two months, awaiting trial for a murder that she didn't commit. A murder that didn't even take place, according to this letter. And you knew it.

India
I found the letter on the kitchen counter.

Tom
Wouldn't Taylor have seen it that morning when she found Lynn's body?

[Pause]

Unless you were there that night.
    You were, weren't you? You went back to the house.
    Cassie was parked on the road that night. She remembered seeing a runner. Her exact words were, 'a few dog walkers and a runner.'
    A late-night runner.
    Not many people run at eleven at night, India. But you do. Locke mentioned that you like running at night. And you were only in Richmond. It would have been easy for you to run to the house.

India

I . . . couldn't sleep thinking about everything that was happening and Bradley's investigation. I knew Mum would still be awake, so I ran to the house to talk to her. I wanted to plead with her to do the right thing and tell you and the police the truth. I wasn't a hundred per cent sure at that point what the truth was, but I knew it was bad because she was so stressed, and I wanted her to be honest for once.

So I ran to the house. The electronic doors in my building are often propped open because the fobs don't always work, so it was easy to sneak out without a record of me leaving. But when I got to the house, she was already floating in the pool. She must have taken the pills outside and got up to go to bed and fallen in.

I found the note in the kitchen. It's total crap, Tom. Mum didn't have cancer. There was no secret battle. No disease. But even in her death she always had to stick to the story.

She must have known it was all about to come crashing down with Bradley's investigation, and the media storm against us all. Dale had just retracted his witness statement, remember? And implicated Mum as the reason. The press were reporting that an arrest was imminent.

So she took the easy way out. Cooking up a lie about cancer. I'm sure she hoped the Bradley investigation would die out too and the truth would never come out.

I . . . was so . . . angry. It wasn't fair that she could dodge all the evil she'd done and leave us with all of her mess.

Tom

So you took the note and hid it because it was all lies?

India

I didn't want her to get away with everything she'd done, even in her death. It wasn't fair.

Tom

Except that's not all you did, is it? Because in taking the note, you framed Taylor. You must've cleaned up the evidence of the pills Lynn had taken too. Did you mean to do that? To set your sister up for the murder of your mother?

India

Oh Tom, don't look at me like that. Please. Don't hate me. I'm not bad like they are, like Taylor and Mum. I wanted the truth out there about Bradley as much as you did. Probably more, in fact. Taylor and Mum had to answer for what they did, and with Mum gone that just left Taylor.

Tom

But you could've gone to the police at any point after the party video emerged, or any point before that with your suspicions about your mum, and Bradley's disappearance. Or you could've just told me everything on day one. I've been coming here for weeks. Taylor has been in prison for months. Why have you waited until now, until I've found every last scrap of evidence?

India

Don't you get it? You're the one that's been talking about justice for Bradley. If Mum's death had been ruled a suicide straight away then where would the justice be for Bradley? If Taylor hadn't spent a single second being questioned and been made to sweat it out in prison for her part in Bradley's death, then where would the justice be?

I didn't have any real evidence of what happened to Bradley. Just my suspicions. It wasn't enough to go to the police with. Taylor would've just denied everything. She'd have pinned it all on Mum.

Cleaning up the pill packets and the glass Mum was drinking from, making sure the police knew about Taylor arguing with Mum that day . . . it seemed like the only way to get any kind of justice.

I was certain Taylor knew about Bradley, and I was right, wasn't I? She lied to the police. She's just as bad as Mum and Dad. She deserved to be arrested. To be put on trial for something. The fact that she didn't get bail and had to spend time in prison is a bonus, I think.

And before you ask, I wouldn't have let her be sentenced for Mum's murder. I knew you'd find the notebooks and the letter. I dropped enough hints.

Tom

You planned this. You planned everything? You wanted me to find the notebooks and the letter?

India

Yes. I'm sorry for misleading you, but you've been brilliant, Tom. Think about it. I knew if Mum's death was ruled a suicide straight away that life would carry on for us. With the key suspect dead, I worried Bradley's investigation would die out too. But if there was some doubt, if there was a question over how she died, then I hoped you'd take it on as well as your investigation into Bradley. And you did and I'm really grateful for that.

I'm sorry if I sound cold or calculating or whatever. It's just . . . I've spent over sixteen years trapped in a life I hated. In a life I didn't want, being controlled by a woman I suspected was capable of murdering someone she loved who threatened to stand in the way of her plans.

This, this unravelling of the truth that you've done, it ends it all. You got Taylor to confess! She's told the truth at last. She never would've done that without the evidence you found and the months in prison being shut way from the world.

Cassie now has the answers she needed; she can move on. And as for us – for Locke and me – there is no coming back from this. I had to make sure of that.

Tom

I need to be extremely clear on this. You framing Taylor for Lynn's murder, me investigating her death in the docuseries – it was all about getting the truth?

India

Yes. I wanted the world to know about Mum and what our lives have been like under her rule. But it was also about justice for Bradley and seeing Taylor under pressure from a police investigation and charged with a crime.

Tom

But it was about the show too? About ending the Lancaster empire?

India

Do you know what I wanted to be when I was a teenager? A chemistry teacher. A professor of some kind. I'm smart. I had the grades.

I never wanted any part of *Living with the Lancasters*. That was all Mum and Taylor and Locke. But I couldn't escape it. I couldn't get away. Mum didn't feel the show worked without me in it. She wanted me to be a model, and so that's what I did.

You asked me once if I ever looked back at my nose job or other stuff that happened and ever felt angry and upset, and of course I did. *Of course*. Who wouldn't? Do you know how many times she visited me while I was being treated for an eating disorder? None. Eight weeks I was in hospital, and she didn't visit once, because in her eyes I'd let her down, I'd got in the way of her plans.

Everything about the relationship we had with our mum was abusive. You said it yourself. It was insane. Taylor and Locke couldn't see it. They loved her so much and did everything she said. So did I.

But now it's all over. The British public hate us. Even our biggest fans have turned their backs on us. We're not famous any more. We're notorious.

Tom
So what happens now? I take this letter to the police, and then what?

India
Taylor will be released from prison and the murder charges will be dropped.

My hope is that she'll then be rearrested for her part in covering up Bradley's death, but whether there will be enough evidence to convict her, I don't know.

I will admit my part in hiding the letter and covering up Mum's suicide. I broke the law when I took Mum's letter and lied about my whereabouts. I left her in the pool for Taylor to find when I should've called the emergency services. I don't like to think of myself as a monster, but I'm not blind enough to consider myself innocent.

I'm sure Locke and eventually Taylor will scurry about on whatever celebrity reality shows will have them for a while before admitting defeat and disappearing into obscurity. And at some point in the future when I've paid for my part in all of this, I hope I'll find my way back to my studies and the quiet life I was always supposed to live.

I know what I've done is extreme, but this really was the only way, thanks to you, Tom. You've done it, haven't you? Just like I knew you would. You found the answers. What really happened to Bradley Wilcox and who killed Lynn Lancaster.

Bravo!

Tom Isaac Investigates: What really happened to Bradley Wilcox?

Episode 16: Who killed Lynn Lancaster? The truth at last! (cont.)

PUBLISHED ON YOUTUBE AND SPOTIFY:
FRIDAY, 24 NOVEMBER 2023

LOCATION: TOM'S STUDY

Tom

Guys, I am not OK. Nowhere close.

I still can't process everything India said today. It keeps coming back to me in these sickening waves of realization.

So Taylor knew the whole time about Bradley's death. She's confessed.

Voice of Taylor Lancaster

But when I touched him, his body didn't feel right, and I just freaked out and went to get Lynn.

Tom

She didn't kill Bradley, but she was complicit in the cover-up, supposedly because Lynn, who was by all accounts a controlling mother, forced her to be.

We know from Taylor's confession and the video that Lynn killed Bradley, probably accidentally, by giving him a spiked alcoholic drink. She did this because she wanted him to stay at the house until the party was over so she and Ed could talk him out of going public about their dodgy dealings. That makes sense. Ed had cultivated a public image of a knight in shining armour out to save youth football, and the fallout from discovering that he was actually corrupt would have been catastrophic.

Taylor found Bradley's body, and Lynn and Ed buried him in their garden and covered it all up, and then all three of them lied about it.

Ten-year-old India captured some of these key moments in her notebook, but didn't understand at the time what any of it meant. Then her dad died and she forgot all about the notebooks.

Twenty years later, Locke releases Ed's party video and inadvertently reignites public and police interest in Bradley's disappearance. India puts two and two together and realizes that Taylor and Lynn are covering something up but doesn't say anything to the police or anyone. Why? Why does she keep what she knows to herself?

Voice of India Lancaster
She was not the type of person you crossed. Ever. It's not just that she would've made things difficult for me, she would've destroyed me.

Tom
So India goes to the house the night of Lynn's death and is first to discover Lynn's body as well as the suicide letter. She was angry with her mum for not being honest even in her final moments.

India saw a scenario where no one would ever know the truth about Bradley, and for what it's worth, I think she's probably right. Without Lynn, the police investigation into Bradley's death would have stalled, and the show and the empire could probably have come back from that.

So India framed Taylor for Lynn's death as a way to make her pay for her part in covering up Bradley's death, and waited for me to uncover the truth. With the Lancaster empire in tatters and Taylor having spent months in prison, India hoped that I'd get a confession out of her, and she was right.

But according to India, she would have come clean before the trial either way.

There's a big part of me that's struggling to wrap my head around Lynn's absolute focus and drive towards fame for herself and her children. And yet, there's something in what India has done that smacks of that same focus. That unrelenting drive. India could've given her notebooks to the police at any point this year, or any time in the past twenty years. Instead, she hid them and waited for this investigation to uncover the truth.

It was more important to India that she made Taylor pay for what happened to Bradley, and to get her past and her story told the way she wanted it to be told, than it was to see the truth out there.

And what about Locke? What did he know in all this? Nothing, it appears. Could he be the one innocent Lancaster among all this mess? I wonder what he will do now. We can assume India will disappear into a life of studying. I doubt Taylor will ever speak to her again. Locke has shown a lot of resentment towards Taylor over the course of this investigation, and I do have to wonder where both of them will end up. Is it like India predicts? Are we destined for a life of seeing Taylor and Locke on reality shows with all the other washed-up celebrities?

This is the final episode of *Tom Isaac Investigates* and we have the truth about Bradley. He was killed by Lynn, and the truth was covered up by Lynn, Ed and Taylor.

We also know who killed Lynn Lancaster. She killed herself because she could see that the truth about her part in Bradley's death was about to come out.

So that's it, TIs. Thanks to our investigation, and in no small part thanks to you and your comments and hard work – especially Wendy Clarke for roping her amazing brother Hal into the investigation. His discovery led us to India's confession that she was downstairs on the night of the party.

We have the truth, but will there ever be justice? Ed and Lynn are both dead. Taylor will certainly be in serious trouble. She was complicit in covering up the manslaughter of Bradley Wilcox. She lied to the police and hid evidence. India, too, will face consequences for her part in covering up Lynn's suicide.

Is that enough?

Maybe the total destruction of the Lancaster empire – the end of the show, their fall from grace, and Taylor's time in prison – is the punishment, the justice we want. It doesn't feel like enough for Cassie or for Bradley, but at this point, I'm not sure what *would* feel enough.

As for me, Mumsie is home now. She's cooking my favourite lasagne as we speak. Snowy is here too. I've missed my girl so much.

There haven't been any more threats, but after a much-needed holiday, I will be doing a bit of digging into them.

You've been watching me, Tom Isaac, on *Tom Isaac Investigates*. If you've enjoyed this docuseries, please like and subscribe, and check out my other investigations too. Until next time, that's it from me.

Tom Isaac Investigates: What really happened to Bradley Wilcox?
Episode 16: Who killed Lynn Lancaster? The truth at last!

PUBLISHED ON YOUTUBE AND SPOTIFY:
FRIDAY, 24 NOVEMBER 2023

276,769 COMMENTS

TI_BiggestFan
You did it again, Tom!!! Well done!! You're so amazing. Love Mumsie xx

Wendy Clarke
WOW! So India knew all along about Lynn, but didn't say anything, and instead framed her sister for murder. She's just as bad as Taylor and Lynn.

> **JulieAlexander_1**
> I don't agree with what India did, but without her, Taylor wouldn't have spent time in prison. I know it's only been a few months but it's still something. And like India said, if Taylor hadn't spent all that time in prison and had her whole life taken away from her, she might not have confessed when Tom confronted her.

> **LWTL_No1Fan**
> Yes! And can we really blame India for her actions considering how messed-up her childhood was? Growing up with a controlling and manipulative mother isn't exactly a great role model. India isn't perfect. She did the wrong thing for the right reasons.

> **Ernie Martin**
> I think they all belong in prison. Bunch of nutters, the lot of them.

Katy Shepard
I'm confused. So who killed Lynn?

> **Wendy Clarke**
> No one. She killed herself. But India found her mum and took the note Lynn wrote so it would look like murder.
>
> **KMoorcroft58**
> So Lynn got the sleeping pills for herself? Why did she get them in Taylor's name? Why wouldn't she get them in her own name? And why did she get them in January before the party video was even released?
>
> **Wendy Clarke**
> Good questions. Tom, what do you think about this?

TrueCrime_Junkie1001
You got the truth, Tom, but is that at the cost of justice? Taylor will be released from prison, the one place she actually belongs. Will any of them ever pay for what they did now? Unlikely.

APRIL 2024

TRANSCRIPT FROM SKY NEWS LIVE
WITH PATRICK MONAGHAN AND
AMBER CARNEY, 10 APRIL 2024

Patrick: You're watching *Sky News Breakfast*. It's eight forty-one on Wednesday the tenth of April. It's now time for the celebrity headlines with Amber Carney.

Amber: The Lancaster family are back in the headlines this week. You'll remember, Patrick, that they dominated the news for most of 2023 after Taylor Lancaster was charged with the murder of her mother. She was later released from prison in December after evidence emerged confirming Lynn's death as a suicide.

Taylor was then rearrested and charged with obstruction of justice, having tampered with a crime scene and lied to police about the disappearance of missing teenager Bradley Wilcox twenty years ago. Her sister, India, was also charged with obstruction of justice in Lynn Lancaster's death. Both sisters avoided prison but were given hefty fines and community service sentences.

Since then, the entire family has kept a low profile. That is until they popped up last month with India signing a one-million-pound book deal, and, rather surprisingly, the entire family – Taylor, Locke and India – moving to LA together.

They're set to star in a brand-new reality show – *Living with the Lancasters: The Next Chapter*. The first episode aired last night on E! Entertainment and follows India, Taylor and Locke as they get to grips with life in America and building their fashion brand, la tierra, stateside.

I spoke with Head of Production for E! Entertainment, Gwen Lipton, late last night.

[Pre-recorded interview]

Amber: The Lancaster family have never made a secret of wanting to build their fan base in America. What makes now the right time for them to do that?

Gwen: The Lancasters are scandalous. They're notorious. And the dynamic of the three siblings finding their feet over here will make addictive viewing for American audiences.

[Sky News live]

Amber: While the new reality show has sparked criticism and anger across the British tabloids and social media, it appears that the scandals of the past year have cemented the Lancasters' popularity in the US, with viewing figures for last night's show already pushing into the millions.

And with E! Entertainment having reportedly bought the entire *Living with the Lancasters* back catalogue for an eye-watering sum, I can say with some certainty that the Lancasters are back on screens and here to stay.

Tom Isaac Investigates: What really happened to Bradley Wilcox?
Episode 16: Who killed Lynn Lancaster? The truth at last!

PUBLISHED ON YOUTUBE AND SPOTIFY:
FRIDAY, 24 NOVEMBER 2023

813,141 COMMENTS

TrueCrime_Junkie1001
I know it's been months since this docuseries ended and I'm not sure if anyone is still checking these comments, but I had to say this somewhere.

Does anyone else think it's really weird that India said in her final interview with Tom that everything she did was to destroy the Lancaster empire, so she had a chance at a 'normal' life, and then as soon as the police investigations are over, she immediately moves with Taylor and Locke to America, buys a Beverly Hills mansion for them all to live in, signs a book deal, and then starts another reality TV show? It doesn't make sense.

> **LWTL_No1Fan**
> Have you watched the show? India has taken on Lynn's role as manager. Taylor and Locke are doing everything she says. It's weird.
>
> **JulieAlexander_1**
> WTF?
>
> **TrueCrime_Junkie1001**
> Tom, what do you think?

To: Cassie_Wilcox@BlueInternet.com
From: Tom@TomIsaacInvestigates.com
Subject: Quick question
Date: 12.04.24

Hi Cassie,

How are you doing?

I know we're meeting up in a couple of weeks but can I ask a question . . . I've just been checking back over our emails and I found the first one you sent me. You said a friend recommended me. Can you tell me who that was? I've been re-watching my docuseries and there's stuff that doesn't add up.

I'll explain when I see you.

Thanks!

Tom x

To: Tom@TomIsaacInvestigates.com
From: Cassie_Wilcox@BlueInternet.com
Subject: RE: Quick question
Date: 12.04.24

Hi Tom,

Sure, no worries. It wasn't actually a friend who recommended you. It was someone on Twitter (or whatever it's called now) who I was chatting to a lot last year when I was trying to get some momentum on #JusticeForBradley. I don't know their name, but it's one of your TIs so you might know them. SyfyGeek90. Actually, they gave me the idea of hiring the cadaver dogs too.

Did you get the signed early copy of my book? You're in the acknowledgements of course! I know I keep saying this, but thank you for giving me my life back.

Before you ask, no I didn't watch *Living with the Lancasters: The Next Chapter*. I can't believe they're just starting again! Sometimes in the night I wake up and still feel the same red-hot rage I carried with me all those years, but I'm working through it and part of that is acceptance. I can't change the past and I can't change who the Lancasters are. Of course, that doesn't mean I'm going to stop the civil case against them.

Hope things are still going well with Hal.

See you in a few weeks. I'll bring pastries!

Cassie x

Text message, 12 April 2024

Tom
Hey Locke, can we talk?
Message failed to send.
Number no longer in service.

Tom Isaac Investigates: What really happened to Bradley Wilcox?
Episode 17: I was wrong!

PUBLISHED ON YOUTUBE AND SPOTIFY:
MONDAY, 15 APRIL 2024

LOCATION: TOM'S STUDY

Tom

It's April 2024. Five months ago, I concluded my investigative docu-series into what really happened to Bradley Wilcox.

I thought we had all the answers. But some things have happened that have me questioning everything. Seriously, I have had a million WTF moments in the last few months and I really need to talk about it.

As you can see from the change of background, I have finally moved out. Mumsie says she's heartbroken, but I know she's glad to get her spare room back really. And I have only moved around the corner. Literally. I can see the roof of her house from my bathroom window.

I haven't quite found the courage to move to Brighton yet, but maybe one day. There's more keeping me in London right now.

But despite the house move and the holiday with Mumsie, I couldn't stop thinking about the Lancasters.

At first, I thought it was because the investigation was so intense and crazy and totally messed-up, but it's more than that.

We missed something.

I missed something. More than one thing, actually. As someone in the comments said recently, it all feels very off. That's because it is. Because . . . deep breath . . . we were wrong.

So I'm back. This isn't a whole new investigation. It's just a . . . a new conclusion. A re-evaluation of the evidence and what we were told.

The series was full of surprises, wasn't it? Not to mention emotional, and at points scary. I mean, hello, we discovered a dead body. And someone was threatening me. By the way, I know who that was, and I'll get to that in a second.

I took on too much. Trying to get answers and justice for Bradley, and also trying to investigate Lynn's death. Everything was unravelling so fast that I don't think I stopped to consider what we were uncovering, and how.

All through my holiday and when I got back, I couldn't stop thinking about what each of the Lancasters said to me and when they said it. There were so many times they changed their story. And that's the key word here. Story. Not truth. Story.

So I went back over all of my notes. I watched my docuseries from the start and I couldn't believe it. I missed something before the first episode even aired. It was something Cassie said in her very first email to me. She said, 'a friend recommended I contact you'.

Someone told Cassie to ask for my help. Someone suggested to her that I start an investigation into what happened to her brother. At the time, I was wrapped up in the MP expenses docuseries, and to be honest, the idea of looking into a historical missing persons case involving Britain's most famous family excited me. So I didn't ask her at the time who it was. Who was this friend?

But I did ask last week. The answer – SyfyGeek90. I'm sure most of you recognize the handle. Because SyfyGeek90 has been commenting and taking part in this entire docuseries. And it would actually make sense for a dedicated TI to message Cassie and suggest my help because you guys are great. And you're always suggesting ideas for future investigations.

Except SyfyGeek90 isn't a dedicated TI. They have never commented on any of my other investigations. So I scrolled through thousands and thousands of comments from this series, and I found every single one SyfyGeek90 made. I told you I was obsessed! It took me hours.

Here are some of their comments:

SyfyGeek90

Tom, have you contacted Taylor, Locke and India as well as Lynn? Where were they during the party? Maybe they know something.

SyfyGeek90

We need to focus on the Lancasters! Taylor was alone in the house the night Lynn died. Tom, when are you going to ask India and Locke about Bradley?

SyfyGeek90

Tom, have you thought about going to the Lancaster home to look around? If India and Locke aren't there then it's empty right now. It would be good to get a sense of where it all happened – Bradley's last known whereabouts and Lynn's death!

SyfyGeek90

Tom, can you go back to the Lancasters' house? You never got to look around last time.

Tom

At first it seems like SyfyGeek90 is just another keen TI, participating via the comments. But not only did they suggest that we should go to the Lancaster house twice, but they also messaged Cassie on social media and mentioned cadaver dogs. Of course, at the time, I assumed that was Cassie's idea.

SyfyGeek90 also suggested to another TI, Wendy Clarke, that she look more closely at the party video. I spoke to Wendy, and she confirmed that SyfyGeek90 even suggested zooming in on the back stairs and looking for clues. I think if Wendy hadn't had Hal to turn to, they'd have suggested hiring someone to look. They wanted me to see those feet. They wanted India to confess to being there that night.

Throughout the docuseries, throughout everything that's happened, one person has been a step ahead. One person has been pulling the strings.

And they even admitted it.

Voice of India Lancaster
I know what I've done is extreme, but this really was the only way, thanks to you, Tom. You've done it, haven't you? Just like I knew you would. You found the answers. What really happened to Bradley Wilcox and who killed Lynn Lancaster.

Bravo!

Tom
And she even said . . .

Voice of India Lancaster
I knew you'd find the notebooks and the letter. I dropped enough hints.

Tom
And then I started thinking . . . if India planned this – for me to take on the investigation into Bradley's disappearance and then Lynn's death – when did her plans start?

And here's where it gets interesting – or scary, even. The Twitter account for SyfyGeek90 was created in January 2023 and straight away all the comments were about the Lancasters. But that's not all that happened in January, is it? Let's not forget that it was also in January that someone pretending to be Taylor called a private GP and got a prescription for Zalpodine.

I now believe that person was India Lancaster, if it wasn't Taylor herself.

I believe everything Taylor, India and Locke told us was a carefully created story. A very clever story. I believe every single thing that's happened, right from the creation of SyfyGeek90's Twitter account and the Zalpodine prescription in January, the release of the 2003 party video back in February last year, the negative press and social media hate, to Lynn's death, and the discovery of Bradley's body – not to mention all of their secrets along the way – has all been part of a plan. That's right: I now believe Lynn's death was murder.

Voice of India Lancaster
When I got to the house, she was already floating in the pool.

Tom
Here's the big thing I missed. The thing that keeps me up at night, that I should have known. I should've asked about. We know India arrived at the house around 11 p.m. Cassie was parked on the road and saw her running past, but didn't realize at the time that it was India.

But Lynn wasn't dead at 11 p.m. The coroner puts Lynn's death at sometime in the early hours of the morning. Lynn was alive at eleven. She would have seen India. They would have talked.

And it wasn't just India at the house that night. We already know that Taylor was there too, and what about Locke? His alibi from his ex-girlfriend, Kelly Lacey, was always weak. He could easily have borrowed her car once she was asleep and driven home, parking around the corner and using the side gate, just like India did.

But we didn't have any evidence. Until now.

Over the last few weeks, I've contacted every single member of the press stood outside the Lancasters' home that night. We already know from the police investigation that the press cameras didn't capture anyone on the road or entering the front of the house.

But it turns out that a woman by the name of Clara Wesley decided to drive to the twenty-four-hour McDonald's for a coffee run at 11 p.m. on the night of Lynn's death. And guess what? I tracked her down and she has dash cam and gave me the footage.

Look at this.

[Pause]

For those listening on the podcast, what we're seeing here is a car journey as it leaves the Lancasters' road and heads towards a McDonald's ten minutes away.

And here . . .

Here. See that car on the roundabout? It's a small Audi and look who's driving: Locke. He was there the night Lynn died. All three of them were. They killed her.

So what was the motive?

Are we to believe that after years of abusive behaviour and coercive control by their mother, the three Lancaster siblings snapped and wanted out? Maybe.

Maybe if you watch the docuseries back like I did, you'll catch glimpses of the hurt and anger towards Lynn.

But if their sole purpose was to kill Lynn and be free from her control, why not stage the suicide and carry on with their lives?

They could've hired cadaver dogs and told the investigation team into Bradley's disappearance that they suspected something, and then they could've pinned his death solely on Ed and Lynn. Taylor could've denied all knowledge of what happened to Bradley.

They could've done all that without the months of media frenzy and social media hate. They could have done it all without me.

Voice of Locke Lancaster
There are some things you can't come back from.

Tom
But what if they didn't want to carry on as before? What if every headline, every social media hashtag, all the outrage, and the scandals and shocking discoveries from my docuseries, what if all of it was a platform, a stage, not to continue as they were, but to catapult themselves somewhere bigger?

Think about it – Lynn had been trying to attract American viewers for years, but the show was too small-time for the US market. That was until one of them was framed for murder and a body was uncovered at their property.

Voice of India Lancaster
We're not famous any more. We're notorious.

Gwen Lipton of E! Entertainment, taken from a Sky News interview on 10 April 2024
The Lancasters are scandalous. They're notorious. And the dynamic of the three siblings finding their feet over here will make addictive viewing for American audiences.

Tom
I know what you're thinking. You're thinking Taylor would never agree to spending months of her life in prison. Of course she wouldn't. But that's because they all assumed she would get bail. Everyone was shocked when she didn't.

Voice of Taylor Lancaster
Like, oh my God, can you believe I didn't get bail? Like, in what world am I a flight risk? I still can't believe it. And it makes me . . . either really angry or really upset, and sometimes both at the same time.
  [Raised voice] I am not going to run away!

Voices of Locke and India Lancaster

Locke
I can't believe they didn't give her bail—

India
Locke.

Locke
Yeah, yeah. I know she's our sister and all that. I guess if you boast about having access to a private jet whenever you want it, the courts aren't likely to let you hang around at home while they get stuff sorted for the trial.

Tom
Notice the way India says Locke's name. She did it quite a few times during the interviews. Like she's warning him. At the time, I assumed that Locke hated Taylor, and India was trying to convince him to go easier on her. Now, listening to the interviews back, I think those warnings are something else. I think India was reminding Locke to stick to the story.

Like I said at the start – that is the key word. Story. I think they cooked up this whole plan, this whole story, as a way to get rid of Lynn, move to the US and start over. And everything they've said and done has been about sticking to that story.

Remember when we got the vibe from Taylor in the first interview that she wasn't taking this seriously? I even said that it felt like she thought it was just the next crazy thing for the show. And it was.

I mean, why else would Taylor ever agree to move to another country with India and star alongside her in a reality show? You don't just forgive someone for framing you for murder unless you're in on it from the start.

And in case you needed more evidence that the Lancasters were all in on it, let's go back to the threats I received. I said earlier that I knew who was behind them. At the time I thought someone wanted me to drop the investigation. I really thought someone didn't want us to find out the truth about Bradley.

Wrong again.

Because of the speed of the investigation and how caught up in everything I was, I didn't take the time to dig into who those threats were coming from. Because if I had, I would have found this doorbell camera footage from the house on the next road, and yes, I did spend a day knocking on every door in a half-mile radius.

Look who pops up walking past this house during an Amazon delivery on the same day someone put the first threat on my doorstep. Locke! And it makes sense. He knew where I lived, of course, from coming over for dinner as a kid.

At first I thought, oh okay, he didn't want me to uncover the truth because he was desperate to get his life back and keep Taylor in prison.

But no. He wasn't trying to warn me off at all. Every time I received a threat it wasn't because I was getting close to the truth, it was because the investigation was stalling, and the threat spurred me on to take action and made me more determined to get the truth, just as Locke knew it would.

So what happens now? Now I've peeled back the layers of the story to find the grimy, manipulative and dark reality? Well, I took my theory and the new evidence I found to Badru. He shared it with DS Ewings and . . . nothing.

India and Locke's presence at the house the night Lynn died, Locke's presence in the area of my house – it's not enough for any kind of warrant or extradition order. Even the fact that Lynn didn't have cancer like she said in her suicide note isn't enough. Because surely the post-mortem would have shown this and it would have been reported in the press. It's easy to see why the police aren't interested in this lie. After all, Lynn has been lying from day one. As far as the police are concerned, the reason for the suicide might not be true, but the suicide itself is, which is the same story India gave us.

The best Badru can promise is that when or if the Lancasters ever return to the UK, DS Ewings will question them on the new evidence I've uncovered. But as it stands, they won't change Lynn's cause of death from suicide. They won't open a murder investigation.

The vibe I got is that the Crown Prosecution Service don't think Lynn's death is a high priority, and to be fair, I can see why. They're not going to win any fans by re-investigating the death of a woman who was responsible for killing two people – Bradley and Ed.

The CPS have already come under fire for wrongly charging Taylor. And the police have also been heavily criticized for failings in both Bradley and Lynn's cases. As far as the police are concerned, both investigations are now closed. The Lancasters are living in another country, and nobody wants to touch this case with a barge pole.

All that's left is Cassie's civil case. She has a legal team looking into getting some kind of justice for Bradley and I really hope she gets it.

I feel . . . I don't know. Empty. Numb. Angry. Stupid. I'm supposed to be the investigator. I'm supposed to uncover the truth. But in this investigation, I was a pawn in a very complex, very detailed long game. A game it looks to me like they've won.

Everything they've done has been about raising their profile and catapulting themselves to the next level of fame, and I fell for it. I helped them do it. It was all just clickbait.

MAY 2024

Living with the Lancasters: The Next Chapter
Series 1, episode 5 (2024)

BROADCAST ON E! ENTERTAINMENT:
TUESDAY, 7 MAY 2024

Taylor
So as you know, I'm dating now! I want to be married and pregnant by the end of this year. And I'm determined to meet my one true love. I'm certain he's in LA. I've been on a few dates now with Chad Healy, quarterback for the LA Rams, and things are going pretty well. American men are so proper. The whole dating thing is much more of a big deal here than it is in London.

And all this sunshine. It's doing me the world of good. Less than six months ago, I was still in prison after being wrongly accused of killing my own mother. I'm so grateful to be here right now, living my best LA life.

Of course, it would be nice if someone in this house – Locke – wouldn't leave the kitchen in an absolute state constantly. I accidentally drank his bulking-up protein smoothie this morning because he left it on my shelf in the fridge. He's drinking the smoothies all the time because he thinks he looks weedy next to some of the American men. He totally does.

I hit the roof when I found out what I'd drunk. I've been working my butt off having a total body cleanse so I'm ready for the Emmys after-party hosted by E! Entertainment tonight. I will seriously *kill* Locke if he goes near my fridge shelf again.

It's a super stressful time at the moment with the opening of the la tierra store just around the corner in Beverly Hills. India is trying to take over all the design stuff, which is totes ridic. *I'm* the designer. She's the organizer. Just look at her. What does she know about trends?

Locke

Yeah, Taylor is dating Chad. He's a good guy and everything, but how long is he going to stick around for once he sees Taylor's temper? All I did this morning was put my smoothie in the fridge and she had a meltdown because she drank it and then found out it was one of my protein shakes. Like, who drinks stuff from a fridge if it isn't theirs? Who did she think made a smoothie for her? If anyone should've been mad, it was me. But she's freaking out because her outfit for tonight's E! after-party doesn't fit. India is currently phoning every stylist in LA trying to find her a new dress to wear.

I still can't believe we're going to an Emmys after-party! It's going to be wicked. Catch me on E! News as I'll be doing some presenting tonight from the red carpet.

India

I am loving life in LA. I love how friendly everyone is. We have so many fans already! It's so lovely to go places and have people be so nice after all the hate we were getting in England. I really hope people come to our new la tierra clothing boutique in Beverly Hills. Taylor, Locke and I have all had so much fun designing and modelling the new range.

I feel like all my dreams are coming true and I seriously hope the younger viewers watching this will be inspired by what we've achieved. If you're watching this and feeling trapped or held back by something or by someone, never forget that you have agency. You can make things happen and change things. You can succeed. It doesn't have to be overnight and sometimes the best success comes after years of planning. Just keep taking steps towards that goal. Be the smartest in the room. Be the one who knows everything. That's what gives you power. Above all, don't let anyone or anything stand in your way.

Credits

L. C. North would like to thank everyone who has worked on the publication of *Clickbait*:

Editor: Imogen Nelson
Copy-editors: Fraser Crichton, Kate Samano
Proofreaders: Lorraine Jerram, Jessica Read
Text design: Dan Prescott
Cover design: Beci Kelly, Anthony Maddock
Publicity: Chloë Rose
Marketing: Rosie Ainsworth
Sales: Tom Chicken, Emily Harvey, Phoebe Llanwarne, Bronwen Davies, Louise Blakemore
Production: Phil Evans
Audio: Gray Eveleigh, Rosemary O'Dowd
Audiobook read by: Sebastian Humphreys, Claire-Louise Cordwell, Carl Prekopp, Florence Howard, Jane Slavin, Ayesha Antoine, Kristin Atherton, Sagar Arya, L. C. North
Audiobook edited by: Tom Rowbotham
Audiobook music by: Kate MacDonald
Agents: Tanera Simons, Amanda Preston
Agent assistant: Laura Heathfield
Beta readers: Zoe Lea, Laura Pearson, Nikki Smith, Maggie Ewings, Kathryn Jones, and Andy Ellingham

L. C. North studied psychology at university before pursuing a career in Public Relations. Her book-club thrillers – *The Ugly Truth* and *Clickbait* – combine her love of psychology and her fascination with celebrities in the public eye. When she's not writing, she co-hosts the crime thriller podcast *In Suspense*. She lives on the Suffolk borders with her family.

L. C. North is the pen name of Lauren North. Readers can follow her on Twitter @Lauren_C_North and Facebook @LaurenNorthAuthor.

If you loved *Clickbait*, don't miss
L. C. North's addictive thriller

The Ugly Truth

"I'm a prisoner. I'm not allowed to leave. There is someone watching me every minute of the day."

Media superstar Melanie Lange has disappeared.

Her father, billionaire business tycoon Sir Peter Lange, says she is a danger to herself and has been admitted to a private mental health clinic.

Her ex-husband, Finn, and best friend, Nell, say she has been kidnapped. They are deeply concerned for her safety.

The media will say whichever gets them the most views – no matter the cost.

But whose side are **you** on? And where is Melanie Lange?

'Fresh, compelling and searing . . . Not to be missed'
Lisa Jewell, bestselling author of *The Family Upstairs*

'#FreeBritney meets *The Appeal* in this addictively unique thriller'
Jack Jordan, bestselling author of *Do No Harm*